PAUL SCOTT

The Bender

Pictures from an Exhibition of Middle Class Portraits

GRANADA

London Toronto Sydney New York

Published by Granada Publishing Limited in 1975
Reprinted 1982

ISBN 0 586 03873 6

First published in Great Britain by
Martin Secker & Warburg Ltd 1963
Reprinted by William Heinemann Ltd

Granada Publishing Limited
Frogmore, St Albans, Herts AL2 2NF
and
36 Golden Square, London W1R 4AH
866 United Nations Plaza, New York, NY 10017, USA
117 York Street, Sydney, NSW 2000, Australia
100 Skyway Avenue, Rexdale, Ontario, M9W 3A6, Canada
61 Beach Road, Auckland, New Zealand

Made and printed in Great Britain by
Richard Clay (The Chaucer Press) Ltd
Bungay, Suffolk
Set in Linotype Times

Paul Scott was born in London in 1920 and served in the army from 1940 to 1946, mainly in India and Malaya. After demobilization he worked for a publishing company for four years before joining a firm of literary agents. In 1960 he resigned his directorship with the agency in order to concentrate on his own writing. He wrote thirteen distinguished novels, including the famous 'Raj Quartet', and also reviewed books for *The Times*, the *Guardian*, the *Daily Telegraph* and *Country Life*. He adapted several of his novels for radio and television.

In 1963 Paul Scott was elected a Fellow of the Royal Society of Literature and in 1972 he was the winner of the *Yorkshire Post* Fiction Award for the third volume of the 'Raj Quartet', *The Towers of Silence*. In 1977 *Staying On* won the Booker Prize for Fiction.

Paul Scott died in 1978.

'Mr Scott is one of those very few contemporary English novelists who can tackle a big theme in a big way'
Jocelyn Brooke, *The Scotsman*

'Paul Scott is a social novelist in the best sense'
Robert Nye, *The Guardian*

By the same author

Johnnie Sahib
The Alien Sky
A Male Child
The Mark of the Warrior
The Chinese Love Pavilion
The Birds of Paradise
The Corrida at San Feliu
Staying On

The Raj Quartet

The Jewel in the Crown
The Day of the Scorpion
The Towers of Silence
A Division of the Spoils

To
Nell and David
and the boys – especially Benedict

Bend: Force out of straightness, impart to (rigid object) or receive a curved or angular shape; arch (brows); tighten up, bring to bear (energies etc); be determined . . . attach with knot; turn in new direction; incline from the perpendicular; bow, stoop, submit (to or before) force to submit; hence, *Bender* n; esp (slang) sixpenny bit, spree.

The Concise Oxford Dictionary

Preamble for Minor Characters on a Hot July Evening

From watering his roses he came back into the twilight of his house, which was open front and back to benefit from whatever cool movement there might be of hot July evening air, and called to his wife, calling her Ma, and found her dozing over her knitting in a room that smelled of honeysuckle, and waking her said: *Where's that boy?* She said: *Click's out. Who's he with?* he asked. *That Gillian Spruce*, she said. He put on his slippers and the light and sat watching the screen until she brought him his supper of beer and cheese and bread and then he said: *So it's that one again. That's right*, she said. *No good will come of it*, he said. *You mark my words. No good will come of it. Perhaps you're right*, she said. He was.

One

'At the age of forty a man is at the crossroads,' Lady Butterfield said; at least, George assumed it was Lady Butterfield. He had dialled her Primrose number, her maid Hilda had answered, she herself had said 'Yes' and her voice (like her person) was as penetrating as ever. But these days you could rely on nothing, so why trust the telephone? Especially this one.

'Actually I'm forty-three, Aunt Clara.'

'That makes it worse, George. What are we to do about you, I wonder? And where have you been? It must be three months since you were in touch and more than that since you came to one of my Thursdays although you always seemed to enjoy them.'

'I've been in the country for a bit.'

'The country? I hope you aren't in any kind of trouble. It is difficult to say whether it's a blessing or otherwise your no longer being married to Alice. What is that clicking noise?'

'I can't hear it at this end,' George said, and tucked in the finger with whose nail he had been tapping the mouthpiece.

'We must talk of this privately. The telephone is all right these days for some things. One can make oneself understood at Fortnum's and occasionally at a box-office, but your problem can't be dismissed like a grocery list or a stall for *Fidelio*. And who knows these days who might be listening? It's gone now but there was that clicking noise.'

'Aunt Clara, it's not really a problem. I rang to let you know I was back in town, and to ask your advice about these two prospects that —'

'Well it is sweet of you. I had begun to think you were gone abroad or were viewing my Thursdays with disfavour. Perhaps you are tired of young people. I am never tired of young people because they represent the future —'

'Oh, yes, I agree.'

'It is Thursday tomorrow. Stay on or come early. I know you were fond of Alice, but from the beginning I saw that you were too alike in temperament for the marriage to be permanent, and I was surprised it lasted as long as it did, especially when no children resulted. You really should be thinking seriously about marrying again, unless of course you want to see that money of your Uncle Roderick's go to your niece. Or would it be your nephew? I never can remember. Which reminds me, your other brother, young Guy, has been coming to my Thursdays recently —'

There was a click, followed by the dialling tone. Finding and inserting another fourpence he dialled Aunt Clara's Primrose number again and got the engaged signal, which suggested to him that she was talking on, unaware of the void into which she spoke. He dialled once more and her telephone rang three times. She answered cautiously, 'Yes?' as if unused to picking up the receiver before her old retainer Hilda had screened the caller. He pressed Button A.

'I'm sorry, Aunt Clara, we got cut off. This telephone behaves rather oddly.'

'I think they get bored and start playing with the switch or whatever it is they use to tap lines with.'

'Who do?'

'Les voyeurs electroniques.'

'What?'

'Les voyeurs electroniques.'

'Oh, yes. You said Guy comes to see you.'

'He is beginning to make a success of his plays. Only on the television. But I fancy it won't stop there. He is still very young of course and there is plenty of time, but I am anxious for him to meet the people who can help him. At the moment he is taken up with an extraordinary girl he found in Islington who doesn't look even a quarter Indian but wears a saree and talks in a most peculiar manner. Her name is Anina, at least she says it is, but as her surname is MacBride one really does wonder. They are obviously living together in Camden Town and she always insists on coming with him. Now George. Guy is too young and inexperienced to shake her off entirely by himself so perhaps between us you and I could find a way of disembarrassing him of her.'

'I'm glad about the plays, Aunt Clara. It must be two years since I last saw Guy. How is he?'

'I think he's a little hurt that neither you nor his other brother – what was his name? Tim? Yes. That neither you nor Tim have been in touch or noticed his name in the press.'

'I never see television, Aunt Clara.'

'Well, and you were in the country, I suppose. And there has only been the one, which I didn't actually see, but the critics used names like Pinter as standards of comparison.'

'Pinter?'

'The caretaker.'

George felt he might sort that one out presently. He said, 'I'm glad he's proving himself, Aunt Clara. If you remember, I did bring him along to see you when he'd finished his National Service.'

'Indeed I remember. And I introduced him to Z, if I recollect.' No you didn't, George thought, you were only going to. 'But two years have made all the difference, it seems. Z is hoping to be here tomorrow, and there's a clever girl I hope will be here who was in that thing at The Royal Court. I want Guy to meet her. My Thursdays are becoming quite theatrical, which I confess is a change from art and politics and banking.'

'Well, I'll do my best to be there too, Aunt Clara, although I'm not sure what heading I come under.'

'Try to be here at six, George. Then we can talk more freely, and perhaps hatch a little plot about Anina. After that I think we must find you a protégée. So many young people need help and encouragement.'

'I don't think I could afford a protégée,' said George. He found it difficult even to afford himself. 'Tim said when I saw him early in the summer that I should get a proper job.'

'Tim?'

'My younger brother. I've never had one really, have I? A proper job, I mean.'

'Oh, Tim. I always forget Tim. I've not seen Tim since he was a boy and his mother brought him for tea at the Langham. His was a pale personality. What did you say he thought?'

'That I should get a proper job. Actually I've got two prospects in view and I wondered whether we might discuss —'

'Goodness knows I did my best for you when you were young. So much depends on what sort of job, George, and after all you have a small income. And what does he mean by a *proper* job? He is an accountant himself, isn't he? One should never believe what accountants tell you. Only the Inland Revenue is required to do that.'

'I owe him two hundred pounds.'

'Is he pressing for it?'

'My conscience is, Aunt Clara.'

'Then repay it.'

'I can't. That's the point.'

'Then he must wait, George.'

'Actually he's been waiting for ten years.'

'If he has waited ten years he must write it off. When your

Uncle Roderick's brother died and Roderick retired from the Indian Cavalry to administer the Butterfield estate he was faced once, only once mind you, with a bad debt. His accountants advised him to write it off. If you tell Tim the debt must be written off you will be talking to him in language he understands and there will be no more trouble.'

'I'll think over what you say, Aunt Clara.'

'Good. And you're still in Pimlico?'

'No. I left Pimlico three months ago. I tried Notting Hill and then living in the country, because people are always advising me to. I'm in Bayswater now, Queensbury Road actually.'

Lady Butterfield uttered a cry.

'Which number?'

'Next door to number fifty. That's let out too. I can see your old area railings from my window. I tried there first and they put me on to this one. They seemed pleasant people.' He waited and added presently, 'Hello?'

'Please tell me no more. I may come and see for myself. But I shall wait until October and the leaves are falling. We'll have muffins and Earl Grey. I shall see you tomorrow?'

'I shall try, Aunt Clara.'

'*Au revoir* until then.'

Two

Returning to her escritoire from the telephone and the conversation with George, Lady Butterfield resumed her station at her Grundig. Since buying it two months ago she had become addicted to it. It was a machine she admired excessively because it never interrupted and spoke, when pressed to do so, with the only voice in the world worth listening to. 'It is a laxative for the mind,' she told her Thursday people, 'and at my age it is wise to clarify one's thoughts.'

Pressed in several places now it played back what she had recorded since lunch.

'... entirely without foundation. The whole secret of living is to be *required* by other people. Not precisely needed by them, because the last thing others wish to feel towards you is gratitude. Actually a bit of old-fashioned fear does no harm, providing it is only a dash, enough to make them consciously square their shoulders before they come into your room. The delight they feel when they discover there is nothing to be afraid of does them all the good in the world. It also puts them at a disadvantage. But between meetings the fear must return. If they are a bit afraid this is proof that they still require you, that they see you not as the essential but as a desirable short cut on the road they have chosen to whatever ultimate end has taken their fancy, although the ultimate end is always the same for each of us, when you analyse it. Power! the exertion of one's will in a manner that will either be submitted to or allowed to flourish unchecked. The moment you become aware that they are about not to require you any more they must be recognized for what they have become: The Enemy; and, if they are worth attacking, attacked at the point calculated to hurt them most. They will then hate you. If you are not required it is imperative to be hated. Only on these two counts does a man or woman exist as a force, as a dynamic personality.'

Lady Butterfield nodded, switched from Play Back to Record, picked up the microphone and said:

'My late husband's cousin's eldest boy George has rung this day after a period of silence, of appearing in fact no longer to require me. His ringing means that he has changed his mind. Of middle-class origin on his father's side, and lower-middle amounting to working-class on his mother's, a poor relation, George had yet one asset which, had he remained penniless, I could have helped him to cultivate – his charm. Unfortunately Roderick's eyes were also open to this aspect of his so-called nephew's personality and although while he was alive I think I succeeded in limiting the expression of his interest there was nothing I could do when he was dead and was found to have willed young George a small income for life. To achieve success through charm it is necessary to remain penniless. He will get no two hundred pounds from me. Does this sound heartless? Heartlessness does not come into it. It is always a question of what is practicable and up here, above the snow-line, only the rarest air is permitted to blow and the coldest light to play upon people and their affairs.

'Below the snowline, unlike in actual mountaineering where the positions are reversed, stimulants are used, artificial aids to breathing, because the air down there is dank. Mist, you might say, only gathers in hollows. It is to my credit that although I had my origin in that mist I never resorted to an artificial aid, but simply held my breath and *climbed*. Up here it was known that my father was a butcher but only down there was this ever thought relevant. All that was truly relevant about his butchery was that he became rich at it and had the sense to do so before I was born. A chain of shops, acres of grazing, contracts with the army and with the leading hotels to each district in which his Victorian beef and mutton empire monopolized the trade, were proof of his sensibility in matters which would affect my future. Still greater proof lay in the self-denial he exercised in order not to decimate my inheritance by encumbering me with legitimate brothers and sisters. I am sometimes persuaded that he was at pains to ensure his one and only acknowledged child should be of the female sex, for so long as a girl had money of the right sort, which is to say enough of it, and available in ample time to give her a liberal education, she could always enter the upper air by hoisting herself up on the hand of an impecunious duchess; as I did. My own duchess was the most expensive of her day. I may confess that I hated her immensely for once referring to me in front of the dressmaker as Miss Porker. My name, let it be known, was Ribbe before it bcame Butterfield – which as was remarked by a servant of Roderick's in my over-hearing seemed to be but a change from meat to dairy. I congratulated her on her ready wit when giving her notice. But, as Her Grace remarked on the morning of my Presentation, "Clara my girl, now that you no longer require me you may hate me to your heart's content without a qualm of conscience. But because what you have required of me has been given you and what I have required of you has been given me, we are equal powers, need not fear each other and shall be friends for ever. At least, we shall have a splendid season."

'As it turned out she was right. We had a splendid season, but she was angry when I declined offers of marriage from members of the aristocracy. I declined such offers because I had divined that, to a man, they wanted my money in order to spend it, whereas Roderick Butterfield, being no longer a young man, wanted to invest it. Can I blame Roderick for no longer being young and for having preferred his Pathan orderly to a bedfellow more in keeping with his sex? Can I blame him for acquiring a knighthood rather than a barony? Think what, with a nudge here and there, he did with our money! And what would have been the point of a barony when having succeeded once he could not summon up again the means to ensure its continuance? We had no child after Bosworth, killed in 1916, and a knighthood was therefore sufficient.'

Lady Butterfield stopped the Grundig for a moment and then continued: 'That George has been at pains to find rooms close to our old house in Queensbury Road is proof positive that he still requires me. The question is: Do I respond or push him back into the obscurity from which I raised him twenty-five years ago? Clearly he wants to come again to my Thursdays because my Thursdays give him the feeling of being in the swim. People not naturally in the swim inevitably think of the swim as essential to progress. They are quite right of course, especially if they are mediocrities.'

Beyond the window that lighted her escritoire, St. John's Wood lay serene in mid-September sunshine. It was twenty-five minutes after three.

Three

The Bayswater telephone was on the half-landing. Directly George picked up the receiver again after ringing off from Aunt Clara, his landlady called from the house's lower intestine, 'Is that you, Mr. Spruce?' He called back, 'I'm on the telephone, Mrs. Morse.' They weren't used to each other's ways yet. Her name was Poulten-Morse, his own was Lisle-Spruce, but there was obviously going to be an understanding that the hyphens cancelled one another out, and in any case there was a limit to the amount of name you could call back and forth on the stairs, particularly if one of you wore a deaf-aid, which Mrs. Morse did, with a battery on her cardigan-ed chest in a bakelite holder that looked like a good hiding-place for a tablet of air-purifier to withstand the rigours of the ground floor and basement: all those damp passages and untrustworthy drains, and the radio playing stale music that rose and fell as the door to her living-room opened and shut.

Investing some money in prospect number one, he fed fourpence into the slot and dialled Regent and then the last and uncrossed out of half a dozen numbers pencilled in under 'Mick' in the pocket note-book which lay open on top of the coin-box.

Somebody, a girl possibly, said without enthusiasm, 'Gerald Flynn Enterprises.'

'Mr. Flynn, please,' said George.
'He's out.'
'Can you tell me when he's expected back?'
'Really couldn't say.'
'Thank you.'
Above the telephone there was a spotted mirror. He glanced into it briefly, putting the receiver back on. Tasks of dignity eluded him. At some point, now impossible to define, his face had ceased to inspire confidence of the right sort, even in bars. But his smile was well weathered and he thought it hadn't yet reached the stage of deserting his eyes to concentrate spent forces round tired teeth.
He turned the pages of the pocket note-book to look up Perce who was prospect number two. He fed the telephone another fourpence and dialled Shoreditch.
'Hallo!'
It sounded like a man interrupted against his will while drinking tea in a cubby-hole, surrounded by rolls of corrugated.
'Is Perce there?'
'You're on to Stores. You want Sales. Are you there?'
'Yes.'
'Hang on.'
Something got wound up.
A faint voice said, 'Sales.'
'There's a chap wants Perce. I'm putting him through.'
'Perce is up in Widnes,' the faint voice managed to say before the line died on them all, and the dialling tone came back.
George returned the receiver to its rest. The Bayswater telephone had now swallowed sixteen of his pennies and wore an air of knowing itself an instrument to give value for money, but already, in three days, he had recognized it as one of the kind reluctant to return fourpence through Button B and not above trying to get away with threepence in full settlement. Twice he had had to rap it sharply to cough up. For a man in his position a sharp telephone was an occupational hazard and at fourpence a time it was as well to know where you stood as soon as you stood there.
He retrieved his pocket book and opened the red and blue-paned door to the lavatory. Water whined through the pipes in the walls of the house like weak digestive juices in old tracts. He opened the door quietly and went up to his first-floor front on tip toe, having paid his rent in advance and being under no

obligation to get waylaid.

Back in his room he went straight to the blistered chest of drawers. Propped against the swivel mirror was the envelope containing the letter from his brother Timothy which had come in the mid-day post and which Mrs. Morse had given him when he got back from The Queen's Head: it being then five past three. It was now twenty-five minutes to four. The letter was addressed care of the bank, and was originally postmarked six days ago, E.C. and not N.W., which meant that Tim had posted it from his office and not from home. The bank had first sent it to Suffolk and Suffolk had sent it back to the bank who had now sent it to Bayswater. The letter inside, in brother Tim's straight up and down handwriting, was done on brother Tim's office paper with the engraved heading saying: Bartle Wallingford & Co., Chartered Accountants. He read it for the fourth time.

'DEAR GEORGE,

I rang your Pimlico number but was told you left last June. I was given a Notting Hill number but the people there said you moved to the country two weeks ago and only gave them the bank as forwarding address. So I'm writing to you care of the bank.

Would you ring me on receipt?

Yours,
TIM.'

There was no actual mention of the two hundred pounds.

He took the letter and sat down in the padded velvet chair which someone with a passion for buttons had upholstered in the late nineteenth century. He took a stub of pencil from his breast pocket. Using his note-book of addresses and phone numbers as a rest and the back of Tim's letter as jotting paper he wrote:

'*Asset.* Income from Uncle Roderick's legacy, at £400 per annum: £7.13.10 per week. *Liabilities.* Rent of bed-sitting room, 51 Queensbury Rd., Bayswater, £3.12.6, not incl gas, hot water or electricity. Bank Overdraft: approximately £74 (reduced from £300 over the last five years). Loan from Tim: £200 (made ten years ago. Not mentioned by either of us for some while now). *Prospects.* Perce would speak Clissold re temporary representation North or Midlands. (But Perce is in Widnes.) Question: And what do I know about Teddy Bears? Mick said to ring if I changed my mind. He was out yesterday. I left my new number. He was out again today. Question:

Change my mind about what exactly? What did he mean, would I object to sometimes wearing a chauffeur's hat? N.B. Alice never trusted him.'

Presently he added:

'Further prospect. Break rule of lifetime and ask Aunt Clara for money to pay back Tim. (And overdraft while I'm at it?) But better to owe bank £74 and Tim £200 than owe Aunt Clara £274? Was she speaking the truth when she told Alice she hadn't left me any money? Suppose she has? How much longer has she got? But I like Aunt Clara. Question: Does she like me? Question: Perhaps Tim has heard of a job he thinks would suit?'

He looked across at the chest of drawers. Apart from the swivel mirror, his war-time regimental hair-brushes, Woolworth's comb, pot of Silvikrin, there was Alice's photograph, taken in her Middle East Red Cross uniform, more than twenty years ago in Cairo, the day he had news of his legacy which they had celebrated by getting engaged.

He had sent Alice a postcard with his new address but it was a long time, several weeks, since he had telephoned her. He wondered whether he should ring her now to ask her advice about his two prospects. But he decided against it. She had heard that sort of thing too often before and for a reason he didn't quite follow, it still being sunny, it was the wrong kind of afternoon on which to talk to her at all.

Four

Clouds that had gathered over the Atlantic before dawn that day had sailed over the West Country at six o'clock in the morning and at three in the afternoon, having ridden full-chested in an easterly direction, they hid the sun over Maidenhead, darkening the river and making it lap the boats, and at four they reached Queensbury Road, Bayswater. The soft September light that had worked its way even through the brittle, yellow net curtains that seemed to George to have been woven from shreds of old loofahs, began to thicken and become more familiarly cataclysmic.

Familiarly, because George fancied often that London, keeping up with the rest of the world's capitals, had gone entirely underwater, and lay submerged from Richmond to Wapping and from Croydon to Barnet. Below the level of the flood the cold-blooded population went about its business, bulging of eye, blown-up of cheek, buttoned of informative lip, sculling through the tranquil murk with cold, crinkly-fingered hands. In time every one of them had become a fish or a skin-diver with harpoon. Those entering the pool from outlying provinces, from abroad, from anywhere indeed other than the world's capitals, gawped, swallowed water and were transformed into fish themselves or speared and sent three times to the surface to sink then without trace or be returned in their Ophelia clothes to their wondering relatives.

'I'll think about all this later,' George said and settled down with a book selected at random from those on the shelf. It was Stendhal, *Souvenirs d'Egotisme*; in an English translation. He flipped through the pages. He disliked books that had their titles repeated at the top of every page. He couldn't help thinking: Did Stendhal have to remember? Dead authors were worse than living ones. When they had gone the works they left behind them began to look like rows of shrunken heads, each with its label. Every time he turned a page of Stendhal, for instance, there was the label, and the book being autobiographical, the black, eyeless but intent little head the label was attached to was undoubtedly Stendhal's own. He sat down, skipped an introduction and began to read. Before he reached the end of the first page he came to words which according to the translator, ran: *Without work the vessel of life has no ballast.*

'I'm sunk,' George said aloud. 'Not only sunk but ruined.' He put the book down, stood up and paced the room, reflecting on the causes of his ruination, which so far as he could see could be whittled down to two: the legacy from his Uncle Roderick and the attack of mumps he had had at the age of puberty. Uncle Roderick's legacy was not enough to live on in any sort of style but it had begun by being too much in the absence of any other incentive to provide an incentive to work, and rot had not so much set in as bloomed creatively like a flower. The attack of mumps, on the other hand, had left him unable to father a child. This had been confirmed to him medically and privately after a wretched affair with a test tube a few months ago. So now, because the capital of ten thousand pounds, invested by unsmiling trustees in mortgages that paid four per cent per annum, could only be touched under the terms of Sir Roderick's will by his eldest child, or by Tim's, failing one of his own, he sometimes felt that even the income was no longer morally his. A man, he felt, should always live under the threat of fatherhood. Put like this the causes of his ruin were money and sex. Which meant that even in a thing as personal to a man as his own ruin he had not struck an individual note.

Putting Stendhal down on the walnut-veneered monstrosity which Mrs. Morse called a teapoy he picked up the leather-bound journal he had taken to the country with the idea of writing things up about the past to pare down his thoughts about the future. In the index under *Butterfield* he made a note: 'Muffins and Earl Grey. Forsyte symbols', and cross-referenced it with 'C' under *Aunt Clara.* He turned now to the fly-leaf on which he had written, in the first flush of Suffolk enthusiasm: 'Notes towards an Essay on the psychological block created by the barriers of class and the scarcity of proper occupations in an affluent modern society.'

The title always gave him pleasure and made up a lot for the fact that he was no longer at all sure what it meant and for the comparative blankness of the pages that followed.

'My Aunt Clara is not my aunt at all. She is the wife of that cousin of my father who was christened Roderick Butterfield and later knighted, and whom my father's side, the Spruce side, the poor relation side, spent most of their mental and physical energy sucking up to. I acquired this habit myself at the age of five or six when I began to understand that there were four important people alive in the world: Sir Roderick and Lady Butterfield, the Bank Manager and the Landlord. Sir Roderick and Lady Butterfield represented God, the other two Mammon. Father wrote out earthly tributes to the Bank Manager on curious little slips of green paper with perforations at one side which separated them from what were called the stubs. At Christmas, Easter and on their birthdays, all of us wrote chatty letters to the Butterfields. These were read by father before being posted. Because I knew that father wrote money away on the green slips I had an idea that all we had left to live on were these stubs and that the chatty letters were somehow connected to an idea of alleviation. I wasn't far wrong. One in about twenty of the green slips went first to the Landlord which made him less important than the Bank Manager who always ended up with the lot (although he returned them much later in batches marked Paid, as if he had been settling father's debts entirely on his own and out of the goodness of his heart). But of the two, Landlord and Bank Manager, it was the Landlord's name that was the more often invoked; for instance, when I kicked a door, broke a window or swung on the gate waiting for the milkman who, unless watched, skimmed cream off our pints into a small private can in the passage dividing our house from its neighbour; our house and that house being at adjacent ends of two blocks of small but respectable suburban villas.

'Lady Butterfield's name often cropped up in the conversations my mother had with neighbours over our North London fence and with callers for tea. With the exception of her name these conversations went over my head so I cannot put my hand on my heart and swear that my mother mentioned Lady Butterfield solely in the cause of social oneupmanship. I honestly recall only one occasion when I felt embarrassed by an unnecessary reference to her. This was when I was sixteen or so and my Uncle Albert (one of my mother's brothers) had brought his fourteen-year old daughter to stay with us while she recuperated from what was called a stomach cough but turned out to be tuberculosis and the death of her. This fourteen-year old daughter said things like "didn't 'arf" and called mother Aunti Vi. Her name was Drusilla and she was the type of girl my mother usually described as being common as muck but in this case didn't. Mother kept her relations in the background and in any case Drusilla was always ailing so I had not met her before. She was a bit of a revelation. He conversation was spiced with references I didn't understand at the time but realized, a year or so later, to have been sexual. I was an innocent youth. I remember mother mentioning Lady Butterfield at high tea. We had given up high tea as a family, but served it if any of these relations could no longer be put off and came for the day. Auntie Ada for instance. I liked Auntie Ada. She had a hat with cherries on it. When Lady Butterfield's name was mentioned I was amazed because Drusilla sniggered. Then I blushed. Later I saw how likely it was that Lady Butterfield was as familiar a link with the upper classes for mother's relations' neighbours as she was for our own, that Drusilla and Uncle Albert might snigger among themselves and to our faces but swank over *their* fences and *their* street corners (of which it always seems to me there are more in south London than in north). As soon as I realized the extent of Lady Butterfield's public persona I cut her down to manageable size and thought of her henceforth as my Aunt Clara, a woman seen but twice in my life and remembered for the size of her hats and the expensive smell of her clothes. Until the age of seventeen I met her only with my mother and father in the public rooms of the Langham Hotel although she told me I was taken once to Bayswater when she and Uncle Roderick still lived there; but that was in my mother's arms and a car hired at Aunt Clara's expense.

'All the year round my father painted pictures for Christmas cards, chocolate box covers and calendars so that although he was a very quiet man he always carried about with him a faint odour of festivity, not unlike the smell of stale Christmas pudding. Mother always took pains to make it clear to us that he was the only professional man in the road and that although financially he had come down in the world (because *his* father had been cheated by a parvenu) he had always done his best to maintain the standards of a gentleman even in a suburban, terraced villa, and had been helped to do so by his closest surviving relative, Sir Roderick Butterfield, who paid the fees that sent me to a private day school called The School House (founded in 1900 for the education of the sons of gentlemen who had gone down but kept afloat mainly by local tradesmen who had come up).

'It has never been clear to me why Uncle Roderick didn't shell out for Tim's fees too. Father paid these himself, mostly much in arrears, and in any case had an understanding with the headmaster which had something to do with cut rates for the second boy. But until it became clear that father would be unable to afford The School House for Tim after the age of sixteen, and that Uncle Roderick never *was* going to shell out for him, the Butterfields were our household Gods. Thereafter mother turned against Lady Butterfield (Tim was always mother's favourite), and it was only then that, from mother, I discovered Aunt Clara's maiden name had been Ribbe, and that she was the daughter of a butcher. This revelation came shortly after the revelation of Drusilla as a blood-relation of mine who said things like "didn't 'arf". The curious effect of these revelations was, however, to make me like Aunt Clara for the first time, because I felt she had risen so triumphantly above her background, and there came a day, when I was seventeen, when I bearded her and Uncle Roderick alone, at the Langham, and set the seal on the first cause of my ruination: this leaning towards a way of life that cannot be described better than in the words of the old saw: Champagne tastes on a beer income.'

The notes on Aunt Clara had got no further than this. George added a note in pencil as an *aide-mémoire* for future development, if ever. '13.9.61. In the three months that have gone since I last saw or spoke to her she seems to have taken up baby brother Guy who, from the hint she dropped, appears to have resumed his playwrighting. No doubt she anticipates some success for him because she had ignored him until now. Find out about this. Guy, born just before the last war, is really a stranger to Tim and myself. He came as a shock to us all, in 1937, when I was nineteen. Tim was sixteen, mother was forty-seven and father was sixty. From that time on we somehow no longer existed as a family.'

In the index of the journal George now wrote under *Tim*: 'Ask Tim to write it off?'

Five

Miss Ada Lisle lay dying in her clean white bed in her clean neat room high up in the eaves of The Grange where she had been housekeeper for over thirty years and bedridden for one. By the bedside Mr. Stainsby, curate of the rural parish church of St. Anne-in-the-Moor, in the country of Devon over which clouds, gathered in the Atlantic, had passed before riding full-chested towards Bayswater, nodded his head and sent up little prayers for Ada Lisle's deliverance. He had heard many times all she had to say about her family and according to his watch it was three forty-five. He wanted his tea, but was equally anxious to carry out his duties.

'George was her first-born,' Miss Lisle said, speaking of her sister Violet, George's mother. 'He came in an air-raid. There was a big window in the kitchen and Vi looked up the day before from her baking, she was making little scones because she had a fancy for them, and there was this zeppelin, it seemed to be coming right into the garden and it wasn't making any sound because the men had the machine turned off. She always said that when she saw the zeppelin she knew the baby would come that night even though he wasn't due for another month. They said afterwards it was the fright of the zeppelin that made the baby come, but Violet told me she wasn't frightened. I wasn't frightened, Ada, she said, because when I woke up that morning I knew it was a different day and I wasn't even surprised to see the zeppelin.

'Oh, and the bicycle, I'm forgetting the bicycle,' Miss Lisle said. When she smiled she looked like Tim (Tim did not know this and neither did she) but when she turned her head on the pillow to collect her thoughts from the patch of September sky outside the window Mr. Stainsby might have noticed that her chin was the Lisle chin which on its men looked malleable, but she was the only Lisle he had ever seen and her chin was simply her chin and nobody else's, even though she had just been talking about George who was born with it instead of with the Spruce chin which looked stubborn.

'And what of the bicycle, Miss Lisle?' Mr. Stainsby said, touching her hand in case she was absorbed too suddenly by the sky she was watching and becoming lost in. It was his first death watch.

'It was Mr. Proctor's who lived next door to Vi and Harry on the attached side. All the street lamps were darkened because of the air-raids and he hadn't ridden it for years and Harry had never ridden one in his life because the Spruces were poor. But well-connected.'

Mr. Stainsby nodded. He knew about Harry Spruce. Harry Spruce had been Miss Lisle's brother-in-law, husband to her sister Violet, father of three boys called George, Timothy and much later, almost as an after-thought, Guy, whose shades were always being conjured in the room high up in the eaves of The Grange.

'The baby was coming, you see, but the doctor wasn't and poor Harry, who was artistic, didn't know which way to turn until Mr. Proctor knocked and said is there anything I can do? They'd not spoken much to Mr. Proctor because he was only a sort of commercial traveller, and Harry was a professional man. He was never strong, Harry. All our brothers were very strong, Violet's and mine, and Harry felt it, they were all in France because of Kitchener, but he wasn't and neither was Mr. Proctor. He was always kind to me, was Harry, and once he gave me five shillings for my birthday. It was all he could afford, and I bought a hat in the Bon Marché. Spruce by name but oak by nature, he said. Now why did he say that? I'm getting muddled.'

'Have a little nap, Miss Lisle, and tell me some other time,' said Mr. Stainsby who wondered whether the doctor was right when he said there wouldn't be another.

Miss Lisle closed her eyes. Now she was smiling at the pictures behind her eyelids which Mr. Stainsby couldn't see but would have found more reassuring than the pictures he thought both of them could see when she stared at the sky.

'I can just see Mr. Proctor,' she said, 'wobbling down the road riding to fetch the doctor to bring little George into the world. Of course I wasn't there. I didn't see my very first nephew until he was six months old. Vi was the youngest but she had children before any of our brothers, but that was because of Kitchener. Vi wasn't there either because she was in bed but I'm sure it was Vi and not Harry told me about Mr. Proctor and the bicycle. She was always full of stories. She made everything dramatic. On the way back Mr. Proctor could hear the shrapnel falling and was almost deafened by the noise of the guns they had up there on the green. It was fenced in afterwards and Harry used to say to George, That's where they fired the guns from, the night you were born. George was a good-tempered baby. Vi said she supposed he tried not to be a worry because of the trouble he'd caused coming a month too soon in the middle of an air-raid. Sometimes I think she took against little George right from the beginning, though. Later it was all Tim. But she's gone, I mustn't speak badly of Vi. There were so many of us and Vi was the youngest. She was always afraid of being left behind and had fancies, and when our mother was dying she said to me, Look after Vi, she's not very sensible, look after Vi, Ada, she may get left behind, and I said I would but it was I who got left behind. Harry would have liked me to go over more often and I liked it there because it was warm and comfortable even if it was shabby, but Vi didn't like me to go too often, my clothes were what she called wrong for their neighbourhood, and I was in service. When little George was a year old she took him to see Lady Butterfield and came home with a silver mug. It was on the mantelpiece. Sometimes I don't think they had enough to eat, and Harry's underwear was all holes, I saw it on the horse the day I went over without saying and there was a row. He was an artist, Mr. Stainsby. He painted Christmas cards and I said, Do you make up the verses, Harry? But he said no, he wasn't clever enough to make up the verses, but he was clever, you know. Every year he sent me a calendar he'd done specially. It was always the same because I said it was the kind I liked, a robin on a gate with snow. I can just see those robins. He made them so real. Sometimes he worked past midnight, but not on the colour. He had to have a good north light for the colour.'

Six

Apart from books that repeated their titles at the top of each page he disliked clocks that ticked audibly and calendars that showed the whole of a month at a glance; anything indeed that reminded him of the indifference of inanimate objects to the continuous whispering draught from time's winged chariot, and in this Victorian bed-sitter everything did. He paused for a moment on the brink of sitting down on the padded velvet chair that belonged like Stendhal to the last century; went over to the window, parted the net curtains with his left elbow and right shoulder and stood, arms folded, watching the area railings of number fifty. Then he gazed at the pavement over which his mother must have carried him more than forty years before. The picture of himself as a babe-in-arms reminded him of Tim as one. Three years the elder, he had spent a lot of his childhood doing what their mother called 'Looking After Tim'. This had become a state of mind as well as a habit of which he did not break himself until he was taken up by Aunt Clara and entered what of her world she saw fit to show him, and left Tim behind.

He sat down and wrote to him.

'Dear Tim,

I have been away and have only just got back to town and thought I'd let you know my new address. It is a long time since either of us mentioned the two hundred pounds I owe you. Although scarcely a day has gone by when I haven't thought about it I have, for no reason that I can put my finger on, become acutely conscious of it during the past few days. But when I consider my affairs I am at a loss for a solution to the problem of extinguishing a debt that I fear in time (barring a change in my fortunes) could come between us. Everything would be simple if I could break into the capital sum whose income alone Uncle Roderick willed to me; but, as you may remember, that sum is held in trust for my eldest surviving child, to be his when I die, or failing any surviving child of my own, for your eldest, or Guy's, failing one of yours. Since I am so far without issue, indeed not even married any longer and with no actual prospect of remarriage in view, it begins to look —'

Here George hesitated in order to consider the inwardness of not telling the truth but writing only around the periphery of a lie.

'– it begins to look as though your daughter, my niece Gillian,* will enjoy the substance whose shadow has led me from the age of twenty-two to live at one remove from harsh reality, led me once indeed into that predicament from which you rescued me with the loan that forms the long outstanding debt I owe you. The fact that today two hundred pounds isn't worth what it was then, even with interest added, a point we never went into, adds insult to injury. Or should it be injury to insult? This is not compensated for by the fact, as I assume it, that today two hundred pounds doesn't make the hole in your resources that it made then.

Because I often quieten my conscience by imagining that this debt is not constantly in your mind it follows that I must apologize for bringing it back to it. But, being no Catholic, and unable to leave the burden of conscience at the confessional – that left-luggage department to which the travellers never return except to bring more bags – I do want to talk to you, soon, and hear your views and, if you have any, your suggestions short of a peremptory demand for immediate settlement which I shouldn't blame you for, incapable though I should be of compliance. As an accountant you must often have advised debtors; and indeed creditors.'

He hesitated once more, partly because he had reached the point where the letter ended short of its *coup de grâce* and partly because he disliked ends of any kind. On a scrap of paper he wrote, trying it out: 'If I owed the money to someone else, I wonder what your advice to *him* would be?' Below this he wrote: 'Write it off' and considered the words with dignity, disapproval and longing. He could not bring himself to add them to the letter which he now wrote 'Yours ever' on, and then his name, George. Without RI after it he thought George was a very undistinguished name.

Having finished he read the letter through. It was not really honest. He said aloud: 'I'll ring first. If he's not at the office I'll post it.'

* See preamble.

Seven

He looked out another fourpence. One of his few virtues, he had begun to notice, was never being at a loss for small change. On the half-landing, the four pennies, two Elizabeths, one George Six and a warm, wafer thin George Five which he had to put in twice to make it stay, went down the telephone's metal throat and clanged in its innards. When he dialled the damned thing actually purred.

'Is that you, Mr. Spruce?' Mrs. Morse called from below.

'I'm on the 'phone,' he called back.

'Bartle Wallingford,' the instrument said into his ear. He recognized the switchboard girl's Lewisham accent. 'Hello, Gwendoline. It's me. Is my brother in?'

'Is that Mr. George? Long time no speak.'

'No, I've been away.'

'He was trying to get you last week I think it was.'

'Oh, was he? How are you?'

'Can't complain. I don't think he's in.'

Everthing was cut out: sound, resonance, breath and heart beat. For almost a minute Bartle Wallingford, the firm of City accountants in which brother Tim was junior partner to old Wallingford, Bartle being dead, was lost to the living world. When Gwendoline opened up again George felt like an archaeologist who, with patience alone, had unearthed an old civilization.

'Millicent says he's not back and won't be. Actually he didn't come in from lunch and Mill was wondering but he rang ten minutes ago and said he was going on.'

'Going on where?'

'To a client I expect, Mr. George. Any message? Or shall I ask Mill to put you on the pad?'

'The what?'

'It's Mill's new system. She tells him messages but people who just ring and don't say she writes on the pad. You could get him at home later I dare say.'

'Thank you, Gwendoline. Don't bother with the pad. I'll try him later at home probably. Have you had your holiday?'

'Yes thank you, Mr. George.'

'Where did you go this time?'

'Excuse me, Mr. George.'

The line became muffled. He heard her say, 'Bartle Wallingford,' and 'I'll see.' Then she was back in full voice.

'We had what's called a two centre. Five days in Venice and seven in Rome and the rest was getting there and back.'

'I hope you enjoyed it.'

'Oh well, it makes a change. The best part's before you go. I'm looking forward to next year now. We're thinking of Corsica. I'll have to say ta ta. They're flashing.'

'Goodbye Gwendoline.'

He could feel Mrs. Morse's presence at the bottom of the well of the stairs and thought it best not to press button B which he sometimes did on the principle that machines, being man-made, ought to be fallible. To ensure that he wouldn't hear Mrs. Morse if she called out he seized himself with a fit of coughing and reached his room wracked and exhausted. He found a threepenny stamp in his wallet, stuck it on the envelope of the letter to Tim and set out for the post.

Eight

When he reached the pillar box at the end of the road where it led into Queensbury Square, the chesty clouds burst. A flash-bulb explosion of lightning lit up that part of the sky he judged to be above Hendon. It looked nearer but he thought of Hendon as one of the few urban districts where Acts of God were still commonplace, so it was bound to be there.

Whenever he posted a letter he felt that he was feeding the poor. There were hundreds of these hungry, scarlet paupers. You came across them everywhere, standing near the kerb, blind and mute; open-mouthed like starving, new-hatched birds. With his hand still retaining its grasp on the letter to Tim, which had otherwise entered the maw of the pillar box, it occurred to him for the first time to wonder why he felt that posting a letter was an occasion of charity while putting fourpence into a telephone was an act of combat. Holding the letter and beginning to consider this he also began to get very wet; and the brass-bound barrels of God whose flash had been seen a few seconds ago over Hendon now reached Bayswater with a long rumble, crashed into some celestial obstruction and fell to pieces just above Queensbury Square. George looked up.

'Why should I be pursued by all this symbolism?' he thought. He withdrew his hand from the mouth of the box, bringing the dishonest letter out to take home and steam off the threepenny stamp. He turned his coat collar up and ran back to number fifty-one.

By the side of the second bell-push from the bottom there was his name printed on a slip of card: George Lisle-Spruce: in elegant printer's copper-plate. His mother had been a Lisle. He had been christened Lisle as well as George but the hyphen was all his own work. In the days when the visiting cards were used friends had nicknamed him Silky, because of the Lisle. Silky no longer went with the card, at least not with the thin strip cut from the one he had saved from the hundred printed. Below George Lisle-Spruce on the original full-scale card there had been an address: The Bucket Club, 343 Sloane Street, S.W.1, and Silky had been appropriate in that context. It was because of what happened at the club that George owed Tim two hundred pounds. Alice had never known about the two hundred pounds, neither had Tim's wife Sarah. Until he mentioned it today to Aunt Clara the two hundred pounds had been a secret between himself and Tim, just as his sterility was a secret between himself and Doctor Honeydew to whom he sometimes felt himself married in view of what, as it were, had passed between them. He had been a fool to mention the two hundred pounds to Aunt Clara. She would probably mention it to Guy, let it slip intentionally, guessing it to be a secret. He could hear her say, 'Guy, remind me. Is it to you or your brother Tim George owes two hundred pounds?'

If Guy was going to make money from his plays perhaps he could be persuaded to lend two hundred pounds in order to pay back Tim? But this was an uncharitable thought. You could not borrow two hundred pounds from a stranger and Guy had always been a stranger: stranger, evacuee child, orphan of the storm and of the bomb that killed their mother and father in the safe green rustic heart of England when he and Tim had been away to the wars. Gone are the old folk, George said to himself, the children are scattered. Who were there now but three brothers and old Lady Butterfield? What, for instance, had happened to Auntie Ada who had gone to the west country to be housekeeper to a family called Bright? There came a time in one's life when one's older relations were more likely to be dead than not.

George, unlocking the front door of number fifty-one, hoped that for once Mrs. Morse would succeed in waylaying him. Why Mr. Spruce, she might say, you're wet through, you could do with a hot cup of tea. But perhaps because he felt beholden to her in anticipation she was nowhere to be seen. The house had not only swallowed her but digested her, extracted her essence. She now existed only as part of its metabolism. On the way upstairs to his room he shivered. He would have to change his clothes, but he knew he wouldn't catch cold. Only Tim caught colds and even he had grown out of them. 'Now just you see that Tim wraps up when you come out,' he could hear their mother say, 'you know what he is.' Now Tim made his boy Andrew take cold baths and his daughter Gillian walks over the heath. Gillian didn't catch colds but Andrew did.

When he had taken off his wet things and rubbed his head with a towel he put on his dressing-gown and made a cup of tea. He drank this and watched the rain coming down. The sky was brightening. In an hour Bayswater would stand mellow and newly-rained-on at the top of uncreaking stairs with its hand on durable banister rails to welcome home the workers of the world. All over the house and all over the district there would be little explosions as tins were opened and gas rings lit. Lights would appear in the windows of young men and women who would go home no more to Bedford or Finsbury Park, or to any of the guilty scenes of childhood. At six he would go out for a modest pint of beer, eschewing, as he had done for several weeks, the gin, because the gin was a specific to hold in reserve, not to be trifled with, an ally only at times of special stress. Beer was enough when problems had not quite cohered into crises: bitter for preference. Drinking it, sitting in ill-lit bars and that autumnal silence which was engendered even on a summer evening by the sight and sometimes the companionship of soft-haired London girls in macs drinking light ale, he could find in himself the likeness of an island that had emerged from urban flood into a kind of Constable country of the mind: temperate well-watered, richly soiled, gentled by calm skies, sung at by modestly feathered birds. From Bayswater, then, the roads radiated only into a rural English night, haywains creaked homeward in the dark along the Edgware Road, and the labourer plodded behind them worthy of his hire as far as Cricklewood.

There was a knock.

Nine

'I was wondering whether you would care for a cup of tea,' Mrs. Morse said, looking in over his shoulder beyond the door he had just opened wondering who on earth.

'How very kind of you,' he said, 'but I've just made myself some.'

'I saw you from my front window running in all that rain. I'd just put a kettle on and I thought poor Mr. Spruce will be wet through and might just do with a cup.'

Her kettle, he thought, must be an old one that had furred up and took a long time to come to the boil, or perhaps it was Mrs. Poulton-Morse who took a long time to come to it.

'Come in and have a cup of mine,' he said, standing back, aware of his bare legs under the dressing-gown and of the way Mrs. Morse's chin seemed to be held up by the hand of an invisible swimming instructor. 'I make rather good tea,' he said, now feeling much the same about his own chin, his eyes held off her battery where it rested in a somewhat compromising position on what was left of her chest. She was an angular lady in her fifties or sixties.

'That is very kind of you, Mr. Spruce, but I mustn't keep you standing. In any case I don't like my people to feel beholden or under any obligation to have me in if I happen to knock.'

'Oh, but please,' he said. 'I shan't take a second to make myself presentable.'

In his curtained-off cooking space (hot plate, sink, ascot and crockery-store cupboard) he put on flannel trousers.

'Do you like your milk in first or after?' he said, carrying a cup and saucer and spoon in.

'First I'm afraid, Mr. Spruce. I know it's supposed to be very non-u, but really it tastes so much better.'

'Actually it's supposed to be better for you as well. The hot tea going on to the milk breaks up the globules of fat.'

'What a splendid cup,' said Mrs. Morse, after sipping. 'What tea is it?'

'Only Co-op 99.'

'I find it difficult to buy a tea I can rely on these days. Do you not find that too, Mr. Spruce?'

'Yes. I know what you mean.'

'It is all to do with the buying and the blending. It is no guarantee, these days, the label.'

'I usually stick to this.'

'My brother was in tea,' said Mrs. Morse.

'Planting?'

'Yes. He managed a garden in Assam. A life much cut off, but full of compensations.'

'The East has its attractions.'

'What we shall do without it I do not know.'

'I beg your pardon?'

'Our Eastern Empire, I mean. It was, you know, what *made* the English middle class. It taught us the hitherto upper-class secrets of government and civil administration. Now we must largely be content again with commerce and science. It is almost medieval, is it not? Merchants and apothecaries. All my young nephews seem anxious to be boffins. They speak you know of ICI much as their fathers and uncles once spoke of The Civil. Seats in the House are somewhat limited after all, and for all that there is a House of Commons, government is now back in the hands of privilege because there simply isn't enough of England to go round, is there, enough to govern, I mean, and what there is is largely spoken for. Not, I might add, that I vote anything but Conservative in the local and national elections. Nor, perhaps I should hasten to explain, do I disagree with the Wind of Change and the end of colonialism. I am with Mr. Macmillan in everything. So far.'

'Quite. I vote Liberal myself.'

'They say it is the coming thing and perhaps they are right. The things at stake between the major parties may become too stark and uncompromising for us English to live with and have to make a choice of. A reduction in the super-tax and a wage pause all in the same year *are* a little difficult to swallow, are they not? Perhaps it will be up to the Liberals to find a better way of explaining why such things are necessary. I suppose it is all a question of Public Relations, or what in my day used to be called A Fair Hearing, although *that* is now referred to as Paternalism. Perhaps it is in the sphere of public relations that the middle class will again find its feet.'

'Another cup, Mrs. Morse?'

'No, thank you, Mr. Spruce.' She gave him back the cup. 'I spoke to my next-door neighbour, by the way, and thanked her for giving you my name. Careful tenants are not easily come by. I'm afraid the amenities are limited and the furnishings somewhat sparse, but they have to serve. I gathered from my neighbour that a relation of yours once owned number fifty. In the old days.'

'Yes. It's why I tried there first,' said George, knowing his stock had risen because he had mentioned Lady Butterfield to Mrs. Poulton-Morse's neighbour and Mrs. Poulton-Morse's neighbour must have mentioned Lady Butterfield to Mrs. Poulton-Morse.

'I'm afraid,' she said, looking round the room, 'it is not what you are used to, but then it is a commodious boat we all of us are in.'

'But I assure you, it's a very nice room. Actually more than I can really afford.'

'Ah, well, yes. Afford. But standards are difficult to lower even when one's income is fixed and the cost of living is not.' She rose from the padded velvet chair. 'We must all of us keep busy,' she said. 'When you told me you had no actual occupation but depended on an income I feared you would turn out to be one of what I call my lonely people, even though *they* are mostly young and out to business. But I am reassured on that point, Mr. Spruce. It is quite cheerful in the house to hear you so much on the telephone.'

'I hope it doesn't bother you.'

'Not in the least. I do confess that the telephone bell is something I am constantly on the *qui vive* for, what, you know, with my deafness and being largely alone all day with my tenants out and frequently finding total strangers using it, strangers that is to say to me, but not to my tenants who themselves are mostly a floating population.'

'I know what you mean,' said George, thinking not only of the flood but of the commodious boat, and of Noah, even of Charon, wondering whether he felt like either.

'It is the sense of oneself being immobile in the still-centre of a spinning wheel that takes most getting used to in this business of letting out rooms, especially if most of one's earlier life was spent revolving in the world of affairs.'

He opened the door for her.

'However,' she said, 'I am more fortunate than most, even if I have dropped out of the race. The pursuit of happiness, Mr. Spruce.'

'Oh, but it's not a pursuit, Mrs. Morse.'

'No?'

'Isn't it more as if it's all round, standing still, but just a bit difficult to stand still with?'

'What an extraordinarily cheery thing to suggest. Now you

have given me something to think about.'

On the landing she said, 'Now just for that, Mr. Spruce, you deserve a stroke of luck. So far I haven't been able to help noticing that all your telephone calls are outward. I shall go back now and think *hard* about someone ringing *you*. With *pleasant* tidings.'

Ten

'Of all Roderick's relations,' Lady Butterfield said into the microphone of her Grundig which was set by the side of her sunken bath in the hour between tea and cocktails, 'Harold Spruce was the least likely. I said to him once: "Roderick, why do you interest yourself in a poor relation who paints Christmas cards and speaks English with an accent that isn't quite, even though it is *nearly*?" And all he said was: "Clara, in our association it is your job to supply the money and mine to make use of it but it is the duty of a gentleman also to look to the kind of riches stored up in heaven." "So long," I assured him, "as you assure me my earthly position is not endangered." I have never believed in God except for the poor, nor in charity except as an expression of force, which is to say a charity to which one may publicly subscribe. In the hospitals of this country, for instance, there is more than one Lady Butterfield ward, and there are several wooden seats set upon public footpaths halfway up the hills upon whose crests old people's home's inevitably rest. Until the war there was scarcely a published subscription list that did not feature my name prominently. What light can the lamp of charity cast from under a bushel?'

Lady Butterfield paused in mid-sponge, reached to her right and pressed switches. 'What light can the lamp of charity cast from under a bushel?' the Grundig asked. She pressed the switch that stopped the machine entirely, and poured a few more drops of Schiaparelli oil into the bath-water. Mr. Grundig's invention was far superior to Mr. Edison's telephone. Mr. Grundig was a force. The voice, by itself, was the ultimate weapon of power. Dilute the voice with the sound of another voice and the power went off the boil. She switched the Grundig on again and recorded two words: 'Pure Power.' Then she switched off. Pure power was a concept that required leisurely and Schiaparelli-scented meditation.

Cooling from her bath in one of her Sheraton chairs with her old lady's feet nestling into a goatskin rug like two lobsters side by side in Neptune's beard, Lady Butterfield continued her recording.

'This nephew of mine, George Spruce, who rang today after a silence of three months, visited with us once on his own at an hotel in London – the Langham I fancy, because we generally stayed there when we came up from Manorlord Mount after we gave up the little place in Bayswater. His clothes were quite execrable although it was clear he had done his best with the means at his disposal. But his hair and his nails were too short and he had an unnaturally healthy look which went only too well with what I might call an open-air accent. When I saw him I hoped Roderick would put him to tea or rubber because he would have been good with the natives. I also feared that he was the kind of boy Roderick might take too obviously under his wing and that sort of thing does not do if there is a family connection, however tenuous.

'For once, though, I saw I had misinterpreted someone's motives. From a letter he had written asking if he could see us alone, without his parents, I had been prepared, almost, to meet a kindred spirit, one born amid those dank and misty hollows who was holding his breath and beginning to climb; but it really seemed that a concern for the welfare of a brother of his which he had expressed in his letter rather too plausibly to rank as genuine was, in fact, quite deeply felt. During the few moments I succeeded in getting him alone I said, "Now, George. Tell me. What is it you want?" Think of it! The opportunity in his grasp! In the eighteenth century he would have said, "Ma'am, I wish to enter the best society and become prominent." But all he did was blush and say, "Now that it comes to it, Aunt Clara, I don't really know." What can you do with a generation like that? The modern young people are much more sensible. For instance his youngest brother Guy, who was born just before the war (an inefficient arrangement which showed why the Spruce side of the Butterfield clan had fallen so low), is quite a different kettle of fish; but then he was brought up in a wholly different environment by his foster-parents in the country and would sell his grandmother for thirty pieces of silver if he knew where to find her. I have some hopes of Guy as a protégé and am not blind to the fact that he thinks me a stupendous and superannuated bore who may nevertheless leave him some money and provide him early on with the financial security from which, in his plays, he can more comfortably attack standards of civilized conduct. How disappointed he will be. But I fancy he is a force. When you recognize a force it is ridiculous to ignore it or contest it. George, I quickly saw, would never become a force. I was very annoyed when Roderick died and I discovered he had left his nephew George an income for life; but it was Butterfield money, not Ribbe, and it has done George Spruce no good.'

Eleven

Later that evening when George had finished Stendhal and something in a tin prepared by a firm called Smedley he saw that if Stendhal had never written his souvenirs no one would ever have known that he was an egotist. In Stendhal's day there was no telephone. He had been unable to ring people up all the time. Writing journals, memoirs and ringing people up on the telephone were the marks of egotism, the only real outlets the true egotist had. They were lone-faced activities. He thought: The telephone is my friend, really. Even the one downstairs.

In time people would have no further need to meet face to face. Smedley's could feed you by post. You could say all that you had to say about yourself (which was the only reason for what was called conversation) on postcards and the telephone; and in memoirs you left behind when you died. In your memoirs you put down all the things you would not even dare to write on a postcard or say on the telephone. And in time, because you saw no other human face, your own face would be revealed. It would come out of its lair like a naked animal, attracted by the sun and a feeling of repose, and no longer ashamed of having no fur.

So many young people need help and encouragement, Lady Butterfield had said. Did they? Surely they were better off without it? Had he, George, not suffered precisely from too much encouragement and help? And who was supposed to benefit from the help, who be encouraged by the encouragement?

When Lady Butterfield had said, 'So many young people need help and encouragement,' the image that had sprung at once into George's mind was of Lady Butterfield twenty-five years before helping and encouraging him. He imagined he could remember the very words of the letter that had set the seal upon his future ruin. He could not of course, but in his mind the letter ran along the lines of:

'Dear Aunt Clara: I should be awfully grateful to you if you could find time to give me some personal advice. May I call on you and Uncle Roderick next Monday at the Langham between lunch and tea? I understand from something my father said that you are staying in London for a few weeks. He does not know that I am writing to you. I had better explain the reason for my request. Now that I am seventeen and quite capable of beginning to earn my living I am naturally anxious to do so at the earliest opportunity, because father's affairs are at a lower ebb than usual. It was not until this year I discovered that it is Uncle Roderick who has been paying the fees to send me to The School House. When I broached the subject to my father of going out to business this autumn he said that this could not be, if only because it would upset you and Uncle Roderick to think of my not continuing a formal education until I was eighteen. I quite see that to leave now might, on the face of it, imply a waste of all your kindness to date. But I am in the sixth form and have reached, so my headmaster says, matriculation standard.

'Tim, on the other hand, although a plodder, lacks what I call the examination mind. I know that my father does not anticipate being able to keep him on at The School House beyond his fifteenth or sixteenth year. What I therefore had in mind was that I might, by leaving school now, pass on the benefit of a free year's education to my younger brother. He has hopes of playing for the first eleven, both cricket and football, when he is fifteen. Please don't bother to reply to this letter. I will telephone the Langham on Monday morning to see whether you have left a message for me. Your affectionate nephew, George.'

Thinking of the letter, trying to recapture both its words and its implications after twenty-five years, one of those implications hit him for the first time; hit him in two felt but difficult to define places; somewhere inside the ribs and somewhere inside the skull. Why had he written this letter to Aunt Clara and not as would have been more fitting to Uncle Roderick?

Twelve

But why did Vi take against George, why was it all Tim, Miss Ada Lisle asked. Mr. Stainsby, back on watch after several hours relief, sent up another little prayer for Miss Lisle's deliverance, which seemed now to be getting closer because her eyes were shut and she had said nothing for a long time but kept moving her lips as if to make them get hold of words to describe the ideas that must be going on in her head.

Why did Vi take against George? But she was always like that. It was always the new toy she liked best when she was little, not like most of us, she hadn't got feeling for the tried and trusted, always running off in a new direction, at least as a girl, it was different when she married Harry. Ada, she said, Ada, all my youth is being kept down, I used to be so vivacious, it's Harry, he's forgotten what it was to be young, think of it, Ada, why Harry's nearly old enough to be my father.

What does it feel like to be old I wonder, Mr. Stainsby asked himself. What does it feel like to be dying? Does Miss Lisle know she's dying? Does she feel lonely to be dying alone at The Grange with all her family gone, or scattered and thoughtless, and the last of the Miss Brights unable to climb the stairs to take leave of a faithful servant? The last Miss Bright was Miss Pamela whose two sisters Georgina Bright and Agnes Bright lay buried already in the churchyard adjacent to the tomb of Hector Bright who had married beneath him and paid for it, so they said, every day of his life in terms of sorrow, sickness and the cross of repentance laid on his thin shoulders by three nagging sisters. The Brights had been coal in their grandfather's day. All my money, Miss Pamela Bright, the surviving sister said, will come to the church. But what of your housekeeper, Ada Lisle, Mr. Stainsby had asked. This was two years ago when Miss Lisle still ordered the household and tipped the tradesmen out of her own pocket so that she could face them. She has gathered riches in heaven, Miss Bright said, not to speak of the bit I don't doubt she puts by from the housekeeping allowance, I was never one to go into detail, she has warm hands which means a cold heart, said Miss Bright who was as warm in all her limbs as a miner's grate. And who, she wanted to know, would stay for so many years in a job that paid her thirty shillings a week unless she were on to a good thing? She is a good woman, Mr. Stainsby replied. You are new here, Miss Bright said, and you are too kind-hearted to recognize cunning.

Ah, thought Mr. Stainsby now, watching the dying face of Ada Lisle, I am glad you are going first and will miss the disappointment of the Will.

Miss Pamela will see I'm provided for, Ada Lisle said soundlessly into her own dark, and I've put a bit by each week out of my thirty shillings since there's been no one to buy little presents for with Vi gone, and Harry gone, and all our brothers and their wives, and their children scattered and not remembering funny old Aunt Ada. It was Kitchener's war, that's when being alone really began. It broke the family up, Mr. Stainsby, and the boys never settled when they came back. Arthur was killed of course, he was in the Engineers, and there was Reggie in the Artillery came back and married little Elsie Spendlove and went off to Southsea and never wrote, and Teddy was wounded at Passchendaele and died the year of the general strike and his wife Cissie married again and we never heard after that. There was only Albert kept up, but then Drusilla died and he and Enid went off to the Isle of Wight, there was a job going in a nursery, he was always fond of a bit of garden and Enid said it was the fresh air he needed, she was afraid it was consumption like young Drusilla's, but it was only brick dust from Mr. Salter's yard. Vi once said, How can he, a common labourer and our father a master builder, and I said, Master drinker, Vi. And we didn't speak for a year. She couldn't bear to hear the truth about some things. You're a lady companion, Ada, she used to say, and I said, Housekeeper, Vi, and cook-general, and glad to get it. She liked it when I came to The Grange because of the address and I suppose because it was too far for me to go over on the off-chance. She came once, when would it be, the summer of '28, and Tim was seven or eight, and George was left back home because she couldn't afford fares for three. I offered her ten shillings but she looked down her nose and only stayed one night because we ate in the kitchen with Mrs. Drayton and young Cora, she'd expected to eat with Them or for me to have what she called a proper companion's apartment. She never had a good word to say for the Brights after that, but they were good to me and Miss Pamela will see I'm looked after when she's gone, poor thing, she can't last with that leg. There's a picture in her room, an officer I think, but she's never mentioned him. There are letters, too, done up in ribbon. I never had letters, Mr. Stainsby. I've never been in love, at least I don't think so. But Harry Spruce was always kind to me and once he gave me five shillings for my birthday and I bought a hat at the Bon Marché. It had cherries on it and little George said, Are they real, Auntie Ada? And Vi slapped his hand before he could even get near them. I thought he was going to cry, but he never cried. He kept looking at the cherries all through tea, Vi wouldn't let me take my hat off even though the pin was killing me, because it wasn't done in the best society to come to tea and not keep your hat on. You've forgotten everything our father taught us, Ada, she said, and I said, That's right, Vi, I never touch a drop. That was the time George said, Was grandpa an awful old soak? and Vi buttoned her mouth up and got that look that always frightened me because I thought the devil had got into her.

Thirteen

George could not get to sleep for worrying about the letter from Tim and his call that day to Lady Butterfield. Had he, honestly, any intention of getting back into that Thursday habit? Whenever you entered that chic St. John's Wood drawing-room there was always the same group of early arrivals standing near the Adam fireplace: young, youngish and early middle-aged men and women holding glasses of martini as though they were At Home with the Borgias. They stood at cocktail-stance, shoulders back and stomachs out. The room itself was furnished in very good taste, which was to say there was nothing in it that should not have been there and nothing absent that should have been present. The trouble was that with the people in the room everything looked slightly questionable so that you felt the good taste never came properly into its own and manifested itself in the main in the form of a somewhat forbidding silence from behind the closed double doors when you were on the other side of them and the room was empty, which you never were; being only invited for Thursdays.

Another thing: whenever he attended Aunt Clara's Thursdays he nowadays felt among those febrile and elegant women like licentious soldiery come to temporary rest at the end of an afternoon's street fighting. He was aware of bristle, sweat and the incongruity of worsted. Did the other men feel the same or were they in a state of cool, smooth comfort; decapillaried, deodorized by Yardley and dressed from head to foot in light-weight man-made fibres?

Tossing on his Bayswater cot he noticed that the house was having a restless night too; its old digestive trouble. 'I am neither Noah nor Charon,' he said, 'but Jonah.' The house was a whale. It lay with its poor, tender belly on the muddy, weed-thick bed of the London flood with its little eyes closed in an agony of concentration, holding its breath while it counted to twenty in an attempt to put a stop to the hiccups. Bubbles must have been rising from all its chimneys.

The people you met at Aunt Clara's were Thursday people. You never met them on any other day of the week and knew from the trend of the conversations which, like exhibitions of average pictures, could be walked in on and out of without making you feel any different, that they too never met each other except in the Butterfield Salon. Years ago you had known the names of the oldest of the habitués and they had known yours but these had been forgotten, having neither rung bells at the time nor become remarkable since. Occasionally a man or a woman would make an appearance, become remarkable and be seen no more in St. John's Wood; at least not on Thursdays. Aunt Clara seemed to see these people on other days. 'I wish you had looked in on Tuesday,' she said, 'X dropped in and was in splendid form, furious with Mr. Gaitskell.' 'Y dropped by on Monday and was most entertaining about her talk with Mr. Nkrumah.' 'Must you go? Do stay. Z may look in on his way to the Snows.' 'A has become an awful bore on the subject of Padre Pio.' 'B told Lord Russell he was using a pin to knock in a sledgehammer.' 'C swears she will never play at Stratford again.' 'D sang a splendid Tosca at the Garden on Wednesday but she was in tears about the conductor when she came in for a night-cap.' 'E had us in fits on Tuesday. He's invented a new game of gifts for authors, but he got stuck over Iris Murdoch because it was a toss-up between a severed head for Christmas and a samurai sword as part of a do-it-yourself Easter kit. He said he'd have to ask Iris which she preferred.'

George sat up and without putting on the light found his bedside note-book, held it slanting into the nocturnal Queensbury Road glow and wrote: Aunt Clara is a bloody liar. Before he put the note-book back again he changed the full-stop to a question mark. Aunt Clara is a bloody liar? He hated to wake up in the morning and find himself face to face with either memories or written evidence of dogmatic statements made in the night before, the closed eyes of someone whom sleep had taught him to dislike, yesterday's cigarette-ends, books opened at a page he had read, cups that he'd the cold dregs of night-cap tea. Before he turned out the light he always washed up, put a mark in the page following the one he had come to the end of, emptied his ash-tray. He also always tried to remember to put a question mark at the end of notes he made during bouts of sleeplessness. The sleeplessness was probably caused by the last minute exertions of tidying up. It was a vicious circle. If he was not sleeping alone he tried to stay awake until his companion had dropped off in order to be clear in his mind whether it was affection or distaste that he felt.

'Every day, make a new beginning,' he intoned aloud. The thought exhausted him and he fell asleep directly to dream again of the letter from Tim and of what it might be Tim wanted him to ring for, and of Tim's wife Sarah, mother of Andrew and of Gillian who looked like inheriting ten thousand pounds, and of his own wife Alice, married now to a man called Sam whom George hoped was kind to her.

In the morning there was another letter from Tim, sent care of the bank.

'DEAR GEORGE,

I'm sorry to have to write to you again but it struck me (*a*) that if you are in the country you might not ring unless I give permission for you to reverse the charge, which I do, and (*b*) that you might not ring even then unless I impress upon you the urgency of the situation. Well, *this* is the situation.

'I'm going to need that Two Hundred Pounds you owe me. I won't beat about the bush. Gillian is going to have a baby. You can imagine what this does to Sarah. Would you therefore telephone me at Bartle Wallingford without delay? Obviously we must meet to discuss ways and means. By the way, Sarah now knows about the money, but I didn't go into details, she simply knows you were in a jam. Well, now I'm in one, in the sense that my daughter is. She was to have sat for her Advanced Level GCE next year, but that's all done with. I have the unenviable job of withdrawing her from the school and explaining why to the Reverend Mother Superior.

TIM.'

Between half-past eight, when the letter arrived, and half-past nine when Tim could be expected at Bartle Wallingford, George made preparations for the day. He shaved, nicked his chin, wondering how poor Gillian could have got herself into such a mess so young, remembering she was his god-daughter – by proxy, true enough, all the way from Cairo, but god-daughter nevertheless. He had never done anything for her. He put on clean underwear and the best shirt he could find, brushed his best suit, polished his down-at-heel shoes. When he had finished dressing he counted his money: a pound note and some loose silver and copper. And it was going to be a gin day. The situation hardly looked promising. At half-past nine he selected the first of the day's pennies and then walked down the few stairs to the half-landing with as much dignity as he could muster in the circumstances.

Fourteen

George swallowed his beer with difficulty because Tim had said, 'What'll it be?' and he had replied, 'Half of bitter,' so as not to impose. Tim had said to the barmaid, 'Half of bitter and a large gin and tonic, please'; and now drank the beautiful opalescent fluid that sizzled between its slice of floating lemon and bobbing burden of ice chunks.

'Who is the father?' George asked.

'His name is Clayton. Christened Alastair but called Click,' Tim said. He had on a dark grey suit that looked new. There were only a few grey strands in the dark brown, close-cropped hair. His face looked squarer than ever, the jaw set against the idea of becoming a grandfather before his time.

'Click Clayton.'

'Yes.'

'How old is he?'

'The same as Gillian. Seventeen.'

George swallowed more beer. Beer, calm and bucolic, did nothing for his ears. At twelve o'clock as he left Queensbury Road for the City pub they had become partially detached from his head in anticipation of needing gin to cope with the interview. And it was now a quarter to one. He was hungry and one gin down. At the other end of the bar there were stools, a white cloth, knives, forks, bread plates with slices of french bread on them, a long two-tiered glass case with dishes of anchovy, roll-mops, pickled red cabbage, egg mayonnaise, smoked salmon, plain yellow cheese, red-skinned cheese and cheese with crumbly blue veins, green olives, black olives, a joint of cold, bloody beef with a crisp fat, a dish of cold roast chickens with their legs tied up as if they were being forcibly converted to a new religion, Scotch eggs, a jar of gherkins, two jars of pickled onions gleaming round and pale in dark brown fluid, a shoulder of cold boiled ham with a lovely greasy, crinkly skin, rows of glistening goblets and little fans of clean white paper napkins.

Tim kept his back to the food and said, 'Well, George. What about this money?'

'I haven't got it.'

'That's what you *say*.'

'You can go and see my bank manager,' George said. 'I daren't.'

'How much do you owe him?'

'Nothing. I owe the bank.'

'I meant the bank,' Tim said patiently.

'Seventy-five pounds. It may be more or less. All I know is I can't cash a cheque yet.'

'It's not yet the third week of the month.'

'I know. I've got a calendar too.'

'You can't have got through your month's allowance already.'

'And a clock that ticks. What?'

'You can't have got through your month's allowance already.'

'It's income, not an allowance.'

'Whatever you call it.'

'I got behind with things.'

'Ten years to be more or less precise.'

'I don't mean the Two Hundred.'

'That's all I'm interested in.'

George sipped his beer. Tim drained his gin and said, 'Have you anything you can sell?'

'If I had would I be wearing this?' He showed Tim his shirt-cuff which was frayed. From the look on Tim's face George guessed Tim thought the shirt had been put on for the occasion. Tim glanced from George's shirt-cuff to his own empty glass.

'Well, you can buy me another of these. Your pockets jingle when you put your hands in.'

George bought him a gin and tonic, mostly with pennies and sixpences. When the girl slid the glass towards him and took his money, scooping it long-nailed out of a puddle, he weakened, said, 'And another half of bitter,' because his ears were hanging on his shoulders.

Tim said, 'You've got to admit I've been patient. You aren't banking on the Statute of Limitations by any chance?'

'The what?'

'Don't pretend you don't know what the Statute of Limitations is. In your Sloane Street days you told me a man could make a living from it.'

'I said people did, not that I did.'

'Yes, all right.'

'There's only one thing I can do. Pay you back so much a quarter.'

'So much a month would be better. So much a week would be better still. Either way the needle's stuck in the groove. It's what you've always said, but I'm sticking out for a lump sum.'

'How much?' George asked, hopeful of compounding a debt, if only in principle.

'Two hundred Pounds.'

After a while George said, 'Why?'

'Because I've got to make it tough for you, George. It was Sarah's money as much as mine.'

'Was it?'

'All our money is on joint account. Savings Certificates, Deposit account and Current account. Joint.'

'What I mean was why do you need it, Tim? To help Gillian set up house?'

'I'm sorry,' Tim said, 'but of course you don't know. Click Clayton is a plumber's mate.'

'Do plumbers do well, then?'

'I neither know nor care,' Tim replied. He had got that saying from their mother. What does Mr. Proctor do? I neither know nor care. A dispiriting thought came into George's mind. He said, 'Do you want me to pay two hundred pounds to help you to set Master Clayton up in some sort of business?'

'What?'

'Business more in keeping with Gillian's social status?'

'Social status?'

'Consulting engineer or something.'

'What are you talking about?'

'I don't know. My ears are dropping off. Master Plumber.'

'I said he was a plumber's mate, not a Master Plumber.'

'The undoubted father of my first grand-nephew or -niece?'

Tim said, 'Who can tell? That is what knocks me. Who can bloody well tell? Do you know what she said? She said, "It just happened." If it just happened with Click Clayton why couldn't it have happened as well with Rod Starling?'

'Who's Rod Starling?'

Tim shrugged. 'One of the others.'

'The others?'

'The others. They are all over the place. Click Clayton, Rod Starling, Rick Wragge, Sandra Hardcastle.'

'Is Sandra Hardcastle a girl or a boy?'

'A girl. She was expelled from Gillian's school last year for smoking.'

'It couldn't have happened with Sandra Hardcastle.'

'What couldn't?'

'You said if it just happened with Click Clayton why couldn't it have just happened with Rod Starling or one of the others.'

'I didn't say that. I was reciting the names of Gillian's set. They know everything. I expect they know more than Sarah and I do. Sandra Hardcastle told me all nuns are sublimated lesbians. Young Andrew says —'

'Your Andrew?'

'My Andrew. Andrew says his form-master is a practising queer. They know it all, but apparently the old thing still happens. That's what I marvel at. When I said to Clayton's father, Well aren't you going to give him something to remember, he said: The young bugger's bigger than me, and I always said as 'ow no good would come of it. He calls Mrs. Clayton Ma and only really cares about his rose-trees. You know the type.'

'They're not denying it, then.'

'Who's not denying what?'

'The Claytons aren't denying Click's responsibility.'

'I don't think the word responsibility occurs to them, but in the way you mean, no, they're not denying it.'

'It's for the wedding, then.'

'What's for the wedding?'

'The Two Hundred Pounds is for Gillian's and Click's wedding.'

'They aren't getting married.'

'Who's decision is that, Click's or Gillian's?'

'It's my decision.'

'What about the baby?'

'We shall have it adopted,' Tim said, not looking at him straight.

George swallowed more beer. He wanted a cigarette but there were only two Bachelors left in the crumpled packet which lay in the dark, fluffy recesses of his coat pocket. He took another sip, pulled the packet out and offered the cigarettes to Tim. Tim took one and he took the last. He squashed the packet and placed it lightly on top of an overfull ashtray on the bar.

'Is your lighter working?' George asked. Tim's lighter was of gold. George did not exactly covet it, but it gave him that drained feeling of pleasure looking at something far beyond his means always gave him: a Rolls-Royce Silver Cloud, or anything in the windows of Asprey's, for instance. He was glad for Tim that Tim actually owned the lighter. He hoped Tim had saved up for it hard and hadn't had it as a gift or bought it on the spur of the moment. Tim had always had it in him to save up for things and never to buy things on the spur of the moment, but George didn't have the heart to ask about the lighter in case it turned out to be a symbol of spend-thriftery, of Tim succumbing to the Age of Extended Credit in the way that he, George, had succumbed to the Age of Dud Cheques when middle- and lower-class men had come back from the wars with commissions, infinitesimal bank accounts and their childhood ways of pinch and scrape utterly depraved by the habit of signing chits and little green slips of paper with the name Lloyds or Grindlays on them. His own little green slips of paper (changed now to pink) unlike those carefully and thoughtfully distributed by their father, had more often been marked 'Refer to Drawer' than 'Paid'. Tim was lucky not to have risen above the rank of Flight-sergeant in the war and never to have gone abroad On Active Service where Drawers tended to be in places awkward if not downright impossible to refer to.

He said, 'An abortion doesn't cost two hundred pounds.'

Tim's eyes became glazed. 'Who said anything about an abortion?'

'These days you can get it on the health.'

'Nonsense.'

'Or you can pay by instalments. The finance companies actually prefer it because of the interest. All you need is a certificate of reduced responsibility and in cases of unmarried girls in the pudding club it's like falling off a log.'

'What's like falling off a log?'

'Proving reduced responsibility, and getting a certificate so that you can do it on the Health in hospital or get a grant-in-aid for doing it in style on the instalment plan in a flash nursing home.'

'What are we talking about?'

'Your two hundred pounds,' George said. He drained his half-pint tankard and placed it carefully on the bar. 'Will you buy me a gin?' he asked.

Tim hesitated, looked at his watch. The strap was gold too. 'You oughtn't to mix them,' he said, but ordered two small Gordons and smiled the bleak smile that reminded George of the times he took Tim to the threepenny Saturday afternoon seats to see films like *The Dawn Patrol* and *Wings*, because it was the smile Tim used to smile on a Friday night as they came past the Capitol and paused to look at the stills and George said: Do you want to see it? Before they went their mother used to say: Just see that he wraps up when you come out, you know what he is. At the box office Tim used to count out his own three pennies and gave them to George like a company director declaring a dividend, with the air, indeed, of a boy not otherwise beholden, but George always bought the bag of toffees for them both unless it was raining in which case the sweet money went on tram fares.

Tim now counted out the money for two gins and tonics, which showed that they had grown up and entered the world of affairs. He said, 'I've got to go soon. What am I to tell Sarah?'

George savoured the smell of the gin. What was Tim to tell Sarah? A man was obligated to his wife when it came to money. He said, 'That I'll pay it back.'

'How?'

'I'll pay it back.'

'When?'

He drank some of the gin. His ears came slowly back into position, one on each side of his head.

'Next week at the latest,' he said.

'What are you going to do, rob a bank?'

That was one of their mother's sayings, too.

'No, I'll see the Butterfield lawyer.'

'You can't touch the capital.'

'I know. I might get an advance on the income.'

'Two hundred pounds would be a half a year's income if your capital's still paying four per cent.'

'I could get a job.'

'You ought to do that in any case. As I've been telling you ever since before Alice and you got a —'

'All right.'

'I've got to send her away, you see,' Tim said.

'Who? Gillian?'

'And Sarah will have to go with her.'

'Yes, I see that.'

'It means keeping two homes going and a woman in to see about Andrew's dinner when he gets back from school.'

'They don't grow on trees.'

'And Sarah will have to come back every other weekend otherwise it'll look as if she's left me. Then there's the direct expense, doctor, nursing home, layette or whatever you call it. It's killing Sarah, you know. But I've got her to see it's the only way.'

'Keep it dark and make no fuss.'

'It costs money.'

'Isn't young Clayton —'

'Bugger young Clayton.'

'Well —'

'Father didn't pinch and scrape to send us to a decent school so that one of his grandchildren should marry a plumber's mate.'

Tim only mentioned their father, but George guessed they were both thinking more of their mother who would have died of shame. How can I show my face, she would have said, where am I to look when I walk out of this house and down the street?

'Mother would have died of shame,' George said and Tim's face went quite blank as it always did if their mother was mentioned because he had quarrelled with her forever about Sarah six months after his marriage and six months before she and their father had died together in the country of the bomb that left little Guy orphaned with both his older brothers away to the wars, Sarah in the WAAF, Alice in Cairo, all strangers to him.

'Well, you know what you're doing,' George said, 'but it's a bit cold-blooded.'

'What's cold-blooded?'

'Sending her away with Sarah to have Click Clayton's kid

alone in some shifty-eyed nursing home that charges double for bringing unmarried mothers to bed of their illegitimate off-spring.'

'She's not marrying the Clayton boy.'

'Does she want to?'

'She's too young in my opinion to know her own mind so why ask her?'

'But has she ever said she wants to?'

'She only shrugs her shoulders. And young Clayton shrugs his. It's the answer to everything you ask their generation. "Like I just got careless, Mister Spruce, like the both of us must 'ave got careless." '

'Where did she meet him?'

'You can't say she met him. They've both grown up in the district. They went to the local primary school. Gill went on to the convent and later I suppose young Clayton failed his eleven plus and went on with the rag tag and bobtail filling in time until he was fifteen and got this job as a plumber's mate. Not even our plumber, so she didn't meet him in the house changing a washer. She can't remember where she first noticed him as she puts it. She says, "Click was just around." Have you ever thought what around means to a father like me with a daughter? Around means the Church Hall, the Youth Club, the swimming pool, the shopping centre, the Italian coffee bars, the pictures, the street-corners, not to mention the road to and from school and the park and the passage called Snog Alley, and Sandra Hardcastle's living-room.'

'If it isn't too painful a subject, where did Gillian and Click —'

'It didn't seem necessary to ask. Knowing would somehow make it worse. And the fact is that I hardly dared ask in case they both shrugged their shoulders and said they couldn't quite remember because they'd been careless in so many different places.'

'You'd say Gillian was taking all this in her stride?'

'She takes everything in her stride, the eleven plus, School Certificate Ordinary Level, tennis and basket-ball and now this. They don't care you see, George, clever or dumb they don't feel any kind of obligation.'

'And Sarah's getting used to the idea.'

'Yes, she is.'

'And you're resigned to it.'

'Yes, I am.'

'And Click Clayton gets off scot-free without even an affiliation order.'

'We don't want an affiliation order connecting Gillian's baby to a plumber's mate.'

'And I've got to contribute two hundred pounds towards this curious state of affairs.'

'Is that quite the way to put it? I'm the one who's spending two hundred pounds, much more than two hundred —'

'You and Sarah.'

'I and Sarah.' Tim paused. 'You are simply being asked to pay back the two hundred pounds I gave you to put back into the kitty of the Bucket Club to save you going to prison.'

For a moment each was silent.

'Buy me another gin,' George said.

Almost, Tim did so. His hand went automatically to his wallet pocket, but then he changed his mind, or noticed what he was doing and stopped.

'George, I'm damned if I will. You'll never get a proper hold of yourself while there are fools like me too damned soft-hearted to say no.'

'I've got a pound in my pocket. I could buy us both a gin, but how do I eat until the end of the month?'

He called to the barmaid, 'Two large gins and tonics, please.'

Tim said, 'You'll have to pay for them yourself because I'm going.'

'Then I'll drink them myself.'

'That's right.'

'Where are you going?'

'I've a one-fifteen lunch appointment at Simpson's.'

'That only leaves you ten minutes to get there, but they keep it all hot under huge silver-plated covers. I want to see Gillian.'

'Why?'

'She's my god-daughter.'

'She doesn't believe in God, neither do you.'

'Oh, yes, I believe in God all right. He made Click Clayton and Gillian Spruce careless and He made me offer you a drink out of my last quid because I don't want you to go until you've bought me a ham sandwich. And He made me want to see my god-daughter before I agree to pay you back two hundred pounds.'

'When I lent it to you did I say: I lend you this money for one week, or one month or one year? Did I stipulate a time for repayment?'

'No.'

'Have I ever said: I want that money back now?'

'You've said it today.'

'That's where the Statute of Limitations comes in, George. The six years during which I can sue you start from today, or if we have to be absolutely accurate about it, from the date of my last letter to you.'

'If you sued me I should deny the whole thing.'

'I've kept the cheque I made out in your name endorsed by you and marked Paid by the bank.'

'Can you prove I've never settled the debt?'

'Can you prove you did?'

The barmaid said, 'That'll be nine and tenpence, sir.'

Tim said, 'Goodbye, George. I'll hear from you within a week, then.'

'Yes, all right.'

'And Gillian doesn't want to see anyone.'

'No. I see. By taking two hundred pounds away from me you're ruining my chances of marrying again and having children of my own and leading a decent life.'

'And I don't want you trying to get round Sarah.'

'No, all right.'

'I've got to make it tough for you, George. Somebody should have years ago.'

'I know.'

'Bye bye, George.'

'Goodbye, Tim.'

When Tim went George fished out his last pound note and gave it to the barmaid. He lined up the two gins and tonics and studied them.

When I am with Tim, he thought, I never talk about the things that matter to me.

But then this was so whoever you talked to face to face. The telephone was better, if you could get a word in edgeways which you hardly could with Aunt Clara, or if you could ignore the sounds of disquiet and disagreement coming from the other end which you seldom could with someone like Tim. Nevertheless next to letters, postcards, journals and memoirs the telephone was the most satisfactory form of communication. Hello, Tim, is that you (he would say). Look, I want to get rid of this burden of two hundred pounds. No, I can't pay it back, I want you to formalize the position that exists, by writing it off. It has got to the stage where I should rather have gone to prison. I know I was dumb with terror at the time but then if you hadn't been terror struck yourself at the idea of having your elder brother in jail you wouldn't have paid the money over. Now you want it back so that Gillian shan't bring a plumber's mate into the family. If you were prepared to lose Two Hundred Pounds to stop having a jailbird brother why aren't you prepared to lose Two Hundred Pounds in the process of avoiding a plumber's mate son-in-law? You are an accountant and you have a logical mind when it comes to economics and the value to be set on things. No, don't interrupt. You aren't going to say anything that will make me think differently because you never do. I can't afford Two Hundred Pounds to help you to support Gillian's and Click's baby. Just how well you were able to afford Two Hundred Pounds to keep your brother out of jail I can only guess but the fact of the matter is you had Two Hundred Pounds you could put your hands on and I haven't, and you'll send Gillian and her mother away to this shifty-eyed nursing home whether you get the two hundred pounds back from me or not. To sue me now for the Two Hundred Pounds you gave me to keep me out of jail will remove the last shred of loving charity that was ever connected to the original giving. Is that how you want it? No, Tim, you're going to have to write that Two Hundred Pounds off. If you sued me and obtained judgment you'd then have to make me bankrupt and no doubt the bankruptcy people would then be in charge of my Butterfield income. But they couldn't *make* me work for my living – I don't say I wouldn't but they couldn't make me – and even a bankrupt is allowed living expenses. What kind of money would be left out of my Four Hundred Pounds a year once the bankruptcy people had had to earmark so much a week for me to live on? How much would be left to settle the debt bit by bit and how many years would it take? When you look those facts in the face your threats about the Statute of Limitations are cut down to size. They are bullying threats. Only a frightened man resorts to bullying. Why are you frightened? You can't be frightened of me, you never were, and mother is dead, Sarah adores the ground under your feet, you have a partnership in a small but reputable firm of accountants in the City, you've kept your nice home dry and your healthy children fed, you've never been politically involved or socially conscious except on the what-will-the-neighbours-think level. You aren't gathering together all your resources like Noah when the Lord tipped him the wink about the Flood. Your fear isn't the cosmic, detached kind. You are just frightened. A frightened man. You were never a frightened little boy. You slept sound, ate solid and smiled your funny smile which made you look a hundred years old, handed out your threepence, caught colds, plodded through school and left it at the age of sixteen with no change of expression, no show of feeling hard done by in comparison with me. You always seemed to know what you wanted. If you know what you want you ought not to be frightened. It's only people who don't know what they want who are frightened.

Fifteen

'"If you don't know what you want, George," I told him,' said Lady Butterfield, speaking obliquely between sips of her lunch-time liquid slimming diet into the neat little microphone that was attached to the Grundig by a white, plastic covered cable that looked like an umbilical cord connecting a small machine to a larger, '"then you had better stay at school as no doubt your cousin Roderick intends."

'At that meeting I was at pains to make three things clear to the boy. One. Whom he called Uncle was cousin. Two. I had nothing to do with overt acts of charity towards the Spruces beyond a tea now and then in the public rooms of the Langham and the cost, if I remember correctly, of a hackney limousine to convey Violet Spruce between her suburb and Bayswater to show me the baby and to collect the silver christening mug which Roderick had at last got down to buying from Mappin and Webb. Three. That it was Roderick alone, having Bosworth no longer to consider, who made an arrangement to assist Harold Spruce to send his elder boy to a local private school and that in consequence he, George, should in no way consider himself beholden to *me*.

'"This little school Roderick sends you to," I pointed out, "will fit you for nothing." Clearly he was puzzled. "Aunt Clara," he said (no use at all to resist that "aunt", it was a symbol for him of self-identification and he was, in his way, charming in spite of his hands and hair) "what do you mean?" I pointed out that unless he went on to a university (which he would not because Roderick wouldn't pay for it) he would be worse off in the future than a grammar school boy, worse off even than a country school boy. A private school, if it was gone to after the age of thirteen or so, was neither fish nor fowl. "You will have no status whatsoever," I told him, "and even a board-school boy has status because his position in society is clearly defined and recognizable by others. If your status is clear you can improve it, but if it is not clear by what standard will any actual improvement be judged?" "I see what you mean, Aunt Clara," he said. He was really very sweet and amenable and I regretted the fact that, as was fairly plain, he would never be a force.

'At this point in our private talk, Roderick came down with his list of fixtures for Lord's. There were some minor matches to which Roderick thought there would be no harm in taking a poor relation. George had been to The Oval or whatever it is called with his father but, as Roderick said, a boy's sense of geography of London must begin in St. John's Wood, after which it may end anywhere it pleases. "But not," I said to Roderick when George had expressed his thanks and taken his leave politely, "in your little flat near the Marble Arch." "Bless me, Clara, what are you saying?" Roderick enquired. It is curious how these little snatches of conversation come back to one.

'Perhaps my enlivened interest in George Spruce, even although I recognized he would never become a force, was prompted by my determination that Roderick should not take him to the Marble Arch. However, I must admit that after he had gone from the Langham that afternoon his personality impinged. He was seventeen and I was fifty. Roderick was sixty-five apart from anything else. It came to me that evening during the second act of Tristan that what George had it in him to be was a charmer, and I thought it only fair to help him to cultivate this aspect of his nature, because charm is a status in itself. There are the Rulers and the Ruled, but mid-way between them come the Charmers. When I considered all the ramifications of the situation I became quite elevated and was glad Roderick had stopped rustling and gone to sleep. There is nothing like a dozing companion and the music of Wagner to aid concentration.'

Sixteen

Harry was most insistent on a good north light for the colour, said Miss Lisle, whose eyes were open because she had got through the night and well into the next afternoon without dying. He was almost finicky about the light you could say. It has to be north, Ada, he said, because north is reflected light and reflected light stays still in the room and keeps level. I wasn't trained for anything you see Ada, he said, I wasn't trained for anything because of my father's note of hand.

Vi always said there was a Mr. Woburn living fat on money that should have come to Harry Spruce but didn't because of Harry's father's note of hand. The Woburns weren't gentlefolk like the Spruces but Harry's father's note of hand was a gentleman's word, so it all went when Harry's father's partner failed and Mr. Woburn called the note in and Harry's father was ruined and his children were put out to work and it killed their mother. People who are born to income, Ada, Vi said, don't understand business, and Harry being the eldest boy it all fell on him. When I think of a man like Harry working and slaving from morning till night, she said, while parvenus like the Woburns never make a hand's stir I could go out and murder somebody.

Poor Vi. Sometimes I thought it was Harry she was going to murder. Sitting there, she said, on his backside in his good north light painting little pictures when Mr. Proctor next door goes off every morning in his car earning good money like a proper husband should.

'Miss Lisle?' Mr. Stainsby enquired because Miss Lisle's lips hadn't moved since last night, only her head moved and her eyes kept opening and shutting, and her legs were restless.

It wasn't a happy home, Miss Lisle told the shade of Mr. Stainsby who sometimes looked like Mr. Stainsby and sometimes like a stranger. We've always been such a happy family, Ada, she said, but it wasn't true, although in a way it was true because when she said it she believed it and what you believe is real in a way, only I don't think I believe in anything any more, so nothing is real Mr. Stainsby. Only I remember I was always fond of Harry and I never had letters or ribbons like Miss Pamela. Miss Pamela will see I'm provided for.

Seventeen

'That autumn when we went back to Manorlord Mount,' Lady Butterfield continued, holding the Grundig's microphone in one hand and, in the other, one of the Floris chocolates for which her lunchtime liquid slimming diet always gave her an appetite, 'I made a few little plans for the following year when George would leave this curious private school of his and launch himself as best he might into what society he could.'

Here Lady Butterfield paused to pop the Floris chocolate into her mouth and having lost her thread switched the Grundig to Play Back without reversing the tape.

'Pure power,' it said almost immediately in Clara Butterfield's own voice. A bit startled she stared at the machine and thought for a moment that it had taken on a life of its own, but realized then that when using it in the bathroom the day before she must have turned the wrong knob and recorded those words far along the tape, in isolation. Its announcement of these words now, Lady Butterfield thought, showed what a remarkable instrument it was and what a force Mr. Grundig had been or was, depending on whether or no he was dead, because the words 'Pure Power' were a splendidly apposite *aide-mémoire*, coming as they did at a time when she herself had become conscious of losing the thread of her argument, of rambling, of becoming – perhaps – enmeshed in the net of a reconjured *jeu d'esprit*.

She turned the machine off and collected her thoughts. When she had collected them she switched it on again and continued.

'Pure power is the power we exercise from a position of anonymity or from an apparently recognizable position which is in fact so ambivalent as to rank as anonymous. My position in regard to young George was certainly ambivalent. In the following July when he ceased to be a schoolboy I invited him to spend a week with us at the Mount. During this week I intentionally put off other people from coming and accepted no invitations. We had recently installed a swimming pool and many a sunny afternoon did I spend, relaxing in the country air at the water's edge, breathing in the faintly soapy smell of chlorine, while George swam merrily from side to side and Roderick dangled his thin white legs in the shallow end and occasionally went in with a hollow sound. Swimming, Roderick always reminded me of a turtle that had been deprived of its casing. By his side George looked, as it were, sprightly. He had a splendid set of genitalia, set off discreetly but to a nicety by little black trunks of the type recently come into fashion to displace those curious garments with holes under the shoulder blades which seemed made for Roderick. I found it pleasant to have him sit on the ground by my chair in his dripping, newly emerged state. He had remarkably handsome ears, was letting his hair grow and curing himself of the habit of biting his nails. He smoked cigarettes with a rather endearing air of not being utterly committed to the mystique of tobacco, but without awkwardness and entirely without the vulgarity of gesture one might have expected of a boy who came from that particular environment.

'He was, of course, somewhat self-conscious of manners, because these were things he had been taught by his mother who picked them up as she went along. It was upon such failings in myself that my duchess was wont to remark although, as she said, my natural ill-temper would always stand me in good stead among the upper-classes so long as I remembered never to vent it directly upon menial persons. In a man, however, manners are most easily remarked if they are not exactly in keeping with a given situation because there are more of them for men to observe than there are for women.

'However, if one is going to acquire status through Charm obtrusive manners are no drawback. It goes without saying that a charmer has risen from a lower level of society than the one in which you find him, although with so many of the upper-classes hard put to it to make ends meet it goes less without saying now than it went without saying then.

'The first thing I had to do was stop Roderick from putting George to Tea, Rubber or Tin – occupations which at first glance he had seemed perfectly suited to because those industries which were such admirable sources of income for Us had to be run by men who actually believed in the spiritual side of the Empire. Boys who had that unnaturally healthy look of the open air invariably had as well this spiritual myopia. No amount of study in the branches of history and economics stopped them from putting on shorts and topee at an early age and being Off, East of Suez in search of that elusive and unwieldy bag of feathers – the White Man's Burden – if once they had succumbed to the lure of the poor man's Disraeli, Mr. Rudyard Kipling. I speak of this social phenomenon in the past tense, naturally enough.

'It was, of course, entertaining to watch Roderick engaging the boy's interest in the Sungei Labong five per cents and the Bukit Kallang Development equity by conducting him on murmurous summer mornings into the vault-like chill of our little palladium museum where the paraphernalia of Butterfield endeavour and Butterfield leisure was preserved by the art of the taxidermist or was to be found in its original state under glass or upon the walls (gone now, alas, like Manorlord Mount on Roderick's Estate-Duty ridden death). Drums, flags, armour and weapons of divers kinds stood guard over rare, oriental, African, Antipodean and West Indian exotica, but it was to the display cabinets of the natural rubber and minerals of the Federated Malay States my husband and my young cousin chiefly turned their attention. When I saw in George's eye the kindling of a stoic passion for all that lay there under the glass I judged the time had come to put a spoke into Roderick's wheel, because George deserved better of this world than a career, especially a colonial one.

'That is the one advantage of charm. With it a man may breathe the rarefied air of the summit without having to employ an artificial aid of approach. Almost, you could say, charm is the masculine equivalent of an impecunious duchess although better because the owner is born with it or acquires it during his upbringing with no cost to his pocket. How fascinatingly simple and clearly defined are the layers of civilized society. Given birth or an acquired equivalent position one may always use if not necessarily obtain wealth because wealth inevitably finds its way to the top. Roderick, for instance, made use of mine. Given enough cows any African savage may be a chief, but he will not be unless he recognizes the truth of this dictum for there are always older chiefs (like Roderick) who had cows and have cows no longer because of vicissitudes and who are waiting to turn his cows to their own advantage. An experience and an understanding of cows are better, any day, than cows themselves. An experience and an understanding of cows, together with cows, render one's position at the top unassailable.

'Down in the very bottom of those dank and misty hollows there dwell those who have neither cows nor experience nor understanding of cows (although among them, scattered like good seed in a bad crop, can sometimes be found the true-born) but it is mostly among the ranks of those in the middle station in life that one looks for the Forces of tomorrow, or – to revert to our simile from the dark continent (dark, alas, no longer) – looks for the young men who are in the process of acquiring cows with their eyes on a fancy head-dress. Men who are Forces but lack birth and position, or charm, needs must seek a career as a means of approach. The man who knows the subtle distinction between doing a job and having a career is a potential Force, and the man who knows the distinction between having a career and being a careerist has practically arrived, but the majority of them get lost by romantic waysides and end up no better than those who merely work, as they call it, for a living.

'Perhaps scarcely one in each half-million of men and women born are destined to be forces. Force does not depend upon class. Force defies class. The Upper-class has always had the sense to see this and has always opened its ranks to admit a genuine Force, such as myself, should that Force wish to enter. Should the day ever come when the English Upper-class closes its ranks to a Force that is thrusting upwards then we shall see the sun catch the sharp edge of the guillotine in all the bosky squares of our ancient city.'

Here Lady Butterfield paused. She was not sure about bosky squares, just a little perturbed by ancient city and more than half ready to scrub the sun on the sharp edge of the guillotine. She could almost hear her duchess say, 'If you mean see our bloody heads cut off, say so.'

Raising the microphone again she said, 'The very latest thing in literary fashion is the satirical cliché.'

And this, having been said, was undoubtedly so.

Eighteen

It was now half-past two in the afternoon and George could no longer put off his visit to the bank if he were to see and talk to Gillian. The bank was ten minutes walk away from the station he had taken up on the embankment near Blackfriars bridge. He had come to the embankment to breathe Thames air in through his mouth in order to get rid of the worst of the smell of gin; and the back of his throat now felt like he imagined the throat of a seagull felt to a seagull that had keened all the way from Southend to Westminster.

It was a cool day, intermittently sunny whenever the pale,

smoky-bottomed clouds drifted away from their moorings on currents that swept them across a widening gulf of blue over and onwards towards Rochester and Gillingham. The doors of the bank were glass, beautifully bevelled and balanced and smoothly hinged but somewhat heavy in the initial stages of opening. Paid in or paid out, money was always given this pause, as it were in gentle contradiction of the slogan easy come easy go.

The interior of the bank was over-heated. There were two courses of action open. He could brazen out the handing over of a cheque made out to cash to a clerk who was new, junior or sleepy; or he could ask to see the manager, which on the whole he preferred the idea of because it rang a change on the more customary note of the manager asking to see him whenever he showed his face and someone at the back recognized it waiting there at the grille, patient, expectant, and hopeful both of money and anonymity, and went on Judas feet to knock at the frosted glass door, open it and say, 'Excuse me, sir, we thought you'd like to know Mr. Spruce is In.'

He took up a position on a broad front, between two grilles, and waited to catch the eye of either one of the two clerks who were being impersonal in the presence of what looked like millions of pounds sterling, but which in the one case he was able to check by adjusting the angle of his head and reading the total of a paying-in book upside down disappointingly said: Two hundred and forty-eight pounds, eight shillings and twopence, which was less than he received in a year.

'Is Mr. Jones in?' he said when the opportunity came. 'George Lisle-Spruce.'

Without really recognizing that he did so, because he was so accustomed to doing it, he watched the clerk's face for the little flicker of nervous apprehension of becoming involved in a situation bigger than both of them; but the clerk was new, and young, and had his life before him, and George hoped that it would be a good life, that he would find a good woman to care for him and keep his collars white and feed him up. George hoped this because the clerk smiled a smile that had no malice in it, no disapproval, no fear, no knowledge, and was thin and slightly grubby with it. It is only at strangers a man can smile nowadays, George thought; he can smile at strangers and talk into the telephone.

The clerk, George noticed, was not even aware of the Look that came on to the face that rose from behind the barrier when he leaned over it and delivered George's message, or if he noticed it, it made no difference because he smiled coming back the same smile he had smiled when going, and murmured something that had a 'sir' in it.

'Mr. Jones,' he said ten minutes later, 'I want you to perform an act of charity.'

'You mean you want some money.'

'Please.'

'How much money?'

'Ten pounds.'

Mr. Jones did not have a clock that ticked audibly. He had a clock that went by electricity. It was mounted on the wall where his customers could see it but he himself could not unless he swivelled round on his green leather swivel chair. Mr. Jones's clock had a slender red needle that went round in time with the seconds. It went round very smoothly, as if in deference to a Winged Chariot which had rubber tyres and was not allowed to sound its horn in a built-up area, especially after lunch. The thin red needle had a look of Time sweeping all before it, which was a change from being dragged, although, when you thought about it, even more cavalier. It was sweeping everything up in order to have things tidy by three o'clock when the clerks stopped giving out money and began counting it, and the building was cleared of all clients except any of those who owned most of the money being counted and who were present and who had the right to sit on here in Mr. Jones's Burma teak office with their feet on the bottle-green Wilton drinking orange-pekoe tea that would come on a tray set with china from Heal's.

I shall delay until October when the leaves are falling. We'll have muffins and Earl Grey.

'I suppose We can manage Ten Pounds,' Mr. Jones said and rang a bell. 'I'll have the Money brought while you Write out the Cheque.'

'Thank you,' George said, who had long ago run out of Appropriate Expressions of Gratitude. He rested his little book of pink slips on the Burma teak table and filled one out with his old Parker 51, the model that had a lustraloy cap and wasn't quite as expensive as the model with a cap of gold, but Alice had given it to him for his thirty-fifth birthday and it was indestructible and knew every stroke of his signature.

The head that appeared round the door a few seconds after Mr. Jones had rung the bell now came back attached to a body that had arms and hands and held in one of the hands ten new one pound notes which were given in exchange for the pink slip. When George was alone again with Mr. Jones, Mr. Jones said, 'I'm afraid we can't Accommodate you again until you've Paid something In. We aren't Alone, Mr. Spruce. We live under the Surveillance of Head Office.'

Mr. Jones always talked in capital letters. The use of capital letters married irony to authority. Banks were full of the symbols of this combination. Above their doors, as above the proscenium arch of a theatre, but invisible, hung the masks of pain and pleasure. Inside the door, on the faces of the staff, there was The Look, The Slight Frown, even The Beam. George had never met The Beam head on, but he had intercepted it at an angle to its line of approach and had even turned his head to get a good look at its recipient.

'I quite understand,' George said, meaning he understood about the surveillance of Head Office and the impossibility of Further Accommodation, but not that he understood why he had been allowed to Draw ten pounds today. He did not actively consider this problem in case it Showed on his Face.

'By the way,' Mr. Jones said, 'was it your brother's play I saw on television a few weeks ago?'

'Oh, you mean Guy.'

'That's right. I thought I remembered his name was Guy and your telling me once he was trying to write plays. So when his name Came up on the Screen I thought: That must be Mr. Lisle-Spruce's brother the one who Isn't an Accountant. It wasn't quite my cup of tea but the Man on the *Telegraph* wrote it up well and so did the Man on the *Times*. Your brother must have been Pleased.'

'I'm sure he was. I haven't seen him recently.'

A hurrying cloud passed over the city on its way to catch the ebb tide in the Medway, so George added, in case Mr. Jones changed his mind about the ten pounds, 'But I expect to See and Congratulate him this evening at Lady Butterfield's.'

The sun peeped through again, lighting upon the smooth Burmese teak and the comfortable Wilton.

'What a pity,' Mr. Jones said, 'that Sir Roderick Tied up the Capital.'

When Mr. Jones started on this tack, which he only did when in a good mood, George always hoped he had some clever suggestion to make about how the law relating to Trustees might be got round, but he never did have: his little soliloquy on the subject of George's legacy never varied and always ended on a dying fall; but this was better than nothing, better than the attitude of the previous manager which had been one of rigid, unequivocal acceptance of the stony laws of property and inheritance.

'But of course,' Mr. Jones continued, 'in those days the income he left you was worth so much more than it is today. I suppose it was the equivalent of what eight or nine hundred a year would be now, and we've got to be thankful that the Capital was in Farm Mortgages and not in Gilt Edged. You can't always rely on Trustees to Sell Out at the right moment and Reinvest Wisely, and as it is they haven't had to consider the problem of reinvestment at all. If the capital had been in Gilt Edged and had been left there the eventual Beneficiary would have been In for a Shock. Not that Anything is Certain These Days, but on the whole I think we've got to accept that Sir Roderick did very well for you, certainly within the terms of reference Applicable Then.'

This was George's signal to rise.

'Tell your brother how much we all enjoyed his play at home,' Mr. Jones said. 'We don't get a very clear picture but it Came Over very well.'

Outside in the cold air he felt light-headed. He had ten pounds in his pocket. Sound was travelling far in search of attentive ears to die on. A draft of St. Paul's pigeons fluttered overhead looking for olive branches. 'The floods are going down,' George said to himself, and smiled at the thought of Mr. Jones one day emerging from his bank and having to pick his way along the barnacle-encrusted pavements.

Nineteen

At a few minutes after three he entered the still flooded underground railway system where the big predators lurked, swooping out of their caves at intervals to shovel up mouthfuls of self-sacrificial minnows. He bought an evening paper on the way in and after the minor inconveniences of the booking hall (slapping a machine to make it eject the ticket that now belonged to him by right) delivered himself to the sliding staircase.

It was not a very good sliding staircase. There was something wrong with the wheels that you couldn't see, and ought not to be able to feel with the soles of your feet but in this case did; and the handbelt moved faster than the stair. He leaned on the handbelt and read the advertisements that went by on the opposite side until his position became untenable. Letting go of the belt he straightened up and mentally counted his money. Change from his last pound note, ten and twopence, plus two shillings and sixpence in pennies and sixpences, less threepence for the *Evening Standard*, less one shilling and threepence for the ticket machine; that gave him eleven and twopence. Add Mr. Jones's ten pounds and you had a total of ten pounds eleven shillings and twopence. Or, to put it another way, ten guineas basic capital and one and twopence petty cash. To put it another way yet he was one hundred and eighty-nine pounds eight shillings and tenpence short of Two Hundred Pounds, and he would get shorter and shorter as the day went by. The only way he could stop getting shorter was by going up and down the sliding staircases for the rest of the afternoon and on into the night until the staircases stopped with a jerk some time during what people called the small hours but which were actually very large and threatening and long and certainly dangerous to be found in half way up a staircase that had stopped moving, with ten pounds eleven shillings and twopence in the pocket, nothing in the stomach and the ears probably floating free, searching for something to adhere to.

You had to let money find its own level. It was no good fighting it. Everybody's pocket had an individual plimsoll line. It was unfortunate that his was scarcely detectable from the line of the gunwale and that he was, in consequence, always awash in any sea that wasn't glassily calm. Money had a life of its own, but it also had a way with it far from mercenary: almost a sense of style. At the other end of his one and threepenny journey to Tim's north-western suburb his money would begin to spend itself right away on a threepenny bus, and the threepenny bus was in all likelihood now a fivepenny one. There was simply no telling what challenges his money would have to face up to and tackle, but better by far the spent bob than the saved half-crown because the spent bob was positive while the saved half-crown was negative. The one had life-force and the other didn't. The other led to several thousand abortive trips up and down a free escalator and a sense of doom at three o'clock in the morning when West Indian porters probably emerged from doors marked private into tiled passages with long brooms and clanking buckets, and every sound told, lived and echoed and relived itself, grateful for any ear, free-floating or attached, reluctant to be squandered on the deaf and the dead and the waves of silence coming from the tunnels where the predators slept. Save me from the small hours, George thought, Especially on the Underground Railway.

At the other end the bus was, indeed, fivepence. After a journey that took him past shops, two churches, a police-station, a garage, and then rows of residences both desirable and undesirable, he got off within a stone's throw of a telephone box which was within sight of Tim's trim white painted house. The telephone was cold. You could tell nobody had spoken to it for hours. He surrendered four warm pennies and dialled.

A female voice announced the number. When he pressed Button A the four pennies were gone, cast back into their native element like birds released from the wrist or fish cast back into the sea, vigorous sprats to catch ponderous mackerel: for this was the other quality about money which had a sense of style; there were unlimited amounts of it and the parts that made up the whole were only free and happy when in the company of fellow parts. You had to let them go if you wanted them to come back pregnant with increase. Each penny sought to emulate the salmon that went back to the river of its birth and swam upstream to spawn in the very spot where itself was spawned. Most of his own pennies seemed to get lost and he hoped this did not frustrate them and that it was only on the journey back to him that they were diverted.

'Hello,' he said, 'is that Sarah?'

'No, she's out. Who's that?'

'That's Gillian, isn't it? This is Uncle George.'

'Oh, hello.'

'I had a drink with your father this morning. He told me about you and Click and I want to see you.'

'Why?'

'Because it must be two years since I did, and I'm your godfather.'

She made no comment.

'Where is Sarah?' George asked.

'Shopping.'

'Can you get away?'

'Get away where?'

'Meet me somewhere.'

'I don't think so. If you want to know, Uncle George, I think I've had old people.'

'How old are *you*?'

'Seventeen and a quarter if it's at all relevant.'

'Your father was out at work at sixteen.'

'What?'

'I said your father was out at work at sixteen. Then he was in the Air Force. By the time he was twenty-one or -two he was married and nine months later your mother was out of the WAAF to have you and she was only twenty. They were very young, not as young as you, but young all the same. From what your father said today, though, I got this feeling you're being treated like a child. You're my child too because you're my god-child. I've never done a blind thing for you as a god-father, so let's scrub what you probably call the jazz. But I thought you might just like to talk to someone you don't know very well, I mean talk to him as a woman.'

He waited for her answer. Presently she said, 'Talk about what?'

'About what *you* think and what *you* want.'

'I don't want anything, Uncle George.'

'There's a coffee bar near your local tube station called The Coffee Counter. I'll wait there until half-past four, just over half an hour. I might even wait there until five. I've got nothing else to do, as you know.'

He put the telephone down. Emerging from the box and going the few steps to the main road he saw a bus half a mile away coming in the right direction to take him back to the tube and walked the fifty yards to the stop to wait for it. Even if Gillian had made up her mind to come right away she would probably have to do something to her face. They would not meet at the stop. The only danger was meeting Sarah. The bus that was going back to the station was coming from the direction of a shopping centre. Fivepence to get here, fivepence to get back, fourpence on the phone; ten guineas left; he was down to basic capital already and threatened with Sarah's presence and recognition: but to turn his collar up would be a gesture of defeat.

Sarah was not on the bus. She probably used the car. He remembered when Tim first bought a car. Perhaps by now they had The Second Car. Seated in the Routemaster, he handed over his last fivepence of petty cash and mentally transferred ten bob from the basic capital to the spending money column. He liked, as Mr. Jones might have said, to Keep the Record Straight, and to Know where he Stood. When he entered The Coffee Counter the clock behind the bar pointed one minute to four.

Twenty

It was at one minute past four o'clock that Miss Ada Lisle became conscious of the fact that she was dying, that she had been doing this for the past thirty-six hours and was wearing holes in the warm little blanket of patience that seemed to be the property of Mr. Stainsby whose face kept coming back either because it sometimes went away or because she sometimes had her eyes shut. The little blanket of patience belonged to Mr. Stainsby, she thought, because he kept adjusting it. It was not quite an actual blanket, more the idea of a blanket. If it had been an actual blanket her feet and legs would not be so cold. Her hands were colder than her feet and legs but that was because she had them resting one on each side of her on the counterpane, but it was because she was dying that her hands, feet and legs were cold in the first place. They needed two or three actual blankets but all Mr. Stainsby had to offer was this idea of a blanket, and this told her that between herself and Mr. Stainsby the communication of physical needs had ended, that Mr. Stainsby thought there was nothing further he could give her in this life because she had gone over the edge of feeling; whereas she hadn't, but could not summon up the means to tell him so; and for this impasse there was only one explanation: she and Mr. Stainsby were already divided by her death which was not only a matter of undergoing certain formalities like ceasing to breathe and leaving her body behind while she went somewhere else and Mr. Stainsby stayed on by the bedside, at a loss.

Mr. Stainsby had been very good to her. She wished that she could do something for him in return like dying for five minutes, coming back for two and telling him about Heaven, what it was, and whether it was, and then dying again and leaving Mr. Stainsby in full possession of the facts. If that wish were granted her would he, she wondered, be in for a shock? What kind of expression would come on to his face if she had to say to him: Well, Mr. Stainsby, I've been and come back and I'm afraid the answer's no for all of us, even for you? Of course he wouldn't believe her. He would pray, but that wouldn't do any good.

Never to pray: that was the thing. She used to pray a lot. Please God, let there be another day at the sea. Please don't let father come home drunk. Please let there be a telegram to say that the first telegram about Arthur is a mistake. Don't let Albert lose little Drusilla. Make Reggie write to us. Don't let Teddie die so long after Passchendaele. Please make Vi not mind when I go over on the off chance, make her kind to Harry and not like Tim better than George. Let not Hector Bright be miserable, and unbend the hearts of Miss Agnes, Miss Harriet and Miss Pamela to him, and please ask someone to write to me and not only a card at Christmas. Look after the soul of our mother. Tell her I try to look after Vi.

She could not quite remember how long it was now since she had prayed. By pray she meant speak to the Lord from the heart and not repeat in church what was printed in the prayer books. She thought that perhaps the last time had been when she heard weeks after about Vi and Harry dying of a bomb in the village they had gone to because of the war and of the baby, Guy, who had come so unexpectedly when Vi was forty-seven and Harry was sixty. Make Them want to send Guy to Devonshire, she had told the Lord on that occasion, meaning the authorities who had Taken Guy Up because his brothers were soldiers away to the wars. Make Them send Guy to The Grange so that I can look after him as my own. But They hadn't been made to want to send Guy to Devonshire but kept him in Dorset with people called Williams; and it wouldn't have done, anyway, because the Miss Brights would never have stood for it unless the Lord had also brought about a change in them; which on the whole she thought unlikely.

I had never seen Guy, she told Mr. Stainsby (who was wondering why she had begun to look at him so intently, and wished she would either speak or be delivered). I don't even know if he's alive, or if George is alive, or Tim. It was only George who wrote after the war, and they were all alive then and Tim had a little girl called Gillian, but even my George stopped writing and in the end I stopped writing too, and it's better, Mr. Stainsby, to remember them as young and safely through the war and with their lives in front of them, and not have to think of them as they might be, in sorrow, need or sickness, because there's enough of it in the world and nothing I can do about it any longer. Even when I used to try to do something about it it all went wrong and there were misunderstandings and rows. You're after my Harry, Ada; that's what Vi said; and flaunting your new hat in front of me because he paid for it. It was only five shillings, Vi, I said. One and eleven's what I pay, she said, you're an old Maid, Ada, and you're after my Harry, after my man who pities you like he does. Don't be a silly bugger, I said, and that tore it. Get out of my house, she said, and never come back. She didn't mean it, it was her temper, but it was a year before we spoke and when we did we never mentioned the row, just went on to the next, and that was about George, only it wasn't a proper row because it was here at The Grange, the time she came down with Tim and I offered her ten shillings to help with the fare.

How's my George, Vi? I said, and she flashed back: He's mine not yours. Yours and Harry's, I said, because she had her shoulder up and that frightened look in her eye, standing at you sort of sideways, shorter than me, shorter than any of us, daring you to say the wrong thing so that of course you always said it because she willed you as well as dared you. That's right, Ada, she said; mine and Harry's but you call him your George because he looks more like our father who you called a drunkard than he looks like my husband Harry who's a Spruce, and you try to make up for hating father by loving George because you're sorry for it now it's too late.

It wasn't a proper row because the Miss Brights came in then, we were standing in the hall and in they came from the village. You could see they were ladies, Vi said afterwards, from the way they held themselves. They're old dears really, I said, and their grandfather was coal. Blood tells, she said when she found we were to eat in the kitchen, money and education aren't any match for breeding, for all their airs and graces the Brights are Trade down to their marrow. Like our father was, I said, and it's right that George has his look more than he's got Harry's, is that why you've taken against him? I loved our father, Ada, she said. And I said, Did you, Vi? But we stopped there. Neither of us wanted a row, and it worried me what she had said about why I loved George and worried her what I'd said about why she'd taken against him. I only loved George because I wanted her to love him more and not make it so plain she liked Tim better, I wanted people to do what was right, Mr. Stainsby, because helping people to do what was right seemed to be one of the things you did when you'd promised to look after them because they weren't very sensible. But I expect it was wrong trying to help her to do what was right, and who knew whether it wasn't right what she was doing in any case, doing already, Mr. Stainsby? I've thought about it often, whether it was true, that I was sorry too late for not loving father just because he was a drunkard and our mother was hard put to it, and not only not loving him because he was a drunkard but because he could be gentle but was only ever gentle to Vi who was the youngest. He cried once when he stood over her cot and I was awake and afraid in the dark corner of the room because he'd hit our mother and I knew our brothers weren't asleep either next door and wished one of them was big enough to stand up to him. Only he cried, you see, Mr. Stainsby, and looked down at little Vi, holding the oil lamp so that it made shadows. He said, my little Vi, and I hated him because he was drunk and had shown violence. Shown violence was what they used to say in the street. Mrs. Lisle, they said to our mother, are you all right, did he show violence? When he stood over Vi's cot I knew he wouldn't show violence again that night, but I hated him because he had already shown it and was able to afford remorse. But was it, Mr. Stainsby, was it because he didn't stand over my bed in the dark corner and say, Ada, my little Ada, that I most hated him?

You must try to forgive your father, Ada; that's what our mother said when she was dying. He came of a hardworking family but got into Bad Company, and his head was in the clouds like Vi's is. Never forget, Ada, she said, that he drank because he loved us all but had no business head and couldn't give us the things he wanted us to have, and now he's gone and left nothing for the boys, and they're running wild, all except Arthur, so it's up to you, Ada, to look after them all, especially Vi because she's not very sensible. And the boys ran wild like she said, all except Arthur who went to night-school and got a job in Mr. Salter's office while the others worked with their hands and I lived in with Vi at Mrs. Sinclair's who was Next Door, and went into service up in Dulwich, and all the boys were in lodgings but chipped in from their wages to help pay for Vi, especially Arthur who said: Let her enjoy being young a bit, Ada. When Kitchener's war came he was the first in. Well I'm in, Ada, he said, how do I look? He was the oldest, but they were all in sooner or later. You must be proud

Ada, Mrs Sinclair said, but I wasn't. I missed them and I was afraid, I had premonitions. I think I knew the actual minute our Arthur was killed. It was at home, on a Saturday, getting on for evening and Vi was upstairs dressing to go out up to the West End to a show with the Belper Girls and Reggie Belper and a couple of friends who were home on leave, not from France, but from Portsmouth. They were officers. Vi had got in with the Belper girls because Gertie Belper asked her to help with tickets at The Assembly Rooms and she sold more than anyone, she was so pretty then, and full of life. The Belpers were big people locally because their father was in the Civil Service and it was through the Belpers Vi met the Craigs who were Printing and Stationery, and through the Craigs she met Harry who was thirteen years older than her and hadn't passed his medical, and he felt it, but Vi didn't, not in the same way. He looks so much younger than he is, it's awful for him, Ada, she said, a woman spoke up on a tram and he had to get out. You should have spoken back and told her you weren't A1, she said. It was funny about Vi and Harry. Before she met him she always talked about our brothers being in France, but after she met him she hardly mentioned them, she was ashamed they weren't officers and kept Harry out of the way when poor Teddy came on his embarkation leave in his rough khaki, he was the last to go across. Come up and help me with my dress, Ada, she called down and I said, Coming, and began to go up with my hand on the rail and half way up it was like one of the boys saying, Hello, Ada, and it was like Arthur saying it. Vi said, What's wrong? And I said, I don't know, and sat on the bed while Vi lit the mantle and said, There you can see better, how do I look, which is what Arthur had said when he came in at the door dressed like a soldier. They tried to give them a good fit in the early days and wanted recruits. It was poor Teddy who looked most like a sack of potatoes. You look fine, Vi, I said, where is it you want help? and she stood close to me so that I could help unpick the tacking threads that had got left in at the waist and which had to come out even though there was a sash to cover them. I've got to look right, Ada, she said, because Cissie and Gertie Belper are always in the mode. It's Reggie and the Craig boys you're dressing for not Cissie and Gertie, I said, but I went on pulling out the threads and where I was sitting I could see right through the door on to the landing and down the stairs to the front door and the letter box where the man would knock if a telegram came. It was the house next door to our old house, and everything was the other way round. I noticed this properly for the first time. When I say properly I mean I noticed it in the way that made me feel left all alone in a house that was the same but not the same. Do you understand what I mean, Mr. Stainsby? The stairs were on the wrong side of the house and Arthur wouldn't ever climb up them again. It seemed to be the house's fault that Arthur couldn't come back. He'd get lost. It was all gas in those days, Mr. Stainsby. You're too young to remember those rows and rows of houses all lit by gas and everything smelling of damp paper. Yes it was all gas. Yellow light on brown paint and green linoleum. Bits of lace at the windows. When you came in on a cold night it was homely, but it wasn't pretty, Mr. Stainsby, not like my nice room here at The Grange.

'What? Still here, Stainsby?' said the doctor who had come to The Grange to visit Miss Bright bedridden downstairs and Miss Lisle dying in the attic.

'Yes, she is still here,' Mr. Stainsby said. He had a talent for misunderstanding things that were said to him.

'I meant you,' said Doctor Barr, 'but how is she?'

'She stares at me,' Mr. Stainsby said.

Twenty-One

'I am sorry to hear that,' Lady Butterfield said. 'How very inconvenient. I had particularly wanted you and Anina to come tonight.'

At the other end of the telephone Guy Spruce muttered something that she heard but affected not to have heard, because she could not tolerate people who did not speak up.

'I said,' said Guy, raising his voice, 'what's so special about tonight?'

'Z hopes to look in. When I told him you would be here he was very interested. He said he thought you might be the coming man.'

Guy, who lay naked on his bed with one arm round Anina smiled and felt warm as well as amused.

'Well, I don't *want* to disappoint you, Aunt Clara.'

'I may have another surprise for you, too.'

'Pleasant or unpleasant?'

'S will be here.'

'I'm sorry. Remind me.'

'She had a small part in that thing at the Royal Court.'

'Which one?'

Lady Butterfield told him.

'Oh, yes,' said Guy.

'She wants to meet you because she thought your piece on the Television was better than Pinter.'

'Who am I to argue?'

'I think she's developing all the time. She's doing that new play about Creon, *Antigone, N.W.11,* for the commercial people next Sunday.'

'Oh, yes.'

'And the BBC want her for I forget exactly, Ibsen I think, or it may be Chekov.'

'It sounds a bit intense,' Guy said, saying It sounds and not She sounds because of Anina there in his arms with one eye open, and suspicious.

'When I told her you'd been commissioned to write two new plays for the commercial people she said she'd like nothing better than to play a part like that of Sally in *A Pram in the Garden.*

'Hall.'

'I'm sorry. My head for titles is bad.'

'Sally Boyd is still in character. Sally was a kind of Antigone wearing a macintosh in Islington.'

'Man, I knew it,' Anina MacBride said from the pillow beside him. 'You're talking about some RADA floozie,' and kicked him hard on the ankle.

'Are you not alone, Guy?' Lady Butterfield enquired.

'Anina has just come in.'

'Shall I rely on you tonight?'

'It's very good of you, Aunt Clara. We're always drinking your martinis. We'll do our best.'

'Then I'll say au revoir, Guy. My love to you both.'

Lady Butterfield replaced the receiver with one hand and ticked off Guy's name with a gold pencil held in the other. Using the base of the gold pencil she dialled another number.

'Hello?'

'This is Clara Butterfield.'

'Oh, hello.'

'I just wanted to make sure you would be here this evening.'

'Well, actually —'

'I've been talking to Guy Spruce.'

'Who?'

'He's very keen to meet you. so I thought I'd let you know he's coming.'

'That's the author of *A Pram in the Kitchen*, isn't it?'

'Hall.'

'Was it? Hall or kitchen, anyway.'

'He's been commissioned by the commercial people to do two or three new plays. He saw you at the Royal Court you know and is looking forward to the Antigone on Sunday.'

'I wish I were.'

'My dear, you sound tired.'

'I am a bit, Lady Butterfield. Actually, about tonight —'

'A good dry martini will buck you up and I think you ought to meet Guy.'

'I really have a bit of a thing about authors at the moment. It'll be such a relief to play Chekov because the old sweet can't interfere.'

Lady Butterfield deliberately kept silent for a few seconds. 'There is interference and interference,' she said then. 'And it would be a pity if you were to miss Z.'

When, presently, the telephone conversation had ended on a note of expectancy, Lady Butterfleld put a tick against S's name which was the second name on a list of two names, the first being Guy's. The list was headed with the word 'Questionable'. Under the two names she now wrote an *aide-mémoire* for future development. 'Because they are being wooed by people in their professions more important than those they knew when I first took them up, S and G are going through a phase of *thinking* they no longer require me, but I know better and can overlook an aberration which I am persuaded is temporary.'

Twenty-Two

At twenty-one minutes to five a tall fair girl came into the Coffee Counter and was obviously Gillian because she had still the north-light look of her grandfather Harry Spruce and the pretty flaxen china blue eye look of her mother Sarah, whose maiden name had been Crooke and whose snapshot in the uniform of the WAAF Tim had sent to George so that George could see what his future sister-in-law added up to on paper. 'This is Sarah Crooke', Tim had written on the back. 'We are engaged to be married.' That was in nineteen forty-one when George was in Cairo wearing on his shoulder tab the two stars of a lieutenant and the insignia of a regiment his commission into which he owed to his own charm and to Sir Roderick Butterfield who had pulled strings on his behalf from eleven a.m. on Sunday, September the third, nineteen thirty-nine until, as far as George could tell, October the first, nineteen forty, when Sir Roderick's own string had been hauled in by God, quite suddenly (so Aunt Clara told him later) in the street, near the entrance to the Cumberland Hotel, so that George never passed near the Marble Arch without thinking of him. 'Indeed, neither do I,' Aunt Clara said when he told her this; which had surprised him because he had not imagined them especially devoted to one another.

As Gillian stood in the artificial light, brushing her longish hair away from her peachy cheeks, looking for him with her September daylight eyes, trying to focus upon the indoor bamboo images surrounding her, George remembered the snapshot of Sarah and the shine he had vicariously taken to her which twenty succeeding years had dimmed because confronted by Sarah in the flesh he always felt himself forced to assume the character of Wastrel, as if she kept a wastrel's cloak especially for him in the hall when he visited them or over her arm if they met away from the neat white house Tim returned to every night of the working week with money in the bank, broad shoulders, and a back that things rolled off.

George stood up so that Gillian whom he had not seen for two years could recognize him. It was the first time he had ever seen her looking like a schoolgirl. In nineteen fifty-nine when she came home late for tea and was reprimanded she was wearing a shapeless pullover and jeans rolled up to just below her kneecaps. The time before that, he fancied, was the time of being late for lunch and reprimanded in a dirndl skirt and Tirolean blouse bought in the Otztal valley; and stretching back from the time of the dirndl skirt were his memories of brief and formal glimpses of Gillian as reprimanded child, not girl, in stiff party dresses worn in honour of her mother Sarah Crooke and in honour of her father's house and his position, and in defence of these against the uncertain influence of an Uncle George invited for lunch or tea but never for dinner because of the dangers of wine with the meal and missing the last train home. But today, with the lush yet tender bloom of pregnancy upon her, in a grey suit that might have been a uniform and sensible flat-heeled shoes, her hair giving her some bother as if but lately freed from the constriction of a grey, brimmed hat with a school ribbon on it, she reminded him of the grey-clad girls you saw in Harrods in January, April and September, full of puberty and mathematics, their eyes wandering free, their limbs following in the wake of mother's: maidens on the brink of adventure and term-time and dazed by the mutual exclusivity of those twin situations, for nothing could happen to them in Harrods, especially in the clothes they were wearing, and at such short notice which was the only kind of notice you felt they would have time for.

Why, George wondered; as his and Gillian's hands slid one into the other in the action described as shaking but in this case nothing of the sort because her hand seemed vulnerable to anything more violent than a limp coming together; why was Gillian wearing clothes like those of the girls you saw in Harrods, when she had already gone over the brink and there was no longer any question of giving her notice, short of long, because what she might have notice of had already happened and she knew much of what there was to know and bore inside her a fruit of the experience of life which the girls you saw in Harrods were only preparing to prepare for?

'I'm sorry I'm late,' Gillian said, now avoiding his eyes because she had done her duty by meeting them straight and true, if somewhat blankly, during the few seconds their hands stayed in contact, 'and I'm sorry about this ghastly rig. It's mummy's. Her waist used to be bigger than mine and it's the only thing I'm comfortable in, even though it makes me feel forty-five.'

'Actually it makes you look fifteen.'

'Does it?' she said, and sat, so that they were together on a padded bench surrounded by twisted cane, hanging ivy and red formica.

'Coffee?' he asked. She nodded. He said, 'Do you fancy anything with it?' She pushed up a lock of hair that fell over her forehead. Her finger-nails were very small and unvarnished. She said, 'Can you afford a cream bun?' But she didn't seem to have picked up Wastrel's cloak from the hall on her way out so he said, 'Two if you like,' and gave the order to a waitress in a black dress whose eyes, outlined, were like the eyes of a doe.

'Do you smoke?'

Gillian said, 'A bit, but not now. I might if the cream bun stays down.'

'Not guaranteed?'

'More or less. Cream buns are my present thing. Although I believe there's an anchovy paste phase in the offing because I had some the other day and keep remembering it.'

'Will it worry you if I smoke?'

She turned to look at him directly for the first time since they clasped hands. She said, 'No.'

He brought out the nearly full new packet of Bachelors that he had bought at The Coffee Counter between his own and Gillian's arrival. While he lit one their coffee and Gillian's cream bun came. It was through the coffee and the cream bun that Gillian at last entered into the spirit of The Coffee Counter whose tangily aromatic warmth was not sufficient in itself to melt the invisible puff-balls of the cool, gusty day which she had brought in with her on her cheeks and clothes and hair. It needed the heat of the coffee and the clinging stickiness of the bun to do that. She raised the white plastic cup steaming to her lips several times and gradually reduced the bun with the edge of her Swedish fork into squashy mouthsful of cream and chocolate: and with each sip, each chew, the early Autumn afternoon diminished in her and her eyes became more like the doe eyes of the waitress; but a doe fallen from grace, watching the fallow deer from a glade not so much safe as recently used and unlikely to be entered again for some time. Only, George thought, in an artificial light or an artificial warmth, does knowledge of the world and its ways really count, and settle on the shoulders like a weight: in bars, and eating places, neon- and shopwindow-lit streets, rooms whose windows were hung with curtains woven from old loofahs, stairways, hot banks, airless telephone kiosks and the slanting tunnels down which you moved on juddering escalators.

'I don't feel old,' George told her, because nothing of interest had yet been said.

'What?'

'I said I don't feel old. On the phone you said you'd had old people.'

'I have. In a way.'

'Why?'

'People who pretend embarrass me and all old people pretend, especially when they talk to young people. For instance they pretend that what's for their good is only for your good which is fantastic anyway because nothing is for anybody's good really, is it?'

They drank their coffee while the ivy grew silently and stealthily in its hanging pots.

'Are you sad at giving up school?' he asked when it became plain it was his turn to speak.

'I'm not sure I know what sad means.'

'Sad means if you lose something you like or somebody you love,' George said, and looked at Gillian to consider in secrecy why her face did not move him in the way Alice's face would have moved him if she had been sitting in Gillian's place, chin in hand, eyes hidden from him by heavy lids far from sleepy. 'But then,' he said, 'I expect you'll answer that by saying you're not very sure what love is.'

'Oh, I think I know what love is.'

'What?'

'Well, it's an extension of unrelated fear, isn't it? I mean most people are basically scared only they won't admit it. The only thing they're prepared to admit to is what they call being lonely, and they see love as what they can have to stop being lonely. It's because I'm not really basically scared that I don't believe in love. I think it's all right about the cream bun so if you don't mind I'll have a cigarette now.'

He gave her one. She leant towards the flame of the match with the cigarette held in hand and mouth as if she were about to blow at something through a tube. The skin of her cheeks looked as soft as that of a child. She leant back, cigarette still held in hand and mouth, and frowned a bit at its lighted end while she sucked in hard. Then she took the cigarette away without lowering her arm, raised her head and blew out a long jet of smoke.

'Why aren't you basically scared?' George asked.

'I suppose because I'm basically existentialist.'

'What does that mean?'

'Well, if you don't know Uncle George, it's much too complicated to explain, but fundamentally it means that here we are sitting at a table in The Coffee Counter, and so what?'

'Oh. Does Click believe in love or is he existentialist too?'

'I'm not sure I want to talk about Click,' she said, and blew another long jet into the air like a smokescreen from a suspicious and vulnerable corvette that fancied it had been sighted by a lumbering enemy battleship. And then, as it were emerging cheekily and pluckily from an unexpected quarter of the artificial fog to get in a broadside, she said, 'I'd rather talk about the two hundred pounds you owe daddy.'

'So you know about that?' he said, when he had more or less recovered.

'They've been going on and on about it at home.'

'Is this why you've come?'

'Well it was your idea, wasn't it, Uncle George? I mean isn't it really why you rang?'

'No.'

Another jet of smoke: but this time blown to one side, shrouding the table from the public gaze. From within this treacherous privacy she engaged him directly, her expression undergoing three distinct [and inherited] changes from that of the grey-clad schoolgirl's: first to the wastrel-accusing look of her mother Sarah, then to the patient look of quiet superiority her father Tim had acquired over the last fifteen years, finally and unexpectedly to the look of Tim's and George's father whose face had every so often been composed into lines of sympathy for people whose problems he had somehow avoided getting mixed up in before going back to his spare-room studio to paint snow.

'Why did you come all the way to the house and then only ring from the call-box?' she asked him.

'How do you know I did that?'

'You can see the call-box from our house. It's what you automatically find yourself watching when you're standing at the phone looking out of the hall window. Of course you can't see who's in the box but you can see them when they come out.'

'Oh.'

'To be absolutely frank one of the reasons I've come is to make sure it was you I saw come out of the box. The other reason is that after you'd rung off daddy rang and asked if you'd been in touch with me or mummy. I said no and he said if you tried I was to steer clear of you. Of course he didn't say why but I guessed it was something to do with the two hundred pounds you owe him, and it struck me as fantastically sordid that you should think there was anything I could do to stop Daddy dunning you for two hundred quid —'

'Yes, but that wasn't the idea —'

'– but you see it also struck me as what I suppose you'd call sad that you should come all the way to the house and only ring from the call-box as if you thought you might be turned away if you knocked.'

'I rang from the call-box because I didn't want to put you off by suddenly appearing wearing my jolly Uncle face.'

'Supposing mummy had been in and answered the phone, though? She'd have put you off. She'd probably have said I was out.'

'Then I'd have been close enough to the house to surprise her a few seconds later by knocking at the door.'

'Not if she'd seen you come out of the box.'

'But I didn't know you could see people come out of the box.'

'Well you can.'

'And anyway I didn't get you here to talk about the two hundred pounds. I asked you here in case there was anything you wanted to tell somebody about Click and the baby.'

'Like what for instance, Uncle George?'

'Like the fact that you wanted to marry him and he wanted to marry you. Your father says that neither of you do anything but shrug. But a shrug might mean quite the opposite of indifference. It might mean you both knew it was useless trying to make your father understand. I was even prepared for you to burst into tears and ask me to stop your father sending you away to this shady nursing home.'

'What would you have done if I had?'

'I wouldn't have thought again about trying to raise two hundred pounds to repay the loan. He only wants it back to help pay for the nursing home.'

'Well there you are, Uncle George. It's the two hundred pounds you're thinking of all the time.' Presently she added: 'Please don't think I'm making a moral judgment. It's simply that I like the facts to be straight. You said I could talk to you like a woman.'

'Yes, you can. After all, you *are*.'

'All right then,' Gillian said. 'Is it true that you only got rid of Auntie Alice because she couldn't give you children and you were climbing the wall at the idea of Great Uncle Roderick's ten thousand pounds coming to me instead?'

George lit another Bachelor. There were now five missing from the pack which meant, at three shillings and tenpence for twenty, that elevenpence halfpenny had gone up in smoke since one minute to four, but this was scarcely worth thinking about when sums like two hundred and ten thousand pounds were under discussion.

'So you know about the ten thousand pounds too,' he said, and almost told her the truth about his mumps and Doctor Honeydew's test tube, and would have done so had she not just then half-surreptitiously undone the waist button of her borrowed grey jacket and relaxed, fractionally, with a scarcely audible sigh of relief for herself and for the embryo left behind by young Clayton like a plumber's spanner in her works. To have told her it was he and not Alice who couldn't have children would have been to render her present position somewhat indelicate, he felt, because the confession would conjure the word sterile and the word sterile, in turn, would conjure the image of the part of him that was and the memory of the corresponding part of Click that hadn't been.

'Alice divorced me because there was no point in going on,' he said. 'I never got a decent job and I was always going on these benders.'

'Your grandfather was a drunkard, wasn't he?'

'The one on our mother's side was. Why?'

'Daddy says you're taking after him.'

'Daddy says a lot, doesn't he?'

'Not usually. Only since he found out I was preg. My being preg seems to have made me remember all the shady things about the family, and he goes on and on about them. In fact he's being fantastically savage, mostly about you Uncle George. I mean he says things like why don't you drop dead before you can marry again and have children, then I should inherit ten thousand pounds when I'm twenty-one and he wouldn't have to worry about my future as an unmarried mother, because no boy would care a hoot how many babies I'd had if I had ten thousand pounds to start him off on his career. Of course daddy only says that because no one ever helped *him*. I mean he had to fight his way up. So you have to make allowances for him, especially just now, because my being preg and about to cost him a thousand pounds means he's got to accept this job he was offered two months ago.'

Twin jets of smoke, one from Gillian and the other from George, met in the air above their heads like clouds of knowing and unknowing.

'I'm going to order more coffee,' George said, 'and then we can take all you've just said more slowly and point by point. Would you like another cream bun?'

'No thank you, Uncle George. I mustn't have another cream bun.'

'Shall I ask if they have anchovy paste sandwiches?'

'No, thank you. I couldn't eat anything else.'

George caught the doe-eyed waitress's attention and signalled refills. Gillian stubbed her half-smoked cigarette and shook her head when he offered her another.

'Now what about this job?' he said.

'Didn't he tell you about it?'

'Not a word.'

'How curious.' She rested her elbow on the table and her chin on her hand and looked at him. 'I suppose he was afraid if he told you about it you'd think he was going to be loaded and wouldn't need the two hundred pounds back. Why do you owe him two hundred pounds, Uncle George?'

'If he's being savage it's a wonder he hasn't said.'

'Well he said it probably saved you going to prison.'

'What do I need to add?'

'Was it a bribe to the police?'

'No. It was to pay back money to the club I worked for. I borrowed two hundred pounds from them without their knowing but of course they found out. I got the sack and a week to pay it back.'

'I think that was awfully nice of them, don't you Uncle George?'

'I suppose it was. The man who ran the club was in the same regiment during the war.'

'You were saved by the old boy net, then?'

'Yes.'

'Daddy says you've always known how to work the old boy net, whereas he's never known any old boys to work it with. What sort of club was it?'

'Just a drinking club. There were a lot of them around after the war. I acted as its social secretary.'

'What had you used the two hundred pounds on?'

'That's it. I can't remember. It had just accumulated all over the place and some of the creditors turned nasty.'

'You've lived an awfully sordid life, haven't you Uncle George? I think daddy envies you in a way because people whose lives are sordid usually have more fun than people like daddy whose life is so unsordid it's hardly true.'

'Tell me about the job.'

'Well if he takes it it involves doing dirt on old Mr. Wallingford and at the age of forty daddy still thinks he can have business scruples and my being preg and about to cost him a thousand pounds means he can't afford them, so finally it's going to be my fault that old Mr. Wallingford will be left without a partner and forced to sell the practice. He's been banking on daddy to carry on when he's too old to go in every day.'

'What about Mr. Bartle?'

'There hasn't been a Mr. Bartle for years and years —'

'So there hasn't. I forgot. I always imagine Mr. Wallingford and Mr. Bartle calling out figures to each other and making dry jokes about the Inland Revenue.'

'I think Mr. Bartle began on his own and then took in old Mr. Wallingford when he was young Mr. Wallingford. Then after old Mr. Bartle died Mr. Wallingford who was old himself by then because it was only about ten years ago took in daddy as soon as daddy passed his final examinations.'

'That must have been a bit more than ten years ago.'

'Must it? Well I suppose you know as much about it as I do, if not more.'

'Not at all. The only thing I know about Bartle Wallingford apart from your father being in it is that they've got a girl called Gwendoline.'

'Isn't that the mousey girl on the telephone?'

'Is she mousey?'

'The one on the telephone is.'

'That's her then. I've only met her on the telephone. We talk about her holidays mostly. She's thinking of Corsica.'

'Daddy says only the weekly wage slaves can afford abroad. This year we went to Seaford and daddy and Andrew spent most of the time in Newhaven watching the cross-channel steamers while mummy and I sat and shivered on the beach. Actually it was in Seaford I first decided I must be preg. I mean what a place to discover you're preg *in*. I mean they have to hold the front up with absolutely gigantic breakwaters and when you're on the beach you feel a bit like a fly crawling over fish in a fish shop because of the slope and everything being bigger than you. I mean in a fish shop the slab they put the fish on slopes, doesn't it, and looks gritty. So I felt like a pregnant fly fantastically lost trying to find its way round huge lumps of grit to get at the cod. I mean one could have approached pregnancy with a kind of *panache* on the Costa Brava. We've only been once abroad and that was to the Tirol, although I went to Rome last year with a gang of nunnery types. We used to slip out of the back gate and go haring off on the backs of Vespas with Roman dreamboats and Mother Mary Francis of Assisi did her nut when she found out. Perhaps the best place of all to find you're preg in would be Rome because of it being the Eternal City and dedicated to the idea of the immaculate conception. I mean as a non-Roman Catholic to find yourself pregnant in Rome might be a very mysterious experience.'

'I want to know more about this job of Tim's.'

'Well it's a directorship in the firm that's always been Bartle Wallingford's biggest and most valuable client, and they want daddy as a full-time financial director and not just as their outside accountant because he did something terrifically clever for them about financial reorganization, and daddy has been dithering about the job because although there are things daddy has always wanted to do at Bartle Wallingford that he can't do while old Mr. Wallingford is alive, he knows that if he takes this job it will leave old Mr. Wallingford in the soup and he thinks as soon as he's gone this company will get rid of Bartle Wallingford and give their auditing to one of these terrifically swish firms of accountants with wall-to-wall carpet, which means the value of the practice will go down and old Mr. Wallingford won't get much for it and will have a creepy old age. But if he stays with old Mr. Wallingford he thinks they'll lose the account anyway because it's only daddy who's kept it going and they won't like him any more if he says no to the job. Actually of course I'm terrifically sorry for daddy because he has this puritan scruple thing which was all right in old Mr. Bartle's day. I mean although daddy's awfully clever about tax angles and things like that he isn't really *with* contemporary values. I think he's also not terrifically keen on this directorship even though it would earn him at least five thousand a year because he's not only worried about the moral thing with old Mr. Wallingford but also wonders whether the board of directors will expect him to be smart as well as clever once he joins them. Mummy says his puritan-thing is due to the fact that he always had to do everything for himself and never got any encouragement when he was young. Nobody helped him to get ahead or thought he was clever or anything but just dull, so of course he thought he was dull too and got this thing about having to work harder than anybody else just so that he could keep level. I mean he went to Bartle Wallingford before the war as a junior audit clerk and just went back there when the war was over and studied and studied, and mummy says, I mean it's fantastic, but she says he *cried* when he got a gold medal or whatever it was when he came top in his finals because he thought there must be a mistake but knew there wasn't and couldn't really grasp it. I mean he was nearly thirty and you'd think by then he'd know what he was capable of, wouldn't you?'

'It's difficult to know,' George said. 'I didn't realize he got a gold medal.'

'It may have been bronze. Of course, I've worked it out about daddy now. You see Bartle Wallingford is *safe* and when people are projecting their puritan-things you always find they're doing what is *safe*, and of course the things they think of as *safe* are usually the things they've always had or worked hard for, and what they've worked hard for usually turns out to be what people went on and on at them about when they were young. And of course that's where daddy is fantastically complicated because according to mummy *his* mother went on and on at him about mutually exclusive things, I mean like being a gentleman even if you are born in a terrace-house in a suburb, and having connections and being several cuts above everybody you were forced to come in contact with but only forced because you were poor, and it being better to be poor and a gentleman with connections than rich and eat your peas with a knife, but all the same having to work tremendously hard and make a lot of money so as to have more than the people who had it but didn't know what to do with it. So now of course with me being preg and about to cost him a thousand pounds he's developed a persecution thing about his past catching up with him because Click is only a plumber's mate and he thinks he has to accept this smart-alec and possibly ungentlemanly job for my sake, and leave old Mr. Wallingford in the soup even though old Mr. Wallingford has always kept daddy's nose to the grindstone and taken more out of the business than daddy and should have made him an equal partner years ago. And all this makes daddy fantastically savage because the situation is so full of contradictions that *nothing* looks safe.'

'It's not true that nobody helped him or thought anything of him. He was always mother's favourite.'

'But it's you who got an income for life, Uncle George.'

'A fat lot of good it's done me.'

'That's exactly what daddy says. I mean he looks at the good it's done you and thinks of the good it would have done him.'

'From the age of three until the age of seventeen most of my time was spent looking after Tim.'

'What happened when you were seventeen?'

'Nothing really. I branched out. I got taken up by Lady Butterfield.'

'I thought it was Great Uncle Roderick who took you up. Was he really a bad lot?'

'What does that mean?'

'It's what daddy says. I mean he had certain tendencies, didn't he?'

'Tendencies?'

'I mean did he ever try to seduce you?'

'Seduce me?'

George watched Gillian's knowing-it-all eyes and pondered this, considering especially the swimming pool at Manorlord Mount, a knee to kneeness on a bench at Lords in front of The Tavern, and a certain moment of hiatus in the palladian museum where all the Butterfield trophies were exhibited in a tomblike splendour that caused goose pimples.

'Actually,' George said, 'I'm not sure. I was a very innocent youth. I didn't know about such things. Not that with Uncle Roderick there was anything to know, as far as I'm concerned.'

'Then I think you ought to tell daddy, Uncle George, because from the things I've overheard him saying to mummy in the last few days I think he thinks – you know —'

'Yes, I see. Tim was always much more sophisticated than I was. I suppose Tim was the sort of boy who would take one look at Uncle Roderick and *know*.'

'But I gather Great Uncle Roderick made it quite clear.'

'Quite clear? How? To your father?'

'Yes. At his little flat at the Marble Arch.'

'Little flat at the Marble Arch?'

'Yes, when daddy went back with him there just before daddy joined the Air Force. I think daddy was hoping Great Uncle Roderick would help him get a commission the same as you, but he got an impression the price was going to be too high.'

'Good Lord.'

'So it seems daddy put two and two together about your commission and about your legacy. But it looks as if he's made five like accountants often do.'

'It's news to me he ever met Uncle Roderick except with mother and father and me at the Langham. It's news that Uncle Roderick had a flat at the Marble Arch, although —'

'Although what, Uncle George?'

'It figures.'

'You liked Great Uncle Roderick, didn't you, Uncle George?'

'He was a decent old boy. He wanted me to go out to Malay but Aunt Clara said it was a waste. She wanted me to go to University but Uncle Roderick wouldn't fork out any more dough, and of course she wouldn't, so nothing really happened at all. She kept putting me on to temporary and rather chi-chi jobs, and then in nineteen thirty-nine Uncle Roderick got me to join the TA.'

'What is that? A Trade Union?'

'No, the Territorial Army. Spare time stuff.'

'What were the chi-chi jobs?'

'Well first there was a commercial photographer in Chelsea. I acted as his assistant until he went bankrupt. After that I think it was the job with the unfrocked priest who ran a travel bureau and left a gang of pilgrims stranded near Lourdes, and that was tricky because I had the telephone to answer in London and the writs to accept when the pilgrims started to trickle back. Or it may have been the job with the wife of the doctor in Wimpole Street who took heroin and walked round the house in bare feet, and needed what she called a personable young man to run messages and act as her social secretary, which of course really meant collecting the stuff in little packages from shady people in Paddington and Victoria and taking telephone messages from debs who wanted curious experiences.'

'It sounds fascinating.'

'I'd rather have planted rubber or mined tin.'

'But you saw life. I don't think daddy's ever seen life.'

'Will you tell me something about Click now?'

'Honestly, Uncle George. I really don't want to talk about Click.'

'Then just tell me this. Are you sure you don't want to marry him?'

'I'm much too young to get married.'

'Did he ask you to marry him when you told him you were going to have a baby?'

'You don't understand, Uncle George. In a modern affluent

society people can afford not to have morals. The question of marriage just doesn't arise because Click's and my status- and income-groups are basically incompatible.'

'Then why don't you want to talk about him?'

'Because I prefer positive to negative thoughts and for the moment all thoughts about Click are bound to be negative. And when I rationalize I have to admit that the main attraction *there* was the leather jacket and the tight jeans, and I mean, well, leather jackets and tight jeans are two a penny, aren't they?'

'Your father said he'd have the baby adopted.'

'Oh, yes. I gather it's fantastically easy, these days, especially if one of the parents has a high IQ which I happen to have.'

'And what will happen then?'

'What do you mean?'

'I mean what is the future as you see it?'

'The future as I see it, Uncle George? Well after I've got this maternity thing taped I suppose I'll go up to university if I can get in, and come down with a second-class degree or even a first and then go into some low paid job with a bit of social cachet in it until some suitable man who's not too fantastically square-drip and is thought of as what they call a coming man decides I'm the girl he'd like to sleep with legally while he concentrates on getting to wherever it is he or his parents have decided it's best for him to go.'

'I'm sorry, Gillian, but I don't believe a word you're saying.'

'Don't you Uncle George? Oh, but it's absolutely true. You see I'm terribly clever academically, I mean like a gift, I can pass almost any general scholastic examination they can think up, but I haven't any *talents*, and although I have nice hair and quite good features I'm not going to be a *rave*. I mean, let's face it, my ankles are too thick already and there's something downright maddening at least to me about the way my quite good features are stuck on my face, so with no talents and no fab vital statistics there's absolutely nothing for me in the world but exactly what daddy and mummy have always pushed me towards, I mean a legal bedding with a young man a few years older who's said to be coming in his profession which I suppose will be advertising or the law or something to do with plastics or chemicals, and if he can point to two generations of middle-class and if he's been to a public school, even just a minor one, or only a grammar so long as it ended with a red-brick spell, then even if it turns out later that he's a fantastic deadbeat or a queer or utterly incompetent in bed or quite incapable finally of earning a decent living, well that will be the boy for Gillian Spruce. I mean, Uncle George, I mean won't it? And even if I wanted to alter my future, well what could I do that would alter it for the better when I have no talents and aren't going to be a rave and when I don't believe in love because I haven't got a fear thing to translate into a loneliness thing and sublimate in a love syndrome, I mean when I'm really basically existentialist and we're sitting here in The Coffee Counter, and so what?'

'Does your father know you're basically existentialist?'

'At the moment all he's interested in is that I'm basically preg.'

'What's your mother interested in?'

'Well for a start, five thousand a year. But not at the price of an illegitimate grandchild and I expect she wonders why she can't have one without the other. I mean she keeps looking at me as if she wished I were a drawing she could rub out and start again. And then she's also interested in what she calls having a happy husband and father in the house which means she bends wherever daddy blows, so of course she's just as fantastically disorientated as he is about Bartle Wallingford.'

'What about Click's parents?'

'Oh I've never met them, but I gather from daddy they're inverted snobs and that Mr. Clayton was only annoyed at our not going after an affiliation order. I mean he takes it as a slight on their financial standing which in their case also means their social standing. If it weren't that they like the money better I expect they'd insist on paying up to prove they can afford to.'

'Aren't you in the least bit fond of Click?'

'Oh yes, I'm fond of him,' she said and drank coffee from a cup George saw was empty from the way it came up too quickly from the saucer to her mouth.

'Do you still see each other?'

'No, we decided we'd better not.'

'Do you miss him?'

'Well I miss him physically, Uncle George, but of course if we lived together his accent and manners and inability to talk about anything remotely interesting would drive me up the wall. Actually it's what I suppose you'd call sad about boys like Click isn't it? I mean Click's basically intelligent, only he doesn't let his intelligence show much because it would mark him out if it got too noticeable and the boys he goes around with wouldn't stand for it collectively. And of course he didn't let it show much with me either because he has this thing about his accent when talking to people like myself. In fact when you have as complicated a thing about your accent as Click it gets so that you don't say much at all unless it ranks as smart, sexy or resentful. Actually the only hope for a boy like Click is to go on being smart, sexy and resentful. I mean he's not smart or callous enough to make a lot of money by his wits and socially he's had it, not going to the Grammar. To someone like me the Grammar's not important but it is to a boy like Click who won't ever speak with what they call the right accent now because he's missed the opportunity of learning it at the Grammar and is committed to tribal rites and customs and smartness and sexiness because of his subconscious resentment at not being able to reject his background which means Click will be an inverted snob too in about two years from now, I mean forever, which could break you up, couldn't it, if you loved him, which I don't, although I like him and I miss him in a way and I suppose it's bad for the baby not to have the father near by during the gestative period.'

'Are you quite content with this scheme to have the baby adopted?'

'Well I can't very well come back from wherever it is daddy has in mind to send me and mummy – Wales I think because they're supposed to be used to unmarried mothers there – I can't very well come back from what's supposed to be some sort of university crammer complete with a baby, can I?'

'Why not?'

'Well it would make nonsense of the whole arrangement.'

'You mean make nonsense of the social deception.'

'It's not my decision that everyone should be deceived.'

'But you're not kicking against it.'

'When you're an existentialist you don't kick against anything. You simply observe and relate observation to experience.'

'How will you relate your observation of the baby to the experience of giving it up?'

She picked up the plastic teaspoon from her saucer and with it rhythmically beat the rim of the plastic cup, watching the spoon and the cup rather, George thought, like a girl-guide watching for smoke from one piece of stick rubbed against another.

'Actually Uncle George, you're the first person who's mentioned that aspect of the situation, but I don't think you need worry. I don't *think* I shall be heartbroken, although I should be very upset if the baby is born with anything wrong with it. I mean then I might feel an obligation to keep it in case it's sent to people who get impatient with it and have to be prosecuted by the NSPCC. I mean you're not told who's got the baby, are you, in case you try to get in touch later, and it would be awful to see reports of people prosecuted by the NSPCC and not know whether the child was your own, wouldn't it? Although as I said, I think I'd only feel that if the baby was a cripple or something. I mean you always feel a child described as in need of care and protection is a cripple of some sort and if your baby was a cripple then somehow farming him out would be like voluntarily handing him over to people who'd get prosecuted by the NSPCC for ill-treating him.'

'I don't suppose it will be a cripple.'

'No. On the other hand any day now you feel the first crop of strontium 90 mutants will begin to appear. What a sell it would be for daddy if my baby came out with two heads. I mean nobody would adopt it then, would they? On the other hand the authorities would help to hush it up, wouldn't they? I expect when the mutants begin to appear the government will put them all in some creepy old stately home with high walls and a guard on the gates and signs saying WD keep out, and everybody will know they're there but nobody will dare say in case they get arrested for negative thinking, I mean long but long before 1984.'

'Are you sure your father is sending you away to have the baby and then get it adopted?'

'Yes, why?'

'When are you going into the nursing home?'

'Oh, not for ages. I mean not until the time.'

'Has he fixed on which nursing home yet?'

'He's looking into it. Why?'

'You won't be going at once into the one he fixes on to have an early examination?'

'You're suspicious, aren't you, Uncle George? I mean you've got it in mind I'm going to be aborted. Well you can forget that. I don't believe in artificially induced miscarriages, not even by gin and hot baths and all those old wives' specifics mummy tried to make me go in for when I first told her. And after all having a baby is a basic female experience.'

'Then why is it costing him a thousand pounds?'

'It's his estimate of the extra amount involved in running two homes for nearly a year.'

It was in George's mind to say: How can you be sure you're not going to be aborted against your will? But he looked at her peachy cheeks and hesitated to make them sweat. She was healthy and pretty and he thought it a shame that she couldn't go back to the convent, escape grey-clad from the incipient dangers of places where things could happen to her because she had gone beyond Harrods; a shame that she couldn't sit on at her wooden knife-scarred desk until to sit there was a discomfort and she had to raise her hand and ask the Reverend Mother to excuse her because her time had come.

'I expect he's exaggerating a bit,' she said, 'about it costing a thousand pounds. I'm sorry there isn't anything I can do to stop him dunning you for your share of it.'

She looked at her watch and said she ought to go now. When the waitress came Gillian took her elbows from the table, giving him free way to deal with the mercenary side of their meeting. Cigarettes, three and tenpence; five coffees at ninepence each (one for George before Gillian arrived); one cream bun at one shilling; total eight shillings and sevenpence, plus a tip of one shilling; fivepence left out of a ten shilling note, the time, fifteen minutes past five and the clouds gathering again over Hendon, Brent, Finchley, Golders Green and Hampstead.

Outside, not far from The Coffee Counter the buses were clustered, double-decked and scarlet. Grim drivers climbed into their cabs, like old crustacea into niches of subterranean rock. Species of fish peered from the bus windows, anticipating movement, a change in the traffic lights or the call, maybe, of the wild from whence the windy currents rippled, fanning invisible seaweeds that swayed rhythmically in standing camouflage to mask the dark mouths of caves thoughts might otherwise enter, unwarned.

'Will you tell your mother and father you've seen me?' George asked.

'I don't think so, Uncle George. After all there isn't much to tell them, is there?'

'I suppose there isn't.'

'Do you think it's wrong not to tell them?'

'No, of course I don't.'

'And it might get you into trouble too, mightn't it?'
'I expect your father would tackle me about it.'
'Well he's cross enough as it is, Uncle George, so we'd better not give each other away.'
'No. Is that your bus?'
'Yes, it is, but I shan't bother with a bus. I'm supposed to take tons of exercise. In fact I'll start walking back now if you don't mind, so thank you very much for the coffee and the cream bun.'
She offered him her hand, which he took, and shook, and then let go of.
'Look after yourself,' he said, 'and good luck to the baby.'
He felt it was a strain for each of them, looking the other in the eye.
'Thank you, Uncle George. It's awfully nice of you to take it so well. I mean as if it were all absolutely natural and not fantastically squalid. Goodbye.'
She turned and was off up the road in her sensible shoes. George saw what she meant about her ankles.

Twenty-Three

In the hope of rousing him again Anina had just drawn a ban the bomb sign, large, in lipstick, low down on Guy's belly.
'You'd better get washed,' he said, 'because you pong.'
And her fingers were still carbonned from changing the ribbon of his typewriter which sat, metallic, on the cluttered table near the window beyond which Camden Town waited to inspire him, clouding over, post-copulatively stony, in the hour before old-fashioned urban neon would blink awake in him contemporary conceptions of classic theatre.
Here I lie, he thought, naked and more talented than Pinter.
Anina went. He waited in happy expectation.
The geyser exploded as Anina lit it and on this cue Guy returned in thought to the play that had begun to worry him. Captions rolled in front of geyser in close shot. Grams played a stylized rendering of flaring gas backed by plaintive oboe. *The Geyser*. Take out. By Guy Spruce. Hold caption and track back. Take out caption. On you, camera two. In close. A girl's eyes. Pull away to reveal the beaten-by-life turn of her mouth. Man's voice off: *A fine thing!* The girl's eyes flicker to the

right, to establish an illusion of space, of a room beyond, from which the man had called. And calls again. *A fine thing I say!*

Guy sat up to light a cigarette. Blowing clouds he listened to the water Anina was now running. *A fine thing I say.* What was a fine thing? Not the geyser but the fact that at last it was back in working order. She'd had it fixed, this girl with the beaten-by-life turn to her mouth and the disdainful slant to her eye.

She'd had it fixed by a man upstairs who sat in his undershirt, showing a hairy chest, and sometimes paused with a hand on the banisters, leather-jacketed, crisp-lipped. She'd had it fixed by the hairy fellow while this other man was out. Now he was back, and creating. *A fine thing, I say. Whaddid ya say this morning? Fix the geyser for me, Joe. Fix the geyser you said. Did I say I wouldn't fix the geyser? Did you hear me say I wouldn't fix the geyser? If I'd said I wouldn't fix the geyser, all right. But you didn't hear me say I wouldn't fix the geyser because I didn't say I wouldn't fix it.*

Pause while camera two holds girl sorting toilet articles in the bathroom. Capable hands; used to doing things for themselves: a shot symbolizing the complaining man's impotence. He can't say: 'I said I *would* fix the geyser,' because he hadn't said he'd fix it. He is useless to her. But they are bound together in some way. By what?

Guy frowned. By what indeed? By their experience of each other? And did the fixed geyser come at the end or the beginning? The end? Yes, it came at the end. It had been fixed, patched up to serve until it needed patching again. Their lives.

Guy stuck the cigarette in the corner of his mouth, tilted his head and looked at his illusion through the smoke. The opening shot would be of the geyser being lit but *not* working. The girl swears, and yells for the useless man. Joe!

But no. She doesn't yell. She knows it's no good yelling, Joe is still asleep.

When the geyser doesn't light she doesn't change expression. She picks up something else that turns out to be broken too. At first glance she is a woman living alone in a world of mechanical contrivances that defeat her. But then will come the first dramatic punch as camera three pans her from bathroom across bed-sitting room, disclosing Joe snoring on crumpled bed: a man about the house.

She opens the flat door to pick up the milk. She lingers a bit, looks up to the next flight. Footsteps. But they're a woman's, not the hairy-chested fellow's. A sense of disappointment amounting to a feeling of deprivation at being denied even the sound of the hairy fellow's footstep. The viewers don't know about the hairy fellow yet. But they wonder, catching the look of anticipation, the look of disappointment.

Yes. Play it like that: subtly, expressively – until the girl and the hairy fellow meet, and he speaks to her for the first time – leather jacket open, showing the undershirt and the curly sexy hair mounting as high as his throat.

Then play it straight on the surface, play it beast-with-two-backs. But underneath let there be a flowing lyricism. Make them feel that all the time she's in the hairy fellow's arms she's imagining those arms as Joe's: the Joe of the beginning, before the rot set in; Joe to whom she's bound.

Guy put on his dressing-gown, palmed his dark five o'clock chin.

A three acter. Two natural breaks. Stylish. The geyser as link.

The hairy fellow fixes the geyser. We don't see him doing it, but we know he's done it. We see him come in while Joe is out and go through the motions of looking at it at the end of the first act. *Needs fixing lady?* Pause. *I'll fix it. Fix anything you want fixing.*

Act Two. Him and the girl, just out of bed. He's relaxed, smoking, half-naked. The girl in her shift. Fulfilled, satisfied. But for him the boredom with her is already there. For her there's now only Joe and the future to think of. Obliquely, sensuously, crab-wise, she approaches the idea of the old Joe by talking to the hairy fellow about her earlier life with him. Beating the fellow's ears in. He hides a yawn. She is torn between the fleshy reality of the hairy fellow and the spiritual reality of Joe.

Act Three. She's been to the store, the supermarket. Hello Joe, I've got chops. She beats Joe's ears in too. Making up her day. Did he get the job? Oh Joe, they don't appreciate you, Joe.

Joe wonders. Watches her. The hairy fellow calls in. Gives her back something he's borrowed. Constraint. Suspicion. The girl wilts. Confronted. Confronted like that with the two images of her love. Gone, the hairy fellow leaves a vacuum of familiar silence. Thoughtlessly she says she'll take a bath. The geyser goes on. Joe's face. He looks up at the ceiling where the hairy fellow is whistling. The girl's face, now. The original shot. Not scared, but beaten by it. The uselessness of explaining. Her eyes. The mouth. And Joe's voice coming in across the sound of the hot water running. *A fine thing. A fine thing I say. Whaddid ya say this morning? Fix the geyser for me, Joe. Fix the geyser you said. Did you hear me say I wouldn't fix it?* Crying nearly, knowing himself cuckolded. He looks as if he wants to smash the geyser. She's not afraid he will, only suddenly full of pity because she knows he hasn't the nerve. Tentatively, like animals, they lick each other's wounds through some small gesture of tenderness. *I forgot your talc*, he says at last. And the girl. Resigned. *It doesn't matter Joe.* And touches her arm. She begins to unrobe. Cut to mid shot Joe. Move in close to him as he watches her naked. He swallows, half intends to speak, to say, *I love you, Lil.* Turns, goes out of the bathroom. Roll captions over working geyser.

Guy went to the table near the window, inserted paper into the typewriter and tapped out the words: *The Geyser*, by Guy Spruce; and then, as a memorandum, the monologue that began, *A fine thing. A fine thing, I say. Whaddid ya say this morning? Fix the geyser for me Joe.*

Going into the bathroom he sat on the hard edge of the tub in which Anina lay, breasts afloat. Only in the skin beneath the breasts was there any trace of her Indian blood; there and in her brown eyes and dark hair.

Her real name was Annie MacBride, and Guy had brought her from Islington, from the house of her Scottish Indian-railways father and Anglo-Indian mother where Guy had boarded while finishing *A Pram in the Hall.* Mrs. MacBride had been glad to get rid of her because at the age of eighteen Annie had taken a fancy to emphasizing her Indian blood instead of disguising it as her mother had always done. She did this by changing her name to Anina, wearing sarees and burning joss-sticks in her oily-papered bedroom. Mr. MacBride had long since ceased to care what happened to her.

So, almost, had Guy.

So he sat on the edge of the bath and looked at her and wondered whether *The Geyser* wasn't too much influenced by Paddy Chayevsky and Tennessee Williams.

Twenty-Four

As George paid for the first of the evening's gins and tonics he thought: I have just been talking to an heiress. Her name is Gillian Spruce.

'You can't tell which way it's going these days,' a man near by said to another man, both drinking brown. 'You can say that again,' the other man said. 'It's what I warned them, isn't it?' 'They don't listen though.' 'Nobody pays them to listen, that's why.' 'You get nowhere talking.' 'You have to carve it up. Look at Spreckley.' 'That's right, Spreckley.' 'Spreckley had it all worked out.' 'Him and Grover.' 'No, Grover wasn't in it. It was Spreckley carved it up. Grover wasn't in it.' 'You don't notice him though.' 'Grover wasn't in it.'

George moved to a side table, but the pub was a small one.

'I told her it wasn't any use,' the big woman said to the smaller woman. 'It's no use, I said, his mind's made up.' 'What did she say to that?' 'Nothing. But she was dead needled.' 'What, nothing? Her?' 'Her.' 'You wouldn't have thought.' 'Made up, I said, and you know what he is when his mind's made up.' 'Didn't she take it off then?' 'Yes, she took it off then.' 'At her age.' 'Took it off and flounced out.' 'Did you ever.' 'You have to laugh though don't you?'

But neither did. George drank up, left the pub and walked back up the hill to the telephone box. He dialled Alice's Hampstead number.

'Hello,' a voice said. Alice. Alice's voice.

'It's George, Alice.'

'Hello, George.'

He pictured the smile that went with her voice and then wondered whether the one he pictured was the one she wore. And how was she standing?

'How are you?' he asked.

'I'm fine. And you?'

'Mustn't grumble. Sam?'

'Sam's fine.'

'Can I see you, Alice?'

'When, George?'

'This evening?'

'Well, no George —'

'Have supper with me?'

'I'm sorry. I'm meeting Sam in town.'

'Oh.'

'You just caught me before I got in the bath.'

'Not even time for a quick one before you're off?'

'I'm afraid not, George.'

'Oh, dear.'

'Some other time. I'd like that, George. It's been a long time since you rang.'

'A long time.'

'Are you all right, George?'

'Yes. And you?'

'I got your postcard, your change of address.'

'Good.'

'Bayswater. Very swish.'

'It's only a bed-sitter. My treat, Alice.'

'What?'

'Supper. My treat. Not on you. Not dutch. My treat.'

'I'd have loved it, George.'

'So much to tell you.'

'Are you on the phone in Bayswater, George?'

They were using each other's names like silent blessings that served for endearments.

'Yes, but it's only a coin-box. I'll ring you.'

'All right.'

'Tomorrow?'

'Yes, but make it after eleven. We'll be late back tonight, and I'll sleep in.'

'I'm glad, Alice.'

'Glad?'

'Glad it's you who can sleep in, now.' He laughed. 'And that it's Sam gets up and goes to work. He still brings home the bacon, eh?' he said.

'Yes. Sam brings home the bacon.'

'Smoked ham sometimes?'

'Sometimes smoked ham.'

'We could have had smoked ham tonight.'

'We'll have it next time.'

'Only guaranteed tonight. I wanted your advice.'

'What about, George?'

'About two jobs I've been offered. Which I should take.' His mouth felt full of old, cold ash: raked so many times in the past. 'Perhaps Sam would help me choose,' he said, because she had met the situation with the familiar, forgiving silence. 'He's a man of the world, isn't he? He could help me choose,' and meant to, but could not say: Choose between two lousy alternatives.

'Perhaps he could, George, but —'

'I'm not drunk,' he thought it fair to tell her.

'I know.'

'I mean I'm not drinking these days. Mick says there's an opening for me in his new set-up.'

'What's the alternative?'

'You never liked Mick. But he's all right. Mick's my style, Alice.'

'I can't advise you, George. Not when it comes to Mick. Neither could Sam. Sam doesn't know Mick.'

'Oh, Sam, Sam wouldn't know any Micks. You don't have to tell me.'

'Don't bring Sam in on it, George. He's sweet and patient, but don't ask him to advise you.'

'I must ask someone.'

'Are you in trouble?'

'No. I don't know. I've got to take one of these jobs. The other's not with anyone you know. Selling stuff on commission.'

'What sort of stuff?'

'Toys. Mostly teddy bears. Cuddly ones. Near Christmas they reckon I could nett twenty quid a week. There aren't any prospects, but it might tide me over.'

'We're half way through September, George. Can you learn the ropes quickly enough to get the best out of Christmas?'

'They say it's easy.'

'Who are they?'

'Two chaps who've done it.'

'Are they still doing it?'

'They're on to something better. It's as I said, there aren't any prospects and I'm over the age limit really. They like young chaps but a man still in the organization, a chap called Perce, says he'll speak for me. You get a car too. It would tide me over.'

'Tide you over what?'

'I owe money to Tim. He wants it back. He's in a jam himself.'

'Tim? In a jam? Tim?'

'It's Gillian. She's pregnant.'

'Oh, no. Oh, no, George.'

'Keep it dark. I've just seen her.'

'Is there anything I can do?'

'I don't think so. Yes. Send her a postcard. A picture postcard saying hello how are you, just casually, but put your address on it.'

'Yes, I will. But why?'

'I don't know. So that she doesn't feel cut off. They're sending her off to Wales soon. Tim's sending her with Sarah.'

'Won't the father play?'

'They don't want him to. He's a plumber's mate.'

'Oh, Lord —'

'They're going to get the baby farmed out by an adoption society or something.'

'How's Gill going to take that?'

'I don't think she's sure. That's why I think she ought to have an escape route.'

'Escape route?'

'If she wants to run away.'

'You mean come here?'

'Well, who knows?'

'I couldn't have her here —'

'You could hold her hand for a night, Alice.'

'Hold her hand?'

'Talking to her you wouldn't think anything was wrong. But how can you tell? If she gets a postcard from you she'll guess I've told you. You may be just the sort of person she feels she wants to talk to. You always liked each other.'

'I wish you hadn't told me, George. I shall worry all night.'

'Look, Alice —'

'What?'

'Ring Sam. Tell him you can't come. Tell him to go where ever it is you're going alone, and then you come and have supper with me. I'm not more than ten minutes away from you. I could pick you up in half an hour when you've had your bath. There's something else I must tell you.'

Her voice rose. 'George I can't. Honestly I can't. I oughtn't to be talking to you now. I ought to be in that bath and getting dressed. Tonight's awfully important to Sam.'

'Business?'

'The firm's New York associates.'

'I'm sorry. I'll ring off then. Not to worry.'

'Oh, George!'

Irritation. desperation; and the dregs of an old habit of affection, of seeing things through together: dying hard.

'Tell me this other thing you've got to tell me,' she said.

'I had a test, Alice. It's I who can't have children.'

He waited.

'Well, yes,' she said eventually. 'It's what I rather assumed. I went to a doctor too. He said I seemed to be all right.'

'Was it Sam wanted to be sure?'

'Sam and I are too old for children, we don't want them, George. It wasn't anything to do with Sam. It was before Sam's time.'

'You mean in our time.'

'Yes, in our time. Ages ago, George.'

'You didn't say anything. Why didn't you say anything? It was one of the things I accused you of, not having children.'

'I knew you didn't mean it. Not really mean it. You always guessed it was you anyway.'

'You should have told me you'd been looked at. Honestly, Alice, you really should have told me. You should have made me go and be done too.'

'Well I was afraid.'

'What of?'

'Of how you'd react if you found out definitely it was you.'

'Yes, I see. No, I don't see.'

'Of course you see. It was one of your big things about the future, I mean knowing your first-born child would inherit ten thousand pounds. When he was born you were going to get a real job and spend the Butterfield income on sending him to Eton.'

'Winchester.'

'Sometimes it was one sometimes the other. If you'd known for sure you'd never have children God knows what would have happened to us.'

'You were wrong, Alice. It would have made me face facts.'

'Oh, George.'

'Well of course it would.'

'How did you face them when you got the result of your test?'

'What?'

'How did you face facts when you knew?'

'It was different then. I hadn't got you.'

'But how many days were you drunk, George?'

Presently he said, 'I don't remember.'

'It was almost the only thing that put you back on the rails when you'd gone off them.'

'What was?'

'This romantic idea of the future having to be worked for because of the ten thousand and Eton or Winchester. Working for it was never quite got round to, but the idea was there. That's why I didn't tell you.'

'At least you could have told me when we had that silly row.'

'Which one?'

'The last one.'

'I suppose I didn't because as soon as it began I guessed it was the last.'

'Why didn't you throw it in my face? I threw it in yours.'

'I hated our rows.'

'Do you and Sam row?'

'No. We've both had our share. Me with you and Sam with his previous wife. George, I really must go now.'

'Alice —'

'Yes?'

'Are you used to it yet?'

'Used to what?'

'Not having each other?'

'Yes, I'm used to it. I really *am used* to it. Ring me tomorrow if you still want to, George. Come and have a drink. Meet Sam again. I don't know – perhaps Sam could help. He knows lots of people —'

'Oh, come off it, Alice.' He laughed to take out the sting. 'I'm not going to butter up Sam. Not Sam of all people —'

'All right. Just ring when you want. Meanwhile I'll write to Gillian. I promise.'

'She's my heir.'

'I suppose she is. But you're only forty-three, George. She's got a long time to wait.'

'Should I have told her she's my heir?'

'No. Why should you?'

'That's what I thought.'

'Goodbye, George. Bless you and take care of yourself.'

'Goodbye, Alice.'

From his pocket he took his loose change and counted out fourpence, the cost of contacting Perce who might be back from Widnes. But there was no answer from either Stores or Sales. It had gone six and the world of commercial affairs had closed down and entered pubs all the way from City Road to Notting Hill.

And he did not want to ring Mick. He confirmed from his

watch that he had time for at least one more drink before setting out for Aunt Clara's: at least one; perhaps two. And he had money in his pocket. Perhaps three. Not beer. Gin.

Twenty-five

At twenty-past six there was an hour yet to go before sunset; ninety minutes before lighting-up time; but the sun was already obscured by a slate grey growth of pink rimmed cloud that bulged solid, twenty degrees above the horizon, touching down behind it in the direction of Woking, Sunningdale and Reading.

City windows facing south-west, high up, jutting above the uneven edges of the metropolitan canyons, became opaline, reflecting the expanse of now clear sky in which clouds other than those making up that low but threatening formation had been torn to wispy threads by brisk winds that whipped straw and orange-papers across the cobbled yards of Covent Garden and blew in gusts along the deserted roads, alleys and passages of the City: Milk Street, Crutched Friars, Threadneedle: winds running for the east coast, to make ripples in muddy estuaries and help stiff-winged gulls to plane effortlessly in the wake of trawlers.

The City was abandoned for the night. In that quiet sector protected by the cathedral cats prowled and carved heraldic beasts stood guard at the gothic doorways of old guild and livery halls whose interiors of cold stone and warm wood benches gave off smells of mice and beeswax. Dustbins and puce-coloured sack, loaded with the day's waste of brown paper, fibrous string and cardboard boxes, stood vagrant over gratings and in the porches of buildings grimy from long survival and apparently blind or indifferent to the tall conceptions in glass and concrete in whose opaque, superior shadows they themselves still continued to house wares and the mystical apparatus of business and the ghosts of a dead race of clerks and apprentices who, under these roofs, had heard the bells of Bow.

As Bartle had: but not Wallingford who now walked lame down Cheapside during this first hesitant leg of the long journey home to his Surrey suburb, going late to avoid the crush, step by step, elderly but dainty, with an ageing man's precision: tap, tap, with a smooth malacca cane; wounded at Gallipoli; a black homburg neat on his head above his thoughtful, droop-lipped face, a worn despatch case (a present from his only child, a daughter, married well into the Law); in the despatch case a draft balance sheet unlikely to be looked at, *The Financial Times*, a muffler (in case it blew up); and *Barchester Towers* to pass the time on what he still called The Southern Electric, but tonight unlikely to be read.

The late Mr. Bartle had heard the bells of Bow, and on such a night as this would walk as slowly home as Wallingford did now, but reluctant to leave, not simply to avoid a crush; and be back at half-past eight next morning; even on his dying day (November the seventh, nineteen forty); a heart attack reaching for the bound, 1938 editions of *Taxation*, alone in the office, because the Alert had gone and partner and staff were sensibly below in the sandbagged basement sipping coffee and saccharin in the yellow light of a naked electric bulb and faced only with the awkwardness when the all clear went an hour later to finding Mr. Bartle there upstairs, dead as a doornail as the Gwendoline of that time had said.

'You will be sorry to hear,' Mr. Wallingford duly wrote to their most reliable junior clerk, Aircraftman Spruce, 'that Mr. Bartle died last week, quite unexpectedly. Only the day before he had referred to you and hoped that you were getting on well. I cannot for the moment say what his death may mean in regard to the future of the firm but naturally I hope for no drastic change but to carry on alone and also to be enabled to stand by the obligation I am under to reinstate you when the time comes and you return to less exciting but perhaps more exacting duties.'

Reading the letter against a bleak November background of frosty airfield wastes Tim had frowned and passed the letter to his mucker – in civil life a baker's roundsman with prospects. His mucker said, 'He couldn't do no less, it's your right, old son,' gave the letter back and added, inevitably as it were, 'Roll on.'

But this Mr. Wallingford had not known (although he might have guessed it, the time being spared to consider) and did not conceive of now on this September evening when he was twenty-one years older (and a stone lighter because time had worn him thin) for tonight nothing of his behaviour towards young Spruce but seemed, in long or short retrospect, fair in employment, loyal in partnership. Heaven could witness (and the bulk of St. Paul's, looming just then at his left shoulder, implied immediate co-operation) that nothing had been undone for Spruce that should have been done, nothing done him that shouldn't have been. He had been easier on young Spruce as junior partner than old Bartle had ever been on him. Had he, for instance, ever said to young Spruce in the hearing of employees anything like: Good God, but you're a fool, Wallingford? After thirty years it still rankled, still quickened the ache in his legs and shortened his patience with his infirmity, revived the ego-diminishing knowledge of old Miss Poole, smirking behind her Remington and a board and glass partition that didn't reach to the ceiling because old Bartle didn't believe in unnecessarily expensive privacy. And Bartle had died in the war when you couldn't get building permits for love or money. It had been 1947 before the partition achieved those final inches that gave more than the room stature; and Matilda Poole, old Bartle's loyal dragon, was dead herself by then, had joined her widowed mother in the family grave at Streatham (from which the deceased father was curiously absent), the one with the angel on it that had looked odd, laid aside to admit Matilda, pointing its marble finger not at heaven but along the gravel path towards the exit of the cemetery on the day Wallingford, for form's sake, attended Matilda's funeral and came away alarmed at the number of relations she had had who might have heard poorly of him second-hand, the women all dragons, and the men uncomplaining in sober clothes.

And it was 1947 – or rather 1946 – when young Spruce came back, bulky from years of airmen's meals, already married and therefore potentially steady, with valuable administrative experience (ground-staff), worth a dozen of the youngsters out of school (although correspondingly expensive); a far cry from the gangling sixteen-year-old Bartle had taken a shine to in spite of the pretentious mother who had come to speak up for him at his interview. They had laughed afterwards, he and old Bartle, at the idea of the mother, but it was Bartle who said, 'That's no mother's boy. We'll have to work him hard, though. That type can turn lazy when they get away from home.'

And work him hard they did. At least Bartle did, tucking him under his wing as if he were the only junior Bartle Wallingford had ever employed. Bartle's own son Barnaby had been both pride and disappointment, rejecting the profession and choosing the Sea. Among the paraphernalia on old Bartle's roll-topped desk strange objects would appear from year to year; and picture postcards that lost their shine under City dust: souvenirs of Barnaby's shore leave. Names of places like Penang, Hong Kong, Honolulu and Rio de Janeiro spiced air that more naturally smelled of Old Jewry, St. Mary Axe and Gutter Lane. In Bartle's office (now unrecognizable, refurnished by Wallingford in the light-oak and green metal favoured by equipment shops in High Holborn and Kingsway) Wallingford had got the measure of Bartle's almost mystical preoccupation with The City, although not a corresponding taste for it. To Wallingford, twenty years younger, Bartle had been 'old school', and what more typical of Bartle and his times than Bartle's stiff, wing-tipped collars, and spotted ties, his addiction to a glass of Madeira after lunch and on his way home?

Wallingford paused, old school himself now, he supposed, and turned off his usual route and picked up the route Bartle used to take, entered the pub Bartle always entered and in the early days of their partnership had tried to get Wallingford to go into with him, night after night, mostly unsuccessfully because unlike Bartle whose wife had died young Wallingford's wife Lesley was very much alive (then as now) and Wallingford's tastes ran more sophisticatedly to Dry Fly sherry from a home decanter and a cosy dinner, with friends, a rubber or two of bridge perhaps, or a quiet supper without friends followed by book and bedtime and formal copulation. He was not wedded to the profession as Bartle had been and came of a family with a bit of money left and not much enterprise, whereas Bartle came from nothing and had always spoken with an accent suggestive of early associations with Walworth, Camberwell, Denmark Hill and Norwood where he acquired property which went to Barnaby (due presently to swallow the anchor and live in Chatham). His share in the partnership went to Wallingford.

The pub was dark and smelled of stale casks and the ghost of Bartle. Wallingford, alone in there except for the barman, drank whisky. There had been a curious codicil to old Bartle's Will: one hundred pounds for young Spruce if he returned voluntarily to the office after the war and continued his studies, to be paid, without prior notification, one year to the day after his re-employment unless of course he had been dismissed for negligence or worse. How surprised Spruce had been, and a bit suspicious at first as if he thought he should have been told earlier.

Fifteen bob a week they had paid Spruce when he joined the firm before the war. He was getting two pounds when he left to go into the Air Force. He knew nothing when they took him on. He hadn't even got School Certificate, let alone Matriculation which meant he had to waste time studying for the articles, which he did at eighteen, but without a premium. Bartle knew the Spruces couldn't afford one, but he believed in the boy. From what Spruce's mother said his schooling had sounded all right until you looked into it. A private school she said, run on public school lines. You couldn't talk to Wallingford who had been to a minor one about public school lines. Young Spruce not only knew no latin, having given it up at the age of twelve, but had also gone home from school every midday for what he called his dinner. No wonder the boy was agonizingly shy and blushed the colour of beetroot if you so much as looked at him.

Wallingford drained his glass and ordered another, not minding tonight that he would miss his train. In fact it would be a good thing to be late. His wife Lesley would say: What happened? in her calm, steady but somehow exasperating way. And then it would be easier to explain. Departure from a fifteen year habit of punctuality would, in itself, prepare the ground.

'Do you remember a man called Bartle?' Wallingford asked the barman, and at once regretted asking in case the answer was yes I knew old Mr. Bartle, was you a friend of his? But the answer was no.

'He used to come in here every night.'

'When was that?'

'Oh, twenty years ago and more.'

'I wasn't here then,' the barman said, conclusively.

Wallingford thought: Tonight I feel my age. I'm sixty-five. If Bartle had still been alive he would have been eighty-five or more; senile, in retirement: as Wallingford himself had been looking forward to being until this afternoon, just gone four, when young Spruce came back so late from lunch at Simpsons.

'There's a potential junior partner for us,' Bartle had said years ago. But Wallingford hadn't been sure. He still hadn't been sure when Spruce came back from the Air Force. The chap hadn't a bean. Two thousand pounds it had cost Wallingford to buy his way in with Bartle and in those days that was money. The only money Spruce had, it seemed (when he sounded him out, unobtrusively, anxious not to put ideas into the chap's head), belonged to his WAAF wife and that not much, and sunk into a mortgage on a house that struck Wallingford as somewhat above Spruce's station and means. There was the hundred pounds from Bartle, of course, and Spruce's gratuity from the RAF: about two hundred pounds in all, probably; nothing from Spruce's parents, dead of a bomb. Nothing. Just Spruce getting his head down and being unexpectedly clever handling old clients, getting a name with them in fact.

But who would have thought he'd get a medal?

They were after him then, all right: the smart firms. Well, if you couldn't find young men in the profession with money any more you found them with brains. 'I've had proposals, Mr. Wallingford,' young Spruce said. He could see him now, still wearing his demob suit after three years, standing there in the light oak and green metal office whose glass partition by then made such a close-knit and satisfactory right-angle with the ceiling, shutting belowstairs chit-chat out. 'Who from?' Wallingford asked, a bit suspicious of a trick, but, on being told, cut to the quick. 'You'll be lost there. They're too big,' he warned, and added, 'You'd better come in with me.' 'It's what I'd prefer,' Spruce replied, so that at once Wallingford wondered why; wondered what could be wrong with a man who'd won a gold medal but preferred a junior partnership in an old-fashioned one-man firm, preferred it to an opportunity with Mark, Pender, Phillips and Co.

And, Wallingford now reminded himself, nobody could say he hadn't treated young Spruce handsomely: Two thousand pounds to buy a one-third share of the profits with payment by deduction from drawings spread over ten years. Fully paid up now. Which meant Spruce owned Two Thousand pounds of their combined capital.

And had walked in, flushed from a long lunch at Simpsons and said he wanted to Dissolve, to join the board of Curtis, Jackson and Bell (Plastics) Limited whom old Bartle had known when it was just old Billy Curtis working in a shed behind a garage in Peckham.

'You're joking of course,' Wallingford said, laying his heavy horn-rimmed reading spectacles on top of the draft balance sheet (now in his despatch case).

'I'm afraid I'm not,' Spruce replied, smelling of brandy which was noticeable because he seldom smelt of anything stronger than Pears Soap and Bay Rum.

'But you can't be serious.'

'I'm afraid I am.'

The brandy had flushed Spruce's cheeks almost as darkly as his agonizing shyness had once flushed them and had gone on flushing them, although to a lesser degree, right up to and inclusively of the moment he announced, in this same office, his medal. And then it had never been seen again, Wallingford realized, until now when through its brandy counterpart it gave him a look of eternal youth; less than frank, vigorous, almost treacherous.

'And what,' Wallingford said, 'is supposed to happen to the Practice?' And, when Spruce did not at once reply, 'What in fact happens to me?'

'I discussed that with Vernon Bell at lunch today,' Spruce said. 'He's talked to Ripley, Coyne and Marples and they're prepared to buy it from us.'

'Who are Ripley, Coyne and Marples?'

'The auditors that Curtis Jackson and Bell are electing next month.'

'They usually elect us,' Wallingford said, snatching a dry, unexpected straw of wit in the sea that he suspected was only keeping him up temporarily, saving him for drowning in the next minute or two.

'Well it's Ripley Coyne from now on,' Spruce said. 'If you agree I'll go and talk to them. They'll want the last few years' accounts.'

'It's not unusual to want the last few years' accounts when considering a purchase,' Wallingord said. 'But I don't understand.'

Spruce said nothing.

'I don't understand what is happening, Timothy,' Wallingford said. They seldom used Christian names because his own was Cyril.

'Here I am,' he went on, 'sitting at four o'clock on a normal Thursday afternoon, considering the curious situation disclosed by the draft balance sheet to the thirtieth of June last of Parton Sons and Nephew (London) Limited, planning to discuss with you whatever connection there might be between the figure of stock-on-hand and the somewhat increased percentage of gross profit to turnover —'

'That's simple,' Spruce broke in. 'The nephew's inflated the value of the stock again. He always does when he wants a bigger dividend.'

'I realize that,' said Wallingford. 'That is simple. That is something I understand and indeed can take care of by a word in the ear of Mr. Parton senior who I am sure will not be surprised because Nephew has long been a cross he accepts having to endure —'

'What don't you understand?'

'Your announcement of an intention to dissolve partnership. The calm manner in which you make the announcement. Your assumption that it should be easy for me to understand what has led up to this astonishing situation I find myself in, on, as I said, a perfectly normal Thursday afternoon.'

'It's simple enough.'

'So you imply. So you keep saying. But I find it far from simple. No, not simple at all. I find it quite the reverse of simple. I see not only a situation I can hardly comprehend but the most enormous complications ahead, looming, yes looming, when comprehension has at last emerged.'

'I am forty years old,' Spruce said, looking not a day older than thirty-two.

'What has that to do with it?'

'I was just saying —'

'*I* am sixty-five.'

'I know.'

'You must grant me a habit of mind, Timothy. Yes, a habit of mind as well as of body. I have little armour to withstand change or even sudden alarms.'

'At the age of forty,' Spruce said, 'a man is at the crossroads.'

'And again, it would seem, at the age of sixty-five.'

'I know you've been looking forward to retirement.'

'I'm glad it hadn't escaped your notice.'

'But I've got another thirty years work ahead of me and I want to spend them in industry not private practice.'

'That is reasonable. Perfectly reasonable. For the qualified accountant these are the two really valid alternatives, a career in industry or a career in private practice.'

'The arrangements we could make would give us both what we want. We sell the practice to Ripley Coyne and Marples, I join Curtis Jackson and Bell and you retire.'

'Retire on what?'

'On what you get from Ripley Coyne.'

'I may be sixty-five, but I don't live in anticipation of an especially early death. To retire from a business continued by a more youthful partner is one thing. You can say, yes, you can say that is possible financially. But to dispose of a business like ours to some quite different firm none of whose partners our own clients may like, and attempt to live on what you'd get for it, that is something else again and no, you can say, no, that wouldn't be possible financially. No, not at all. Not at all possible.'

'We don't know yet what Ripley Coyne and Marples have in mind as a purchase price.'

'Indeed we don't,' Wallingford said and, upon inspiration, added, '*We* don't. But do you?'

'No, I don't. I don't *know*. But Vernon Bell thinks the whole thing might be done first of all on the lines of a merger, with you continuing for a while, making sure our clients are happy under the new regime, and then retiring presently.'

'Got rid of as soon as decency permitted.'

'Do you want to go on working for ever?'

'I said got rid of as soon as decency permitted.'

'I heard you.'

'Got rid of.'

'Pensioned, not got rid of.'

'It's remarkable.'

'What's remarkable?'

'The things that can go on respecting one's future without one's slightest knowledge. They must want you badly.'

'Why do you say that?'

'Well isn't it obvious? I'd say it's obvious. You seem to have worked over every possible inch of the ground in anticipation of my objections. Not you alone, no. You and young Vernon Bell. Putting your heads together. You and Bell. Heads together over lunch at Simpsons not only today no doubt but countless times before. Heads together over lunch at Simpsons while I am left here, in ignorance, coping with the firm's business, mulling over, yes mulling over the ba'ance sheet of Parton Sons & Nephew. Rigged stock included. Rigged stock included, I say,' and accompanied saying it with a bang of an ebony ruler on a light-oak desk with green-leather top discreetly decorated with a gold-filigree edging.

'And Ripley Coyne & Marples,' he continued, encouraged by

what he believed to be a look of dismay on young Spruce's brandy-flushed face at the bang of the ebony ruler. 'Ripley Coyne & Marples. Who are they? Where do *they* spring from?'

'I thought everyone had heard of Ripley Coyne & Marples.'

'You thought everyone had heard. What does that remark suggest? That I ought to have heard? That I'm out of touch perhaps? But my point is quite a different one. The name of Ripley Coyne & Marples is not exactly foreign to me but I say again where do they spring from? What are they to do with our oldest and most valuable client Curtis Jackson and Bell, whom Mr. Bartle knew long before you were born when it was just old Billy Curtis working in a shed behind a garage in Peckham?'

'I've told you what they are to do with them.'

'When Curtis Jackson and Bell was just old Billy Curtis their accounts were Bartle Wallingford when Bartle Wallingford was just old Bartle. If two firms ever grew up together you can say Curtis Jackson and Bell grew up with Bartle Wallingford. But of course I am out of touch. Oh, yes, a long way out of touch. I keep forgetting that it is *you* who have dealt almost exclusively with Curtis Jackson and Bell for the last year or two —'

'The last ten years.'

'So naturally you must forgive my curiosity if I ask what has happened, if I ask what has gone wrong, if I ask why after sixty years Curtis Jackson and Bell have become dissatisfied, so dissatisfied that next month they propose to elect Ripley Coyne and Marples in our place. Could it be that Tom Bell's son, your friend Vernon, has another friend, someone whose name is either Ripley or Coyne or Marples and has promised to transfer the account at the earliest opportunity? Are you all masons, I wonder? Old Bartle was a mason. Could some of that distressful aroma have rubbed off on to you, Timothy?'

'I have nothing against masons, but I find the reasoning behind your suggestion offensive.'

'*Do* you. *Do* you. Offensive. And I am not supposed to find offensive your casual suggestion that we dispose of Fred Bartle's firm and pension me off in order to ease your way on to a board with Master Vernon?'

'No, you're not supposed to find it offensive. We are talking about business, but you keep making the whole thing so damned personal.'

'Oh, I'm sorry. I apologize. Please forgive me. Obviously I must stop looking aghast at the prospect of a penurious old age —'

'Penurious!'

'– and start looking at the affairs in terms of a brilliant career for you in plastics.'

'I suppose we should carry on as we are, then, with me doing eighty per cent of the work and taking thirty-three and a third of the profits and eventually shouldering the liability of a sleeping partner who costs me a fortune.'

'Ah. Ah. Now we're getting at the truth. The next thing that will come up is the firm's name, I don't doubt. It will come out that you harbour resentment because we agreed not to change it to Bartle Wallingford and Spruce.'

'It wouldn't have hurt you.'

'You should have said so at the time. Between partners there is nothing if there isn't a frank exchange of ideas and views.'

'You have always had a talent for not listening to any that don't correspond with yours.'

'If there's one thing I dislike it is lack of frankness.'

'When in the past twelve years have we adopted any of *my* suggestions?'

'It's the rock all partnerships founder on. Lack of frankness.'

'Your whole attitude towards me has been one of distant superiority.'

'Bartle and I had our differences, but we always discussed them frankly.'

'Distant superiority and not-so-distant annoyance because clients like Curtis Jackson showed their preference.'

'I should have followed my instinct and let you go when you made out you'd had an offer from Mark, Pender, Phillips.'

'I *did* have an offer.'

'But I allowed myself to be persuaded by poor old Bartle's opinion. Even though he was dead and gone. "There's a potential junior partner for us," he once said, and I took that into consideration.'

'You took my examination success into consideration, and the fact that clients —'

'I should have followed my instinct, but there you are. There's nothing in partnership if there isn't give and take, if you're not capable of giving weight to an opposite view.'

'I'm sorry you regret taking me in.'

'Can you expect me not to when I'm faced with this dissolution?'

'Dissolution is only a word.'

'So is ruin.'

'Now you're being melodramatic.'

'And what about our loyal staff?'

'What about them?'

'Are Ripley Coyne and Marples going to employ them?'

'That's the sort of detail I haven't gone into.'

'How can you call it a detail?'

'How can I go into that sort of detail before you and I have reached an agreement?'

'Agreement? A dissolution strikes me as the opposite of an agreement. What about young Gregson? And Mathews? And Wilson?'

'What about them? Is there any reason to suppose Ripley Coyne could take over our clients and not expand their staff? Surely it goes almost without saying that Gregson and Mathews and Wilson will automatically go over with our clients?'

'To make sure the clients are happy, I suppose. For how long? I ask that. For how long? What happens when Ripley Coyne decide they can cope with the extra volume of work without the expense of three extra audit clerks? And what about my Miss Crayfoot and your Miss Maple?'

'Millicent would come with me anyway.'

'What about Gwendoline? Do Ripley Coyne put in an extra telephone exchange to accommodate Gwendoline?'

'She can easily get another job. And knows it.'

'Only last week she was getting excited about her next year's holiday.'

'Gwendoline is always excited about next year's holiday. She can hardly wait to get back from the one she's on.'

'What will she say when she gets the push and has to search for another job with a firm that will respect her next year's arrangements?'

'I can't order my life on what Gwendoline will or will not say or what her next year's arrangements are.'

When old Matilda Poole slipped on the stairs and broke her ankle we paid her full salary all the time she was away, and sent her to the Isle of White. But that was in the old days. That was before your time.'

'From what I remember of Matilda Poole the firm wouldn't

have dared do otherwise.'

'Before your time. In the days when people were treated with consideration. The days of old Bartle. Old Curtis. What do you young chaps know about the private ethics of business? It's all make, make; grab, grab. Look at you, Timothy. Twenty-five years ago you wouldn't have said boo to a goose. And now you're telling me what I've got to do.'

'I'm sick of this,' Spruce said, leaning suddenly with his square hands splayed upon the green leather of the desk. 'Sick of this and sick of you. I've had to work for what I've got. Bloody well work. Work like hell. I sweated blood before the war and sweated blood after it and if I stay on here I'll go on sweating blood so that you can sit back like an old city gentleman because you were well enough off to buy yourself into a business Fred Bartle built up from scratch and you came near to ruining during the war.'

'Don't talk to me about the war. Ah, now, don't you talk to me about the war —'

'Skulking down there in the basement just because the alert had gone and poor old Bartle up here, dying alone because there wasn't anyone to help him.'

'Now that I won't stand for. I won't stand for it, Spruce.'

'That's what they said. That's what Matilda Poole said.'

'I don't care a bugger what old Matilda Poole said,' Wallingford shouted. 'And if I was skulking, so was she. She used to sit down there in the basement with her spare typewriter, saying, "There's no time to be idle, Mr. Wallingford." It used to get on all our nerves, that typewriter, clack clack clack. I tell you I carried the whole weight of this business from 1940 until the unfortunate day I took you in as my junior partner —'

'You were always keen on that word junior.'

'—the whole weight of it, Spruce, and never knowing when you got here whether you'd find the building still standing. Records lost, businesses ruined, old clients ringing up in tears because everything they owned had gone up in smoke —'

'Oh, Christ —'

'I had to be guide and counsellor, clients in tears I say. Chaos everywhere. Picked your way through broken glass many a morning. While you sat back having a rare old time, like all you youngsters that were in uniform and never heard a shot fired in anger. But quick enough to come back and talk about reinstatement rights.'

'You never heard me talk about reinstatement rights.'

'Coming back, fed like fighting cocks. It wasn't like that in the previous lot. Biscuits and bully we had then. No reinstatement rights either, even if you were lucky enough to have come through Verdun or Passchendaele —'

'Or Gallipoli.'

'And Gallipoli. Families ruined. Profiteers everywhere. Twenty thousand pounds my father lost between 1914 and 1918.'

'My father never had twenty thousand pounds to lose.'

'Twenty thousand pounds. So much for my going up to Cambridge. So much for my career at the Bar. Practically every penny that could be spared put aside to help me into some kind of partnership some day. You don't think I didn't sweat blood too? And something you probably wouldn't understand. No, no you wouldn't. But accountancy was a marginal profession for me. I can hardly expect you to understand, and no doubt it sounds ridiculous, yes ridiculous, but a profession in which you find yourself junior partner to men like Fred Bartle – brilliant, yes I don't say not brilliant – but bless his heart hardly speaking the King's English, well, set that against your upbringing and expectations and see where it gets you.'

'It gets you a comfortable pension from Ripley Coyne and Marples, and Mark Ripley is Charterhouse and Cambridge, so honour should be satisfied.'

'Is he!' Wallingford said. 'Which college?'

Spruce flushed deeper. He didn't know. 'I don't know,' he said.

'These are things you ought to know,' Wallingford said, instinctively turning the social screw. 'Curtis Jackson and Bell, for instance. Old Curtis was nothing, but the grandson is Rugby and Jesus. Jackson is Jewish and stinking rich and so it doesn't matter what else. Bell is county and young Vernon is Winchester and Balliol like his father before him.' He added, 'I hope you're not stepping out of your class. You may think Vernon Bell accepts you at face value and is too much of a gentleman to look into your pedigree, but believe me it will have been done.'

'I was sixteen when Mr. Bartle first took me along to their offices. They know my pedigree.'

'So long as you realize it. More power to you. It's your brain they're after. I hope it's elastic.'

'What is that supposed to mean?'

'Industry isn't private practice.'
'Are you talking about professional integrity?'
'In a big firm like that you have to be a member of the team. That's what I'm talking about. It's Jackson who calls the tune where *you're* going. Curtis has the patents, for what they're worth now, Jackson has the money and Bell is a gentleman. Brains, money and class. Remember that, Remember that, I say, you're not taking them anything they haven't already got. You're not filling a gap. Your contribution isn't going to be a unique one in their experience.'
'Well, they're paying five thousand a year for it, to start with.'
Wallingford endured a brief sensation in his belly like the one in a lift, going up.

He felt it again, two hours later, towards the end of his second whisky. Five thousand a year took the fight out of you. He could remember nothing of their quarrel after the sum was mentioned. The quarrel had petered out. There was no arguing with five thousand a year.
He ordered yet a third whisky. 'One for the road,' he said, and smiled bleakly at the barman who smiled bleakly back and wondered whether the old man was a fruit hanging about for a wandering sea-going lad making his thirsty way west from the docks.
Five thousand a year. Wallingford thought. And Spruce was barely forty. Irresistible temptation. The whisky tasted metallic, like gold coins. It's peat-smoke smell conjured an ambience of Town and Country and hound's-tooth cloth that extinguished the beer-cask whiff of black-coated, stripe-trousered, hard-worked Bartle.
I have not been a success, Wallingford thought, as if admitting fault in a People's Court; blind to realities I have clung to out-moded ideologies. I have been guilty of false assumptions, of bourgeois interpretations of the class structure in our capitalist society. Believing as I did in the cult of privilege and not in the cult of brains and personality I failed to see in young Spruce what Fred Bartle saw.
He drained his whisky, sealing the confession in.
'Time I was moving,' he said to the barman, nodded a goodnight and, collecting his despatch case and stick, made off, turning into Ludgate Hill which ran down to the old course of the The Fleet, now a sewer, hoping to pick up a cab to Charing

Cross, tapping his good-soldier way with his back to Mercantile London, his face towards Chancery, Temple and the Law whose medieval turrets still held prisoner the pale Rossetti faces of his lost Edwardian youth.

The wind, although he did not know it, had changed direction and the bank of south-west cloud which neither he nor the barman had seen was held arrested and beginning to thin out on top as a breeze from the south took command of its destiny and direction. Behind the spire of St. Mary-le-Strand, as the cab he had hailed and now sat in moved towards Aldwych, the opal sky, flecked with lost kites of cloud so high they were yellow with sunlight, created an illusion of darkness not yet due, of a sun about to break through again to frisk the leaves of the plane trees and the blown spray of the fountains which marked the beginning of august, classical, Establishment London.

In the courtyard of Charing Cross station, historically endowed by the monument to Queen Eleanor in her progress, it promised a fine evening; and Wallingford, paying off his cab, was already making calculations in preparation for a meeting with Ripley Coyne and Marples, rendered inevitable it seemed, not by Spruce's action or his own impending acquiescence, but by the press of time from the clocks and Whittington chimes of London, the weight of water in the shadows of her bridges, the caress of air that married stone, bred nothing, but sometimes coaxed, as drugs will coax from prisoners, unpalatable truths, like the truth of being old and tired and glad, almost, of rest in prospect.

'It's Spruce I'm sorry for,' he told himself. 'When Curtis Jackson and Bell pile on the pressure.' And he spoke the truth, elevated enough to do so by the blessed respite from boredom afforded by the day's drama, and felt in his pocket for his first-class season ticket, his passport to Surrey, his gabled, lattice-windowed house; two acres, a strip of land attached worth quite a lot per foot of frontage, money in the bank, a careful wife with private means, respectful tradesmen and a woman for the rough.

Twenty-six

'Worry never got anyone anywhere, Con,' Miss Maple told Miss Crayfoot.

'It's all right for you, Mill,' Miss Crayfoot told Miss Maple who was younger by five years, Connie Crayfoot being thirty-six, the prop of a widowed mother who loved her married sons and daughters more than she loved Connie and would, Connie knew, be sitting alone in Wimbledon staring out the new Slim Jim 21 inch, begrudging her the monthly night Up West with Mill: a beefberger, chips, American fruit tart and espresso at The Wimpy, followed by seats at The Plaza or the London Pavilion, the Odeon Leicester Square or the Ritz, or the Empire, or the Leicester Square Theatre, or The Warner; the old Gaumont in the Haymarket having become a grey-stone shell. Tonight it was *The Brand of the Beast* and *Paranoia* at the London Pav, cert X; no one allowed in ten minutes before the end; so they sat on at The Wimpy over an extra espresso, dutch treat, subconsciously inhibited by the sluggish beat of time, consciously and almost as fearfully excited as presently they hoped to be by *Paranoia* by the row between Connie Crayfoot's Mr. Wallingford and Millicent Maple's Mr. Spruce which Miss Crayfoot had got the drift of from behind the board and glass partition sealing her off, ostensibly, from partnership privacy. Because They had shouted.

'It's all right for you, Mill,' Miss Crayfoot said, stirring her coffee and easing her tweed-skirted knees under the narrow ledge which held the remains of their meal and brought their noses within a few inches of a wall papered to look like bricks from Holloway jail. 'I distinctly heard Mr. Spruce say "I'll be taking Millicent." '

Millicent Maple absent-mindedly squeezed the ketchup bottle: a red plastic tomato whose nozzle-stalk was clogged with brown, petrified bubbles. 'Are you sure that's what he said?' She wanted Con to repeat it. She couldn't hear it often enough. It was due to her.

' "I'll be taking Millicent," he said.'

'Well I don't know, Con. Sometimes I think I need a change. I'm thirty-one you know. I've been here ten years.'

'I've been nearly twenty, Mill.'

'Mr. Spruce has changed recently,' Mill said. 'All these new systems. Like putting people on the pad. It's become – I mean – as if he felt he couldn't quite *rely*. In the old days as soon as he came in he used to say, "Anyone rung?" and I'd tell him, but now directly anyone rings I have to get off my chair, carry my note-book into his room, write them on his pad, walk back and carry on typing. And you can lose the drift, can't you, Con? It's an awful waste of time and if he'd had his way I'd have had to type out messages as well as people who'd just rung but I said to him, Wouldn't it be better if I just put people who ring on the pad and *tell* you messages when you come in? So he said all right, all he'd been trying to do was cut out the chat and save both our times, but he made it sound unfriendly, saying chat like that.'

'He wouldn't be taking you with him if he didn't value you, Mill.'

'And another thing. This new craze he has for making records of telephone conversations. It all takes time. Directly he's rung off, down goes the buzzer, down goes my work, up I get, in I go. "Telephone record," he says, before I've sat down even, "Vernon Bell to T.S." Then the date. Then the time. And not only what was said but what he calls his interim appreciation. Then back I go and have to type it right away and it's not as if it can go straight on the file, he has to see it first, top *and* carbon, and that means a paper clip. *He* says in case it suggests a line of thought but it makes me feel he doesn't trust me to take down. And it all has to be filed. It all adds to the filing, doesn't it? And young Betty has more than she can cope with as it is. I know you don't think much of young Betty but she's the best junior we've had since Mabel.'

For a few seconds they considered the fate of Mabel; two months gone, morning sickness, afraid to tell Mum; and Dad strict.

'It's ever since that twenty page report for Curtis Jackson and Bell he's been different,' Millicent continued. 'It nearly killed me, Con.' (Con nodded, because she knew.) 'I typed that report six times, top and eight carbons, which won't take in those old machines, and meant typing each page *twice*. And six *times*, the whole thing like that, before his Lordship was satisfied with it.'

'But you must say this, Mill, it was the best thing ever put out by the firm,' Miss Crayfoot said: and her soul prickled like a witch's thumb, for she dreamed sometimes of Timothy Spruce tenderly removing her glasses in the passage outside the loo, in the living-room at home, in summer meadows and on the kind of dunes where People loved Players. 'I felt then,' she said, 'that one day he'd be Off to Pastures New. As soon as I read it I thought: My old Mr. Wallingford had better Look Out.'

'I don't say,' Mill said, 'that if it came to a toss up between them I'd choose Mr. Wallingford. It's just that I think Mr. Spruce is getting a bit too big for his boots.'

'Oh, but I like to see a man get on,' Connie Crayfoot said; for she now accepted her unmarried state as permanent whereas Millicent Maple still harboured hope and, therefore, resentment; could adore and detest almost in the same breath. 'I've known Mr. Spruce so much longer than you, Mill. I remember him coming back from the Air Force,' when she was only twenty-one, already in Mr. Wallingford's confidence and working with Matilda Poole who knew all, both of them hearing more from behind the partition which in those days didn't reach the ceiling. 'There wasn't anyone like young Mr. Spruce for work,' she said, 'and old Miss Poole said it was just the same before the war. "First in last out," she said, "that's always been young Mr. Spruce." The office I mean, not the Air Force. And shy, Mill. You wouldn't think of him as married with children. The other clerks used to rib him about the shadows under his eyes —'

They giggled a bit.

'—but it was burning the midnight oil,' Miss Crayfoot went on. 'And Mr. Wallingford never really appreciated him. He often took the credit for work Mr. Spruce had done. Oh, no, Mill, you can't really blame your Mr. Spruce if they've come to grief. It's always been the same. I *know*. If it hadn't been for Mr. Spruce we'd have lost the Curtis Jackson and Bell account *years* ago. No, I like to see a man get on, not that I'm sorry for Mr. Wallingford. For all his faults he's a gentleman born and over the years I suppose you could say he and I have reached an understanding, although of course you never have the chance to keep up your speeds with someone as set in his ways as Mr. Wallingford and I must say, Mill, I had a bit of a cry before we came out, thinking of what it might mean.'

'Perhaps it will all blow over.'

'Perhaps. How's the enemy?'

'We've got five minutes yet.'

'But I don't think it will, Mill, blow over like you said.'

'I can't imagine Mr. Wallingford losing his temper like that. Banging a ruler.'

'It's what first made me stop typing.'

'And he said nothing when you went in?'

'Not a thing.'

'Of course Mr. Wallingford has dignity.'

'Yes, but he's a bit of an old woman. He was always scared of Mr. Bartle, so old Matilda Poole said.'

'Did she? You never told me that before Con. Of course it's what I've always said about Mr. Spruce, isn't it? I mean that he was always scared of Mr. Wallingford. I must say I do like a man to stand up for himself.'

'Oh, Mr. Spruce stood up for himself today all right, Mill. He told Mr. Wallingford a few home truths, I can tell you.'

'I think there's trouble at home.'

'Oh? With Mr. Spruce you mean? What sort of trouble?'

'Well. It's Gwendoline who mentioned it first. She said is everything all right with Mr. Spruce, he's always asking for a line. And once she cut in without thinking and it was Mrs. Spruce, but all she heard was something about how could they afford all that extra cost.'

'The extra cost of what?'

'Gwendoline didn't hear,' Mill said. 'She's very good about not listening. And then Mrs. Spruce was always ringing *him*. And yesterday that brother of his rang and again this morning. And Mr. Spruce went off early to meet him before he had lunch with Mr. Bell Junior at Simpsons. He was late back yesterday and late back again today and as soon as he got in he rang home. Gwendoline said Mrs. Spruce was out but he talked to young Gillian and before Gwendoline had disconnected she heard him say: Has your Uncle George been on?'

'The brother was always a trial,' Miss Crayfoot said, beginning to sort out her handbag.

'He sounds nice on the phone,' Miss Maple said, absentmindedly noting that the lining of Con's bag was grubby.

'A bit la-di-da if you ask me, Mill. Before you came and I was sharing Mr. Spruce with Dotty Barnes when he first became a partner, the brother was always on the phone, and once he came without an appointment and Mr. Spruce was terribly embarrassed because Master George had been drinking. And Jacqueline Pratt put in a complaint.'

'Who was Jacqueline Pratt?'

'The telephone girl we had before Gwendoline. Of course Jackie Pratt hated it if men *didn't* make a pass at her and so we all guessed she only complained about Mr. Spruce's brother making a pass because Mr. Spruce never made a pass at her himself. And Mr. Spruce must have told his brother never to come to the office again because he never has. He only rings.

'That reminds me. I meant to ask but clean forgot.'

'Ask what, Mill?'

'About Mr. Spruce's brother. I mean apart from Mr. George. It was early in August when Mr. Spruce was at Seaford. We were getting a bad picture on commercial and switched over, and there was one of those queer plays. You know – the sort without any plot, that make you feel you're being got at in a way that isn't quite nice. And I wouldn't really have noticed because I had this cardigan on the needles —'

'It's nice, Mill.'

'I'm not sure about the colour. It's worked up brighter than the ball. But at the end it said somebody Spruce. It was Mum noticed it and you know what a sense of humour she has. She said he wasn't at Seaford at all but had gone on the television and changed his first name and I could face him with it when he came back. Of course I wouldn't of done but I looked it up in the *Radio Times* and meant to ask if it was a relation.'

'One of the actors?'

'No, I think it was directing or designing. But it's so many weeks ago I can't remember.'

'Now wait a minute, Mill. That rings a bell. Now why does it ring a bell? I believe there was another brother. But it couldn't have been could it? I mean if Mr. Spruce had a brother on the television we'd have all known about it wouldn't we? Like Helen's famous boyfriend.'

And again they paused, remembering Helen who came between Mabel and Betty and had a boyfriend who said he knew Bruce Forsyth, Adam Faith, Eric Robinson, Malcolm Muggeridge and Hughie Green.

'If we go now we'll be just right,' Millicent Maple said. She took out her purse and gave Connie Crayfoot her half share of the bill and of the sixpence to leave under a plate.

Leaving the Wimpy they entered the grand canyon formed by the watersmeet of Coventry Street, Haymarket, Lower Regent Street, Piccadilly, Regent Street and Shaftesbury Avenue. Above Swan and Edgar's the sky was the colour of pale violets crushed together with their leaves, and was clean, as if washed by rain that had since fallen upon the town, changing in form to crystals from the spectrum, to create from roof level down a rainbow magic of advertisement.

Miss Crayfoot and Miss Maple walked arm in arm, handbags in the crooks of their free elbows, hatless, but with scarves on their heads, in duster coats that resisted showers, both of them wearing spectacles that seemed to keep the features of their faces held together in a bright-eyed effort of concentration on the matter in hand: the scented, padded dark, and *Paranoia*, when at last the teasing poster of a sombre, dark-eyed man, razor in hand, climbing steps in front of his ape-shadow would be revealed in motion, induce catharsis and close the gap not Mr. Spruce nor Mr. Wallingford could fill.

'You get the seats, Con, I'll get the chocs,' and they came apart, like a conjuror's rings, to deal separately with their purses. They would settle up later, in the tube, in a carriage used all day by smokers, and Con would get out first to change trains, and leave Mill wary on her own, avoiding the merciless eye of a lad sitting opposite with his legs too far apart.

Twenty-Seven

'May I speak to Mr. Lisle-Spruce?' Gerald Flynn said into the telephone.

In the days when George was called Silky, Gerald was called Mick. Since then he had taken on a stone and very often more than he could chew except in the way of women for whom his appetite was unflagging. 'My trouble's tail,' he would confide. Male friends of short as well as long standing were never greeted with Hello! but with a tap on their shoulders and a gin-pickled stage whisper: Well Boy? Are you getting it?

'I'm afraid he's still out,' the telephone said. 'Actually he's not been back since he went out this morning just before twelve.'

'Who'm I speaking to?'

'Mrs. Poulten-Morse. His landlady.'

'Are you expecting him any special sort of time?'

'I really couldn't say but he's usually in in the evening.'

'Would you tell him Mick rang?'

'Nick?'

'Mick. M for monkey.'

'Of course. You can rely on my telling him the moment he comes in.'

'Thanks love.'

He swung himself on a creaking swivel chair to return the telephone to its rest and face the pale thin man who sat on the other side of the new second-hand desk on a new second-hand visitor's chair with an air of being ready to opt out of any situation others might try to get him into.

'That friend of mine's not in,' Mick said.

'I don't like it.'

'So it'll have to be you, old boy.'

'I don't like it at all. Not one little bit.'

'You keep saying that.'

'Lisle-Spruce? I've never heard of no Lisle-Spruce.'

'Wrap it up now, Charley. See me in the morning.'

'So long as you know.'

'I know. You keep telling me. You don't like it. Be a good boy and wrap it up for now. It's going on eight. I've got calls to make. On your way out tell Elfie she can go. I'll lock up. And Charley. Don't forget your titfer.'

Charley retrieved the chauffeur's hat from the desk and went through the half-paned door with the letters Private showing backwards, into the main office where Elfie sat doing her nails and reading *Boyfriend*, her hair piled up like Bardot's, surrounded by crates and cardboard cartons. The room smelled of new paint and the bulb hanging from the ceiling had no shade yet.

'He says he'll lock up.'

'I'm waiting for Len,' said Elfie without looking.

'Suit yourself,' said Charley, and went on out of the second half-paned door with the letters Gerald Flynn Enterprises, Wholesalers, Exporters and Importers also showing backwards: on to the lighted landing, down the darkling stairs and out into an alley where there was a smell of gutters.

A few minutes later, still walking, Charley was in Great Portland Street going past locked slide-away doors through whose windows second-hand cars at fancy prices stood parked in mortuary silence.

Here, north of Oxford Street, night falls more quickly than it does south to the river, east to Ludgate Hill and west to Marble Arch. In dark stretches beyond that roughly defined area of lighted pool a man or woman, drowned, might float undiscovered until morning; and within the pool dead eyes reflect the sparkling phosphorescence and are not distinguishable from living. London is no place to die, at night, in the open.

Twenty-Eight

'You do me proud,' said Sam, kissing his wife Alice, five minutes later than expected but still with time to spare; for Sam was a careful man who hated rush and liked, as in this softly-lit, expensive cocktail lounge, to savour his dignity and skill, his prospects and his luck; and saw to it that schedules were never tight, business dinners which Alice must attend so timed that they had together the slow minutes it took to drink a quite, companionable martini. And in this pause the perfect opportunity arose to brief her if she needed briefing, to set the tone, recapitulate the end and rehearse the means of establishing accord, Sam's private word for Deal. Likewise he had attempted with his first, Rose-Anne, who never seemed to see the point or share the pleasure of it in the way that Alice did; thin and graceful, beautiful beyond his expectations now that carefully, step by step, he had rebuilt her confidence, re-taught her how to dress and hold her head up. These were things which in his heart he knew she must have had and known before her first disastrous marriage, and he would not for the world have taken credit for what he had not done, only for what he had.

'It's you,' she said, 'you who do me proud. Dior did the rest.'

'Is it that one?' he said, smiling gravely, with delight. 'I never know the difference. Only notice the effect.' He offered her a cigarette. 'John,' he said, giving her a light, 'the one you haven't met,' and paused long enough to be sure she had brought the cigarette holder that went best with her evening-bag, 'is the new vice-president.'

'*Vice*-president.'

'He comes from Boston, and so won't call you Alice right away.'

'John *Kennedy*.'

Sam smiled, pleased both by her improving memory and with his impending joke. 'Yes, but no relation.'

He put his hand on hers to signal a different train of thought and a special surge in the constant flow of his affection. 'What time is the car?'

'I said eleven but warned him it might be later.'

'Good,' he said. 'I've ordered dinner. I hope I've chosen right.'

'You always do.'

'No. Not always. But if it comes off it's effective. It leaves the right feeling. We'll see. Fingers crossed. But I'll tell you how we begin. Smoked ham with melon. *Jambon de Parme.*'

She blew a gentle drift of best Virginia tobacco smoke. 'I shall like that,' she said.

He nodded, then looked at her full, struck suddenly by something that was back in her eyes, that had been absent for many weeks, that he had not realized had been absent until now, the moment of its revival: a look of tenderness that mirrored an experience of sorrow but transcended it. Tonight its light outshone the small glitter of modest diamonds above the mould of her breast. She was complete, a triumphant amalgam of his image of her and her image of herself.

'Now they are here,' he said, seeing from the corner of his eyes, even as he watched her, their entrance.

Twenty-Nine

Sarah Spruce ordered minestrone to be followed by Osso Buco, and Tim the same, with a carafe of red Tuscan; and now they turned to one another, side by side on a green velvet padded bench that ran the length of the narrow Italian restaurant they called Theirs, her right knee in close proximity to his left under the stiff white table-cloth. They raised glasses of gin and tonic.

'To us,' said Sarah.

'To us,' Tim repeated.

Warm smells of sunny cooking mingled with those of napery and ice-cubes. The carpet was a comfort to their feet. Whenever the door opened air entered from Soho and was presently expelled again by the fan that whined on a low note high up in the window above the level of nylon net curtains. Opposite them a man and a woman, fingering green-stemmed goblets, watched the table-side ritual of *pêche flambée*. To their left was a man alone with soup. To their right three men talked earnestly over *tournedos*, the odd man out among them, facing his companions, occasionally watching Sarah: which Tim marked but did not resent, safe as he had her by his sheltered side, in long wedlock and her going-out dress of bobbly wool, a mixture of grey and charcoal that flattered her china blue eyes and once-flaxen hair now more the colour of corn stooked out after a thirsty summer.

'What shall I wear on Sunday?' Sarah asked, setting her glass down. They were promised for lunch in Sunningdale with Vernon and Minerva Bell.

'What you've got on is nice,' Tim said, 'but why not something new?'

'Do you mean it?'

'Yes. Take the cheque book for a walk tomorrow.' Because she had so few Tim got pleasure from her new clothes.

'Five thousand a year man,' Sarah said. 'You need at least two new suits.'

'Presently.'

'And that old briefcase is a disgrace.'

'I'm not getting rid of *that*.'

'You could keep stuff in it at home and have a new one for town.'

'Perhaps. We'll see.'

Apart from the five thousand a year from Curtis Jackson and Bell there would be his share of what Ripley Coyne and Marples paid for the practice.

'I've been thinking, Sarah. We ought to sell the house.'

'I'm all for that. Where would we go?'

'Move out a bit.'

Sunningdale, or somewhere like it, was not impossible.

'When?'

'What's wrong with right away?'

'Nothing. Except. Well. Could you cope with so much virtually alone?'

'I don't know,' he said. 'We could scout round together the weekends you come home, and I could scout around myself the other weekends. On the other hand —'

'What?'

'Well, you could come up *every* weekend, now, couldn't you?'

The fares looked less expensive.

'What about Gillian?'

'She'll be all right. At least she will be for the next three or four months, the time that matters.'

'Yes, I suppose so.'

'Mrs. Williams said she'd keep an eye on her whenever you came home for a day or two.'

'I know. It seems awful leaving her on her own though.'

'I think you'll have to,' Tim said. 'Not only because of looking for a house but because of what the firm and especially the Bells will think.'

'I know.'

'What are we going to tell them on Sunday?'

'What do you think we should?' Sarah said, treading water.

'We ought to tell them something. The idea of the crammer is out. They'd ask its name.'

'We'll just have to say she's been overworking for the GCE and I'm taking her down to distant relations.'

'Ought we to say relations?'

'Perhaps not. Why not though?'

'They'd wonder why you stayed with her instead of leaving her with them.'

'Tim. Do you think we ought to say anything definite? If we tell them where I'm actually going it might turn out that they know the district. That sort of thing can become awkward.'

'Yes. You've got a point there. On the other hand when you've gone and they ask where you are they'll have to be given some idea.'

'You could say I'm taking her from place to place, visiting relations and friends.'

'Yes. I think that's what we'll have to say. We'd better say it on Sunday.'

'Suppose they say they know the perfect place for Gillian to get well? Suppose they've got a cottage somewhere and offer it to us?'

'We'll have to get out of it.'

'I know,' said Sarah. 'But they might insist. I've only met Minerva that once at the party when they were all giving me the once over without either of us realizing it. She was terribly nice but she struck me as a terrific insister. I mean terribly kind but awful to say no to.'

Tim put his hand on hers.

'You mustn't be scared of people like Minerva.'

'I am a bit.' She finished her gin. 'I hope I'm going to be a help to you and not a drag. In my WAAF days I could have dealt with twenty Minervas but I seem to have lost it.'

'I bet Minerva Bell would give anything to have your looks and your figure.'

'Thank you. But she's got something I'll never have. Tremendous poise.'

'Tell you what.'

'What?' Sarah asked.

'I'll ring Vernon tomorrow and say I've changed my mind and ask old Wallingford to forget what I said today.'

They laughed and the minestrone came.

'In all the excitement,' Tim said, ladling soup, 'I forgot to tell you. I saw George.'

'When?'

'Just before lunch.'

'How much did you tell him?'

'Well I didn't mention the new job. I'd told him all that mattered in my letter.'

'What did he say?'

'He said he'd pay it back.'

'He never will.'

'I know. But I put the wind up him.'

'Keep it that way.'

'I mean to.'

'You've got to think of yourself now, Tim.'

'That's roughly what I told him.'

'How was he looking?'

'Seedy. His shirt cuffs were frayed.' Tim, soup finished, put down his spoon.

'Poor George,' Sarah said. 'If he'd been a man you could count on we could have asked *him* to look after Gillian at weekends. I mean he's got the time, and he *is* her godfather.'

'If George were a man you could count on he wouldn't *have* the time. He'd be in a job,' said Tim.

'I suppose you paid for the drinks.'

'No, I made him pay his whack. He tried to cadge an extra gin and some grub but I wasn't having any.'

'That must have shaken him.'

'I think it did. You know what, though?'

'No?'

'Well you'd guess. About Gillian. He leapt to the obvious conclusion for him. About why I wanted the two hundred quid.'

'What obvious conclusion?'

'An abortion,' Tim said, his voice lowered for the occasion.

'Yes I *could* have guessed. I suppose he made a joke of the whole thing.'

'More or less. He said he wanted to see her.'

'I hope you squashed that.'

'I did. Actually I half expected him to offer to act as a go-between – you know, work the two hundred off as a fee for getting her to that sort of person.'

'George would never stoop to that.'

'Wouldn't he?'

'I'm sure he wouldn't. Even his worst enemy couldn't call him mercenary. In fact...'

'What?'

'Well. Although he's an awful waster and an idler and he makes me flaming mad he's basically good-natured, isn't he? I mean he's got a streak of generosity you can't shut your eyes to.'

'He seems to shut his own eyes to it without much difficulty. I suppose Gillian forgot to tell you I rang this afternoon?'

'You rang? When?'

'Directly I got back to the office from lunch with Vernon. I told her to keep out of the way if her Uncle George rang or called. She was supposed to pass the message on to you.'

'Well she didn't. But then she was out when I got back from shopping and she'd only just got back when you rang about meeting you in town, and there was all the excitement of getting ready.'

'Do they know why we're celebrating?'

'Andrew doesn't. But I think Gillian guesses. I didn't tell her because she was in an odd mood when she came back from her walk.'

'Oh?'

'I wasn't going to tell you until later, Tim, but I'd better. She said she'd been thinking and had decided that when the baby was born it would be better if she didn't even see it.'

'Is that a good or a bad sign?'

'Bad.'

The carafe of red Tuscan was brought and Tim tasted it selfconsciously.

Sarah said, 'What about Andrew's school if we move?'

'Yes. That's a problem, isn't it?'

'Unless we can send him somewhere better than a local grammar?'

'That's what I hope,' Tim said.

'It's going to be difficult with Andrew,' Sarah said. 'Perhaps if we have definite plans to move he won't wonder so much about Gillian leaving the convent and going away with me.'

'I wonder how much he guesses? Have you noticed how little he says to her?'

Sarah nodded. 'He *has* been quiet,' she said, 'but I thought that was end of holiday gloom.'

'Perhaps it is,' Tim said. 'But we've got it to face. In some form or another. Will he swallow it? I mean she looks so damned healthy. And is it fair to worry him with a fib about her not being well and needing country air?'

'He's still only a child, Tim. We can't tell him.'

'He knows more about the birds and bees than you think.'

'I should hate him to know about Gill.'

'I know.'

'And we agreed to keep it from him.'

'I keep wondering what he'll think of us if he finds out after it's all over.'

'You mean will he ever trust us again?'

'Or Gill. I don't know. It's a hell of a mess, isn't it?'

'I feel it's my fault.'

'Don't be silly.'

'I'm not being silly, Tim. Somewhere along the line I've failed her. Coming up on the train this evening it struck me that she hasn't got anyone she feels she can turn to.'

'Now you're being ridiculous. Come on, drink up and forget it. We're celebrating five thousand lovely smackers a year.'

'When she was quite a little girl I was always finding fault with her. When you were working so hard at night I threatened her terribly if she made the smallest sound. And later. Always reprimanding her about something. For being late, for being untidy, for being forgetful.'

'Well she was all those things.'

'But so was Andrew.'

'Andrew's a boy,' Tim said. 'You expect boys to be late and untidy.'

'I never punished Andrew like I punished Gillian. I expect you've forgotten that awful time when Gill smacked Andrew when he was still in his carry-cot and then when I smacked *her* and asked why she'd done it she said because Andy was making a row and interrupting daddy downstairs. And all I did was smack her again and say Andrew was only a tiny baby. No. I've never punished Andrew like I used to punish poor Gill.'

'You make it sound as if Andrew's always got off scot free.'

'No, I don't mean that. But it's you who've seen to that. If anything I've always protected Andrew from the consequences of his actions, I suppose ever since the night Gill smacked him in his carry-cot I've protected him from Gill and protected him from you.'

'Darling, you mustn't upset yourself. You couldn't be expected to anticipate the arrival on the scene of Master Clayton. And *that* is the *point*.'

'But I feel I should. I should have insisted on Gillian bringing him home so that we could see what sort of a boy she was going out with —'

'That sort of thing is never done these days —'

'But I feel I didn't do it because I didn't care enough. I made her grow up so quickly, Tim. When she said tonight about not even wanting to see the baby —'

The Osso Buco came and Sarah turned away to open her handbag. She blew her nose on a tiny lace-edged handkerchief.

'Spinach for madame?' the waiter said.

'No thank you,' she said, without looking.

'One thing I forgot to tell you,' Tim said, when the waiter had gone. 'When I had the battle royal with old Wallingford. He said I harboured resentment about the firm not being called Bartle Wallingford and Spruce.'

'Oh, how petty,' Sarah said, snapping the clasp of her handbag and facing her front again.

'It shows you, though, doesn't it, how much it's been on his conscience. Bartle Wallingford and Spruce.'

They laughed. Tim pressed her knee with his hand under the table.

'I love you,' he said in a low voice.

'I love you, too, Tim,' Sarah replied.

They sipped more Tuscan, tackled the Osso Buco.

The meal, the occasion, their situation side by side: these, if nothing else, were a vindication of the years of their marriage.

Thirty

'She's on her way out, Stainsby,' said Doctor Barr, adjusting the coverlet over Miss Lisle's chest, then turning to put things away in his leather case, bending close to it because the bedside lamp was dimmed by a square of silk: the night-light not of the dying but of the Watch. The window was uncurtained and beyond it darkness showed. Rain, ridden in again from the Atlantic, came in gusts against the panes. The gas-fire was turned low, its orange light reflected in an old pudding-basin set in front of it half-filled with water that had gathered dust on the surface and by morning would be all evaporated unless Mr. Stainsby remembered to replenish it, which he likely would, being a restless man with thin hands happiest when engaged.

'How long do you give her?' he asked, forgetting it was in God's jurisdiction, not Doctor Barr's, Miss Lisle's hours rested.

'Ah well, with these old people. Who can say, Stainsby? But I've given her something to ease the passage and I doubt she'll see morning. What of you?'

'Of me?'

'It's good of you to give so much of your time. But will you see it through?'

'Oh yes, indeed. Poor soul. Lonely enough in all conscience without my deserting now.'

'I think you can rest assured that she's gone beyond such mortal cares, Stainsby,' said Doctor Barr whom death affected poetically. 'But nobody should die deserted should they? Now I must go down and see Miss Bright.'

'They promised me a flask of tea. Do you think you could look in on the kitchen and remind them?'

'By all *means*,' Doctor Barr said, stressing the last word and so reminding without meaning to both men of Miss Lisle's means, the small tin box whose hiding place in the wardrobe Miss Lisle had taken care to point out to them every so often so that if anything happened to her no one would be put to the trouble and embarrassment of searching. Both of them had seen the contents too, having each on separate occasions brought the box from the wardrobe to the bed at Miss Lisle's request and sat beside her while she explained its intricacies.

First there was the copy of the Will, drawn up a few years back by Mr. Took whom she had Spoken To in the hall after one of his visits to the surviving Miss Bright. The Will appointed Mr. Took her executor and instructed him to pay her just debts and funeral expenses, and then the sum of Five Pounds to each of her three nephews, George, Timothy and Guy Spruce and the residue of her estate to the parish fund of the rural parish church of St. Anne-in-the-moor to be applied towards the cost of the Sunday School outing first falling after the date of her death and a yearly wreath of poppies for the war memorial in memory of her brothers killed 1914–18 (including Teddy who lingered until 1926).

After the Will came her life insurance book, paid up monthly at the rate of fivepence a week. This, she hoped, would cover the cost of her funeral and a wooden cross with her full name Ada Lavinia Lisle, her date of birth, February the first 1882 and, of course, the date of her death. She also expressed a wish for a word or two of verse, something suitable, but to be decided upon by the vicar or the curate of St. Anne's. Should the life insurance money be insufficient (and she had no objection to interment in a coffin of pine, oak being, in more than one sense, a luxury) the the balance might be found from her only other asset, her Post Office Savings Book, which carried a balance of seventy-three pounds four shillings and twopence. However, she hoped that this would not prove necessary because she would like to think that at least Fifty Pounds could be paid to the parish fund after the three bequests of Five Pounds each had been distributed. Apart from a few sentimental tokens such as cards from old birthdays and far-away Christmases (including one of a robin on a gate with snow) the only other item of interest to Mr. Took (as she explained separately to Mr. Stainsby and Doctor Barr) was a slip of paper on which she had written in ink the last known address of her nephew George.

'But no one must be sent for,' she had always insisted.

So no one had been sent for and Mr. Stainsby, watching Doctor Barr closing his bag, said, 'I am divided in my mind. Whether it was right to respect her wishes.'

'Which wishes, Stainsby?'

'Her wishes not to send for the nephews.'

'They'd need tracing first. There'd not have been time, would there? Ah, no, Stainsby. Better like this. Now don't you think so? A flask of tea, wasn't it?' He paused, taking his leave of old Miss Lisle by looking at her where he had left her. 'Well we all come to it. Yes, now, we all come to it. But Miss Bright lasts well. Oh, my goodness yes.'

When he had opened the door on to the small landing high up there in the eaves of The Grange he muttered something about These Stairs which Stainsby didn't catch: but Stainsby heard his footsteps going down until, at the second turn, linoleum gave way to carpet.

Thirty-One

'But why N.W.11?' Guy asked, his voice raised somewhat to defeat the many other voices in Lady Butterfield's crowded drawing-room.

'It's Golder's Green,' said the actress Aunt Clara had just faced him with.

'Is Creon Jewish?'

'No. But stinking rich in a suburban way.'

'Are you playing Antigone?'

'The sister. Of course it's her brother's reputation Antigone wants to bury not his corpse. The first scene is driving back from the Crematorium. We filmed it last week and got beautifully mixed up with the cars arriving for the real thing because Larry kept us hanging around hoping it would rain and look like Harry Lime.'

'Who's Larry?' Guy asked.

'Larry Bate.'

'Didn't he direct that Australian play?'

'That's him. He came over with it. Most of us wish he'd go back.'

'Is the play as much a stinker as it sounds?'

'I thought you were looking forward to it,' the girl said blowing smoke in a way that reminded Guy of Auden's line about a train engine shovelling steam over its shoulder. He thought she was about thirty. She had the undusted look of a girl producers kept forgetting to take off the shelf. On the other hand her eyes, being the eyes of that kind of girl, trained not to look too interested in anything, seemed not unlike the eyes of a girl who might make something of *The Geyser*.

'I was looking forward to you in it, not to the play. Aunt Clara told me you liked *A Pram in the Hall* by the way.'

'Yes, I did. I didn't know she was your aunt until she introduced us just now.'

'It's a family tradition to call her Aunt. She's only a distant cousin really.'

'You're Welsh aren't you?'

'I was born in London but brought up in Dorset and one of my foster-parents was Welsh. My accent is strictly hybrid.'

'Lady Butterfield says I've met your brother, but I don't remember.'

'George?'

'I think so.'

'He calls himself *Lisle*-Spruce,' Guy said.
'You meet so many people here.'
'She says he's coming tonight.'
'Don't you get on?'
'Why do you say that?'
'The way you said he calls himself Lisle-Spruce.'
'George is all right in an old-fashioned seedy-fringe way. He's much older than I am of course. Anyway I've not seen him for a couple of years.'
'Have you any sisters?'
'No. I've got another brother. A solid suburban type. He's older too. And I've not seen him for five. I don't really know any of my relations.'
'What happened to your parents?'
'Well when the war came I was only a toddler so they evacuated to Dorset to be safe from the bombs, only they weren't. Something to do with a German plane that had been shot up losing its way and off-loading.'
'Were you in it?'
'No, it fell on a cinema in the local market-town. I was back home in the village with the people we had rooms with.'
'What about your brothers?'
'Oh, they were in the Army and Air Force.'
'As much difference in age as that?'
'Yes. I must have been a shock to everybody. Of course my parents never had any money and I've worked it out that they'd stopped buying contraceptives because they thought it was safe. I don't suppose my brothers ever quite believed I'd happened. Anyway when my parents were killed I just stayed on with this couple, Mr. and Mrs. Williams.'
'What about after the war and your brothers came back?'
'Tim was married to a WAAF and George was married to a girl he met in Cairo.'
'Didn't your Aunt Clara ever take a hand in your welfare?'
Guy looked across the crowded St. John's Wood salon to see how safe it was to say what four of Lady Butterfield's martinis had encouraged him to say.
'Aunt Clara is only interested in successful or potentially successful people.'
'Oh, good. That means I'm a potential at least.'
'If you look around you'll notice one thing. There's nobody in the room above the age of forty-five. That's the limit. After that you can't rank as potentially anything.'

'Is your brother George a success?'

'No. And he's nearing the limit. But then he has a private income from Uncle Roderick Butterfield. They say he only married this girl in Cairo because he was out there when Uncle Roderick died and there was a provision in the will for the money George gets the income from to go to his children if he had any, otherwise to Tim's or mine. And the last time I heard of him he was just getting a divorce because he and this girl from Cairo hadn't had any kids and there weren't likely to be any. At least that was the impression I got. Not that George is totally self-centred. About three years ago he did try to get Aunt Clara to help over some plays I'd written during national service, but she wasn't having any. But directly *A Pram in the Hall* came on and got these notices she was on to me.'

'Through George?'

'No. George has been out in the cold. *She* says because he just stopped coming. But it's odd he should be coming again tonight, isn't it? She'll probably introduce him to people he hasn't met as Guy Spruce's brother. She wrote to me at the BBC and said, Surely you are my nephew, Guy, do come and see me. So I did. How did she get on to you?'

'She *said* Ken Tynan had mentioned me, but I think she must have meant she read what he wrote. Actually it was Larry who first brought me here. And of course she got on to him over that Australian play. But so what? The martinis are good. And there are only a few theatre people come. Which is a change. I get tired of shop, don't you? But perhaps that's because I'm no longer *sure*.'

'Sure about what?'

'That I'm any good.'

'That shows you are.'

'Of course with a real part I feel differently. But that hasn't happened since the Royal Court.'

'Aunt Clara told me you'd have liked to play Sally.'

'Who wouldn't?'

'You really liked it that much?'

'I thought it was very nearly a great part. If you don't mind my saying *nearly*.'

'What made it not?' Guy asked, draining his martini and adding smoothly, 'I mean in your opinion?'

'I don't think she'd have given way to the man to quite that extent.'

'Why?'

'Because she saw right through him.'

'Bert?'

'Yes, Bert. The whole feeling as she came down the stairs and then stood watching him, well, I thought what you were saying was —'

'Life must go on.'

'Yes. But why did it have to go on on Bert's terms?'

'It has to be Bert's terms because he is the weaker.'

'I don't see.'

'It's the weakest who calls the tune.'

'But Guy – if I may call you Guy – I don't agree because surely —'

'In *that* environment it's the weak who set the pace. It's part of Sally's strength as a woman that she sees that. She's strong enough to face the future on Bert's level.'

'Because she loves him?'

'Partly. But the element of self-preservation mustn't be overlooked.'

'Well you see that's what I was looking for and it didn't quite come over.'

'The lines were there.'

'What were they?'

'Well. You remember how Bert stands over the pram and says: Him! Him!'

'Meaning the baby.'

'Only symbolically, because the kid's upstairs in the cot. But: Him! Him! That's what Bert says, and then —'

'—he threw the pram blanket on the floor.'

'Exactly. A gesture meaning destroy the kid *but* also himself and her too. And Sally says: Please Bert.'

'Well?'

'Well, that's it. Please. Please Bert. I mean she submits to his violence but is also trying to save the kid, and that means saving herself, which is where the self-preservation comes in. Actually though, I know what you mean because Lisa didn't say please in just the right way, although she got it in rehearsal.'

'She made it sound flabby when it should have had steel in it?'

'Steel? Yes. But flexible. Much the same sort of difficulty arises in the thing I'm just beginning to work on for the commercial people.'

'Tell me about that.'

'I'd like to.'

'What's it called?'

'The Geyser.'

'The Geyser.'

'And in this play it's even more the things that aren't said that are important.'

'I wish you could get into a quiet corner with the little man who wrote *Antigone, N.W.11.* We have to say everything twice.'

'I don't think a quiet corner with him would give me much of a kick. Are you doing anything for supper?'

'Yes. Something called cannelloni.'

'What?'

'It's a sort of pasta in a tin. But there's only enough for two.'

A tray of steady martinis appeared at their elbows held by a little woman called Mrs. Braithwaite who was a friend of Lady Butterfield's maid Hilda. She had a way with glasses that meant not a drop spilt. She had once been Nippy of the Year and had a certificate at home in Kentish Town rolled up in a drawer with marriage lines that had gone wrong, and was happiest in a crush of people where she was obliging for fifteen shillings and a hand with the washing up.

Recharged, Guy said, 'I meant have supper out.'

'I know you did. And I was explaining why I'd invite you to share my cannelloni but can't because it's only enough for two.'

'I see. You're not on your own.'

'Oh I'm on my own. But you're not are you? Aren't you with that fascinating girl in the saree?'

Guy thought she said 'fascinating' but the word might have been 'fantastic'.

Thirty-Two

'What part of India do you come from?' asked a young man with a long neck who was said to show promise in the Foreign Office.

'Islington-pore,' Anina said. Her nipples showed through her turquoise-blue saree. Her hair, dyed blue-black, was back-combed into a tall beehive. She wore gold sandals, no make up except for white lipstick but her eyes were outlined in black and shaped to look like the all-seeing eyes painted on the walls of Nepalese temples.

'Islington-pore? Where is that?'

'You best go by tube. Change at King's Cross for the Angel. Are you English?'

'Yes. Don't I look it?'

'Your trousers are too narrow. I wasn't born in Islington-pore.'

'What did you say about King's Cross and the Angel?'

'It's where you change.'

'You mean if your trousers are too narrow?'

'Have another of these,' Anina said, putting her fourth empty glass on Mrs. Braithwaite's rock-like tray and taking a full one.

'Mrs. Braithwaite,' the young man said, following suit, 'has a certificate in Kentish Town for balancing trays.'

'Well, sir, you've got a memory haven't you?'

'I have a wide memory, but narrow trousers, and I'm going to the Angel by way of King's Cross.'

But Mrs. Braithwaite was gone and Anina's attention taken by Lady Butterfield.

'Anina,' Lady Butterfield said. 'This is Guy's brother George.'

'Hello, Anina.'

'Hello, George. You don't look like Guy's brother.'

'I am though. Where's Guy?'

'He's in a corner with a girl called Antigone. May I tell you the story of my life?'

'She was born in Islington-pore,' said the young man from the Foreign Office.

'He's got it wrong because he's had too much to drink. I come from Islington-pore but I was born at Number Three Railway Cuttings. Man, like I mean, way out there in Nehru-ville. You dig that crap?'

'No. I'm too old.'

'You can't be too old if you're Guy's brother. Perhaps you're his father. Guy digs my idiosyncratic brand of Kooky talk but then Guy's a genius-man, chatting up Antigone, big deal.'

Lady Butterfield led the young man away to talk to a women who showed promise somewhere.

'You're stuck with me now,' Anina told George, 'and she's cross with you for being late. As soon as we came she said: I want you to meet George but he's not here yet. And that was hours ago.'

'It's only just on eight. There's lots of time.'

'I think I like you, George. Are you as sober as you look?'

'No.'

'Time for what then, George?'

'The story of your life. You said may you tell it?'

'That was to get rid of Buster. I call him Buster because he doesn't look as if he could. Also to prove to her.'

'Prove what?'

'That I should be discouraged. Discouraged from coming. I live with Guy. Like I make the bed and empty the pot and do his washing and change his ribbons and he got me for twenty quid.'

'Twenty quid?'

'It's what I worked it out at. His board and lodging in Islington-pore came to twenty quid only it was less than twenty he got me for because they charge five quid a week all found and it only costs them two. So it was twelve quid he got me for. Little lost-boy. Little genius-man. Making that Rada floozie. Only like it'll be a laugh.'

'What'll be a laugh?'

'Because he didn't wash it off.'

'Didn't wash what off?'

'The ban the bomb. I drew a ban the bomb on him and if she sees it tonight she might.'

'Might what?'

'Ban it. I mean like laugh. And little lost-boy doesn't like you to laugh. Genius man's got no sense of humour.'

'Why do you call him little lost-boy?'

'Because he had a sad time. Like I mean as a boy.'

'I'm not sure,' said George, 'that I know what sad means.'

'Oh sad, sad means like what, like I used to feel thinking of Nehruville. Sad means like the wallpaper when it's yellow and goes like brown islands and you think of ships.'

'You're too young to be sad.'

'But that's the best time. I mean like I remember way back, way out there in Nehruville in Railway Cuttings, I mean crying because small and grandma black.'

'And that was best?'

'You can't be sad except when you're like young because when you're old everything is funny. Which is why Guy is little lost-boy.'

'You mean he doesn't see the joke yet?'

'That's what I mean. But I know what you're thinking. Like because I'm not even as old as Guy is, how come I see the joke while genius-man pulls a long-face?'

She pulled a long face.

'I think you're absolutely adorable,' George said.

'I cost.'

'You told me. Twelve pounds.'

'No. More than that. Old masters cost. Likewise young mistresses. Each year a bit flakes off. And that adds. Like *craquelure*. I had a friend in Islington-pore that was a painter and he told me about *craquelure*. The more *craquelure* there is the older the old master is which is why when you forge an old master you have likewise to forget the *craquelure* to match, and that's more difficult than anything because genuine *craquelure* is the gift of time and who ever forged time and got away with it? Come close and get a look. Can you see my *craquelure* just beginning? How long will it be before my *craquelure* is as good as Mona Lisa's?'

'A long time.'

'But each second it adds. It adds and it costs. The joke is I don't cost yet like Antigone costs. Her *craquelure* is more advanced than mine. And doesn't that make you laugh, George? I tell you another thing make you laugh. I never could take home this man who was a painter because my mother had a rule, no niggers, likewise in that house in Islington-pore there was no picture to be found of grandma who made me cry in Nehruville because she was black. I mean like my childhood was sad but now it is funny and genius-man was like happy but don't now know why except it must all have been a mistake, so is sad thinking about his happy childhood that ought to have been unhappy, and that is no way to end up looking like the Mona Lisa.'

'How is my *craquelure* coming along?'

She flapped her hand at a drifting puff of cigarette smoke and peered closely.

'Your *craquelure* is just fine, George. You have the best *craquelure* of anybody in this room. Like you were made all over of that glass they put in cars in front of the driver and someone had taken a hammer and hit you like in a sensitive spot, like I mean one of the knobs about the base of your spine.'

'Do I look like Mona Lisa?'

'You look like her brother.'

'I didn't know she had a brother.'

'Yes, she has a brother, but he's still waiting for an old Master. I mean they're sitting there smiling at each other because it wasn't little old Da Vinci that painted Mona it was Mona's brother and he never been able to look in a mirror to do a self-portrait because when you look in a mirror it is a very serious matter. Shall I tell you a secret?'

'Please.'

'Mona's brother was hoping Picasso might make an old master of him yet but he's lost heart and it seems there's only John Bratby left to look forward to, which would like wipe the smile off anybody's face.'

'Were you an art student?'

'Why do you say *were*?'

'Because of your *craquelure*.'

'The answer is anyway no. Unless you count lipstick.'

'Lipstick?'

'White on Clarence Rockefeller Brown and red on Guy. But I haven't got any talents. Have you got any talents, George?'

'None whatsoever. Nor any vital statistics. You're one up on me there. And do you know how lucky you are? Never running the risk of discovering you're pregnant in Seaford?'

'But it is a terrible terrible thing not to have any talents.' She looked into her drink, sipped it, looked into it again and then up at him, puzzled. 'Where's Seaford?' she asked.

'Near Newhaven.'

'I remember Newhaven. From that town one day two summers ago Clarence Rockefeller Brown and I rocked across the channel way out to Dieppeville, with two bands going but half of us sick and not wanting to know. He held my head going and coming even though he was crazy for that music, even though that music was jumping in him, he kept there at the rail and held my puky head. Why, that sweet man could have had me when I didn't cost at all.'

'Why do you say it's terrible not to have any talents?'

'Well, now, take again that sweet man, Clarence Rockefeller Brown.'

'Who is Clarence Rockefeller Brown?' asked the young man with the long neck who showed promise at the Foreign Office and had appeared again.

'Now you know that you shouldn't be back again talking to me, Buster-man. You know it was only allowed because George hadn't showed, but now George has showed I'm supposed not to mix any more because I make all the other women in this crazy-crazy room look like top grade probation officers and any man talking to me look like he's the type who'd never ever defend his sister from rape being too likewise engaged to notice. Except George can talk to me. Because George is the kind of man who makes any woman he's talking to look like she got rape over long long ago and has led like since a blameless life. So make him go away George.'

'But I honestly do want to know who Clarence Rockefeller Brown is.'

'He is an expert on *craquelure*,' George told him.

'What on earth is *craquelure*?'

'It's what happens when one of the nobs on your spine gets hit in a sensitive spot.'

'Really? I must tell my old mum she's got *craquelure* then, not a slipped disc, but if Clarence Rockefeller Brown is an osteopath she's already met him because she said only last weekend that she's run through the whole lot.'

'He is, like, a kind of osteopath,' Anina said. 'He will hold your head and turn it this way and turn it that way very very very gently and you will feel the music in his fingers, but I have not seen him for a long long time and since then my *craquelure* has made like considerable advances.'

'There is an argument developing about Bahrein,' said Lady Butterfield speaking from behind and using the young man's sharp elbow as a fulcrum upon which to tilt him in her direction, 'and it is your opportunity to prove to us all what an extraordinarily clever young man you are.'

'I know not a thing about Bahrein. Belgrave is the man for that.'

'He isn't here. So come along and sing for your supper.'

'You must come closer to me, George,' said Anina, 'so close that nobody but nobody will dare to interrupt us again in case there is, like, revealed in parting, something disreputable.'

George went closer and leant. She smelt of musk.

'Only don't sniff me like I was a dog. You got to accept I'm Mother India tonight and parts of me are untouchable.'

Mrs. Braithwaite came to their side.

'If we take two drinks each,' Anina said, 'it will look as if we do not trust each other with one hand free. Like this, gradually, we build up a picture of underprivileged behaviour.'

They each took two drinks.

'And man! If only we could manage a lighted cigarette in

our months and a canapé in each hand full of wine-tasters for glasses, this would be like in a cellar full of wine-tasters for two wine-tasters to swallow instead of spit, and not say pardon.'

'There's a ledge just behind you. With the help of that we might cope.'

'But George, sweet-George. Like I will not hesitate to hasten my own end. But whyfor should I let you hasten yours, inevitable though it must be?'

'What is my end and why is it inevitable?'

'Because you are like at what genius-man says is the age-limit.'

She hesitated, one of the glasses almost at her white lips, and stared at him through her lamasery eyes.

'Oh, George. Sweet-George. Have I run one? Have I like opened too wide my bloody mouth? I mean again for godsake. As upon innumerable occasions. Not least to my ma and pa on the subject of Clarence Rockefeller Brown, returning now Jamaica-side by way of *rive-gauche*.'

George drained the martini in his left hand and began on the one in his right.

'If Clarence Rockefeller Brown had not had any talents he would not have gone Jamaica-side by way of *rive-gauche*. Like he would have gone steerage from Liverpool all that watery way without stopping and now be working the old plantation drag and not considering crazy-nice things like spatial relationships. Or maybe he would not have gone back Jamaica-side yet. Either by way of *rive-gauche* or by way of without stopping from Liverpool. Because if he had not had any talents he would like more have been punching your ticket on the bus from Angel to Newington Green. Because if you are not privileged upper-crust like Buster-boy then you must have talents and if you do not have talents it is a terrible thing but it is more, like, a terrible thing for a man not to have talents than it is for a girl not to have talents because if she has those all the same like vital statistics then as you so very very sweetly wisely said she is unlikely ever to find herself pregnant in Seaford, but only in Cannes. And I regret, sweet-George, that my vital statistics are not of that calibre to rate Cannes, they being more vitally statistical in regard to a Camden Town jag, which same town little-lost-boy, big genius-man, is all the time outgrowing with Antigone there, who is a girl with both talents and vital statistics and will make Cannes if it like kills her. Which is the reason why this is positively my last appearance in this crazy-crazy room, in which I have not been happy until now.'

Anina finished the drink in her right hand and began on the one in her left.

'Why haven't you been happy?'

'Because I have been frightened in this crazy room, sweet-George. Let me tell you one thing I have told no living man. When first I came into this room, this other time that is the very first time of all and we have spent a happy lifeforce afternoon and dressed up in our personality-attire to visit with rich Aunt Clara whom genius-boy calls old drag but like might be useful in the top-climb months to come, when I come into this room there are two things I notice even although on the way we have had liquor to like get with it before it got with us, two things I notice and it is like they are connected because the first thing I notice is Guy going away from me even though we are still standing very close together, very very close with our arms touching, but he is going away from me in his traitor gut being at that ins-tan-tan-eous moment ashamed of my saree from Nehruville and what my face and hair look like, even although it had been agreed on the very doorstep that a little matter of *épater les bourgeois* was about to take place. And man, the second thing that I notice and do not believe is exactly disconnected from the first, and it is that I do not have it in me to walk into this room wearing what I am wearing and looking how I am looking, I do not have it in me to do it and get away with it.'

'What is it you'd have to have in you to do it and get away with it?'

'Man, you think if I had like since discovered what it was I would be telling you how I feel without it?'

'Do you look the same this evening as you looked the first evening?'

'Yes, sweet-George.'

'And how many times have there been in between?'

'Two three other times.'

'And always looking like you look tonight?'

'Yes, sweet-George.'

'So even if you think you haven't got it in you, you come looking just as if you thought you had.'

'I come just looking, sweet-George.'

'Looking for what it is you think you haven't got in you?'

'Once it was for the john. Why sweet-George is it, can you

like tell me, that in houses like Aunt Clara's house you cannot direct yourself unerringly to the can? Now this I have like celebrated over and even chat-talked genius-man into consideration of.'

'What were the findings?'

'Findings. Findings. This is a word like a bell. I do not precisely remember the findings excepting that according to little lost-boy the soap in rich people's houses smells different, even in the gents. But it is remarkable about the waywardness of their johns. And it is like nothing to do with rich, like it is to do with class. Let me explain, sweet-George. I have been in the houses of very rich people who are rich because they have talents or vital statistics and in such places you have but definitely to wet your finger and hold it up and you may then go like without hesitation following the wind blowing from looward and presently drop anchor. But in the houses of people who have both money and class it is like of no use to wet your finger and hold it up because someone will simply stick upon it a canapé filled with *paté de foie*. Because people of breeding and with the means at their disposal are anxious only that you should not faint with hunger and collapse upon the Aubusson, and it does not occur to them that the john could be on your like list of requirements. Or is it like I mean a test of your pedigree that you should be able to find the john without asking and without losing your way and ending up in the linen-cupboard? Is it that upon entering their houses you should at that same moment be like acquainted with the fact that the interior is designed by Sir Joshua Pot, circa seventeen ninety-three, and in consequence be like aware that this old drag but always put the loo the fourth door on the right, turn left at the top of the Adam staircase?'

George put his weight on to another foot. 'You're making me want to go,' he said.

Thirty-Three

Then they should like go together, Anina said, and led the way towards and through the open double doors.

Below them now from their right the staircase described a descending arc to the ground floor and mounted from their left by a parallel arc to the floor above. A chandelier of glass pendants hung in the well at eye-level, suspended on a chain that went on, upwards, out of sight. To their right at the near end of the broad corridor a sash window, with dark blue damask curtains drawn back beneath a fringed pelmet, revealed through its elegant panes a plane tree lit by street-lamps. To their left the corridor, guarded at arched intersections by bronze statuettes on malachite pedestals, led to a corresponding window through which nothing could be seen of the outside at all, only a reflection of the inside, and of their distant selves standing by the balustrade. The walls of the staircase and corridor had been done over in an ivory emulsion paint. In the corridor where the wall met the ceiling there was a band of moulding and this was painted pale blue. The ceiling itself was pale green, but both these colours were darkened by the yellow light of electricity burning steadily in the filaments of bulbs plugged into brass brackets which were rendered in the shape of hands holding lanterns aslant as if for the benefit of revellers returning from a rout. The corridor was carpeted thickly to each wall, in blue darker than the damask curtains; and on this carpet Anina stood in her gold sandals and peacock saree.

'I usually go to the one downstairs,' George said.

'That is because you are a man. If you are a woman it is very essential to go upwards as like a distressed damsel in search of a turret and not downwards as like a fireman making haste.'

She moved to the foot of the stairs leading to the floor above and arriving at it subsided gracefully, as if that had been her intention, on to the second step, in a sitting position, still holding her two empty glasses: raised like votive offerings.

A man's voice said, 'Hello, George.'

It was Guy: his black hair falling in a short-cut Roman fringe. Gone was the incipient dandruff look of hair trained by continual combings of anxious scholarship fingers not to lie down. Gone too was the look of the wide-bottom trousered provincial-user. Everything he wore now would have a label on it saying Made in Italy.

'Hello, Guy,' said George, holding out his hand and having it taken by a hand whose cleverness had somehow been proved in the face of all kinds of opposition, both fixed and mobile. 'And congratulations,' he added, meaning on his play and not Anina, which Guy did not for a moment seem to get the wrong idea of.

'Thank you,' he said. Time was when 'Thanks' had sufficed.

'I didn't see it, but my bank manager did. He asked me to say how well he thought it came over. In fact I think I owe you a drink.'

'Oh, why?'

'I fancy it was having a Brother on the Television that made him Accommodate me. No doubt he's After your Account.'

'My overdraft,' Guy said because this was the kind of thing that was always said in palatial surroundings, particularly to people like George.

'I'm helping Anina to find the ladies' loo.'

Guy looked at her and then back at George. The movement of his head released a little puff of masculine cologne.

'How much has she had?'

'Why? Is she rationed?'

'No. Sloshed,' Guy said and moved to the staircase. She looked up at him. She smiled.

'You'd better give me those glasses before you break them.'

She held them out but withdrew them when his hands were about to touch them.

'No. Like I will not give these very valuable glasses to you, lost-boy. Like I will only give them to sweet-George who is helping me to find the loo and afterwards will help me to find a taxi as soon as you have given me a one pound note to enable me to part company with the driver-man in a sweet and pregnant spirit of accord.'

'All right. Give them to George. Only do it now.'

She surrendered the glasses. George went away and put them carefully on the pedestal belonging to a bronze girl wearing something diaphanous in a high wind with her arm raised to hail, perhaps, a passing chariot. Returning he heard Guy say, 'I'll have to go alone.'

'This is not to worry you, genius-man.'

To George Guy said, 'Are you really finding a taxi for her?'

'Won't she be going with you?' George asked.

'I wanted her to cook supper for a guest —'

'He means Antigone. In this context guest is a word of like rich significance.'

'—but she's not in a condition to play hostess. So I'm taking the guest somewhere else.' He turned again to Anina. 'Come on. I'll put you into a taxi. George has better fish to fry.'

'Give me a pound, little lost-boy. You are like admiring to hand me down these softly-softly stairs while all time I am just crazy to make like up them in the opposite direction.'

'How are you, by the way?' Guy asked George, putting a brotherly hand upon his brother's arm and, at the same time, giving his other hand to Anina to lever her up with the strength and superiority of his youth.

'All right,' said George. 'I saw Tim today.'

'The loo is downstairs,' Guy said as Anina rose. She swayed a little, like Cleopatra making land after too long on her barge.

'Do I genius-man like presently have to spell it out? That john which I require is a carpeted john. Moreover it is like heated. Not that it is an ostentatious john. It has not for instance like the john in the apartment of Solly Gluckmeyer a little circlet of mink nor is there a television set let alone a machine that dries with jets of like delicious hot air. It is an exactly proper john with comforts but no degeneracy. I have forgotten the precise door which you require to turn the knob of but sweet-George will see I come to no grief and afterwards he will help me find a taxi and tell the driver-man where to take me and come back to fry his fish.'

'Who's Solly Gluckmeyer?' George asked.

'Mr. Gluckmeyer,' Anina said, letting her finger fall gently on George's chest, 'is the gentleman who will make little lost-boy rich because he is about to pay five thousand pounds for the right to make a very very beautiful serious film of *A Pram in the Hall* and if genius-boy here were also a gentleman he would be about to do his best to get poor old Antigone a very very beautiful and serious part in that picture only like I know he will not even mention to her that this very serious and beautiful film is about to be made because he would prefer for all the beautiful parts in it to be played by very very serious and Top People like Albert Finney and Joan Plowright, but if Mr. Gluckmeyer were the kind of producer who could interest Albert Finney and Joan Plowright in acting in one of his beautiful and serious films he would like be paying genius-man thirty thousand beautiful pounds instead of five serious ones.'

'Five thousand sound beautiful as well,' said George to Guy who was looking compact, handsome and disengaged from a close relationship. With one blow Guy, living, had become worth half of what George was worth dead.

'Anything looks beautiful until you think of the tax,' said Guy with the narrow smile of a man whose short-term worries had given way to long. 'You saw Tim. How is he?'

'All right. Certain problems.'

'In all this sad world,' Anina said, 'there is not man, woman or child unproblemed. A pound please, lost-boy.'
'Where's your bag?'
'With my coat.'
'And where's your coat?'
'Downstairs in the little room, full of *chinoiserie*.'
'Have you got your key?'
'It is in my bag.'
He gave her a pound note. She gave it to George.
'Sweet-George will look after my pound note and give it to the driver-man being sure to tell him to give me correct change minus one shilling when we have arrived at my pre-destination.'
With the pound note only just left her fingers and held by George, Aunt Clara joined them.
'The heat and the noise,' she said, by way of comment and forgiveness both, 'but you are in demand, Guy.'
'Personally or professionally?'
'You are young enough not to distinguish,' she said and led him by the arm.

Thirty-Four

So George went up the stairs behind Anina like a man sunk to borrowing a pound from his young brother's mistress, and as they mounted they entered inch by inch the cooler air of private quarters he had never seen, there having been no occasion. There was light in the second floor corridor but it struck dully and not glittering on the eye and the further end was in shadow. The faintly ammoniac smell of the unknown came from doors half opened on to darkened rooms; and the stairs continued in a narrower and less graceful way to a floor above which sent down impressions of neither light nor warmth.
'It's at this other end,' Anina said, heading somewhat unsteadily for the gloomy section of the corridor.
He followed her and doing so felt himself pass into the buzzing little world of semi-drunkenness whose ground made itself known by being a fraction of an inch lower than his feet seemed to expect. One gin and tonic before ringing Alice. Three double gins and tonics between ringing Alice and coming unchanged, hands and face washed only, to Aunt Clara's.

Three of Aunt Clara's martinis.

And worry.

And two lousy alternatives.

Which in the hour between Alice and making for St. John's Wood had evolved definitely into three.

And then into four.

The fourth having always been there.

Like the third floor of Aunt Clara's house.

From which no light came.

Nor warmth.

'This is it,' said Anina at the second door tried. 'Have you by chance a penny?'

'Isn't it free?'

'Nothing is free, sweet-George, consequently I am beholden unless I like leave a penny on the ledge.'

She pulled a cord, reaching into the darkness to do so. There was a grating and then a click and light exploded at the far end of the cherry-red carpeted john whose mounted pedestal, now illuminated from above, looked a long way off, and closed for the night like the vault of a bank.

She pressed another switch. Strip lighting flickered and then held steady over a hand basin and mirror and brought up the glaze on the lavender coloured tiles that covered walls and ceiling. A partly opened sash-window disclosed a night of black velvet, very close, so that it seemed a miracle it did not spill in over the clean ledge which held nothing but a tin of Sanilav.

Anina considered her reflection in the mirror. 'Man, I look like a clown,' she said and held her hand out. George gave her a penny, closed the door on her, and considered his situation.

I can't afford it, he thought – meaning his pride which kept on coming back to his breast like a bird to a weather-beaten crust in a garden of hungry cats.

He had never yet asked Aunt Clara for *money*. He had never been on the road with a case of samples. He had never worn a chauffeur's cap and did not get the significance of a chauffeur's cap in relation to working for Mick. But these were three of the alternatives. The fourth narrowed his vision of the corridor in which Aunt Clara all at once appeared, having climbed the stairs in search, it looked, of some kind of assurance: a remarkable woman going on eighty, strong in the bone, meagre in the flesh, pickled in the vinegar of wealth which made her sour but kept her wholesome.

'It's good of you to cope,' she said as he went to join her. 'She's never been *drunk* before.'

'There's always a first time, Aunt Clara.'

'Is she being sick?'

'I don't think so.'

'Guy tells me you are putting her into a taxi. That is sweet of you, George.' She patted his arm. 'We must find you someone, you know.' She patted his arm again, more peremptorily than affectionately. 'As your protégée.'

'I don't want protégée, Aunt Clara. I want two hundred pounds. Is it worth two hundred pounds to have my clever brother permanently disembarrassed of Anina?'

'What are you suggesting, George?'

'I'm taking you up, that's all.'

'You've been drinking again, and are talking nonsense. Unbrushed too. Just look at your suit.'

'Am I to stay on?'

'Stay on?'

'On the phone yesterday you said come early or stay on. But I couldn't come early.'

Looking at Aunt Clara he was conscious of there being between them no shared sense of history, or of time even, although something was occurring which later might be placed in relation to a time and pass, thus, into what could be called a record of their relationship. Was it by any chance that elusive abstraction, the moment of truth?

'I thought you weren't coming at all,' Aunt Clara said. 'And you can hardly stay on in the state I see you're in. In fact you had better take Anina all the way home. It's only to Camden Town.'

'And then?'

'You can get the tube and go home to Queensbury Road and get a good night's sleep.'

'Shall I ring you tomorrow?'

'Of course you may, if you want to.'

'No, it's if you want, Aunt Clara.'

'You make us sound like people who can only be pressed into one another's company by a third force.'

'I think this is true —'

'Now what is *wrong* with you, George? You quite ignore me for three months, you change your address without a word, you ring without warning to seek my advice on a situation I'm not clear about, and then arrive too late for us to talk privately and too drunk to stay on.'

'Oh, not drunk, Aunt Clara. I hold my liquor pretty well. You've often said so yourself.'

'I can't say so tonight, George. You must go with Anina and may ring me tomorrow. But please be quite clear in your mind that I can't give you two hundred pounds.'

'I meant lend, not give.'

'I thought you were telling Tim to write it off?'

'Aunt Clara, I *can't*. You've no idea how complicated things are for him at the moment.'

'Things are always complicated for all of us. And borrowing two hundred pounds from me to pay Tim back simply complicates them more. No. Tim must write the two hundred pounds off and if he can't afford to do so after all these years plodding away in his suburb it's hardly your fault.'

'Isn't it?' George asked, feeling dangerously encouraged.

'I think part of your trouble, George, is that you've never completely outgrown that morbid sense of obligation to him.'

Now just you see that he wraps up you know what he is.

'I remember the time you offered to give up a year's schooling for his benefit, but I should have expected by now you'd see that Tim is quite capable of looking after himself, in his own way. And I don't doubt that he has always rather resented your few advantages over him.'

'He forked out, Aunt Clara, when I was in trouble.'

'There is no such thing, George, as the utterly altruistic action. I neither know nor wish to know what kind of trouble it was, but I'm sure you wouldn't have to look far to find a reason why Tim thought it worth two hundred pounds to keep you out of it. And whatever reason it is that now appears to prompt him to dun you for repayment after all these years you ought not to be blind, George, to the fact that you are forty-three, still not settled, still childless, and in danger of seeing a not insubstantial capital sum going to one of Tim's children. If you rule out the unlikely gesture of a bomb-in-the-post there is very little he can do to ensure that it will and I'm not trying to give you the impression that he duns you consciously with the idea of putting obstacles in the way of your remarriage. Nevertheless, while you are worrying about how and where to find two hundred pounds you are being deflected from what ought to be your main purpose.'

She looked him over.

'If you had not let yourself run a bit to seed, George, we

might yet have found you a comfortable woman with a bit of money. You have been a disappointment to me, you know. In spite of all the help I tried to give you when you were at an impressionable age, you are still hankering after what you'd call an honourable occupation and hankering to be loved for what you are. There aren't any, and one never is. You were a charming boy, and are still a fairly charming man, but it is too late. What a waste.'

'Which should I do first, Aunt Clara; look for someone young to help and encourage or someone to marry? Or is it one and the same thing? Was that in your mind?'

'Really, George. Have you no way at all of standing on your own feet now and deciding things for yourself?'

He considered this, as a man might consider from the end of a platform he'd run the length of the last coach of a train that had left on time.

He said, 'It seems I haven't, Aunt Clara. And yet —' and he made a rare gesture, placed his hand on her shoulder, '—I often feel very hopeful. At times like that I brim over with expectation. And it seems that nothing is too much for me.'

'Partly I blame Roderick for leaving you an income. Partly I blame Alice for not keeping you up to things. Alice was a mistake, George. She had no ambitions for you beyond a settled home. But the main fault is in you. You can't get it out of your head that there is some kind of higher authority. And your appeal to it is invariably sentimental.'

'There aren't many people who have been helped as much as I have been helped,' George said, vaguely aware that neither of them was for the moment quite listening to the other and at the same time vaguely on the alert for anything significant she let slip. Conversation that took this kind of monological turn was like a length of watered silk. Holding your end up you had yet to endanger your hold on it by twisting it this way and that to get glimpses of its random pattern. Less gin would have been a help although without it the conversation could scarcely have got started, it being an Age when, sober, no adult said anything worth listening to. Half-drunk it was difficult to hear. Drunk, it did not matter. How many martinis had Aunt Clara had? 'I have been helped more than anyone I can think of,' he went on, 'and I've been taken up a lot with thoughts of how this sort of thing can be repaid, but it can't you know, Aunt Clara. It really can't. You see first you have to want to do what people want to help you to do, but so often they decide for you and help you to do something before you're even quite sure what it is. Please don't misunderstand. I am very fond of you.'

'Take Guy,' Aunt Clara had already started to say, 'I have some hopes of Guy. It has always been my concern to show young people that there is no authority higher than their own ambition.'

'He is worth half as much alive at twenty-four as I would be dead at forty-three.'

'Of course he has been luckier than either you or Tim, brought up like that away from the influence of Family.'

'Do you think he is kind to Anina, Aunt Clara? I don't think he's at all kind to her.'

'Whatever abilities were latent in the Spruce side they seem to have cohered in Guy and taken the form of this talent for the drama. He says he thinks he got it from his mother. I can't think why.'

'Yes, but is he kind to Anina? Isn't that a test of character?'

'I doubt he will ever fall into the error of a sentimental appeal.'

'He is on my conscience. I think he's on Tim's too. We never mention him except in passing and that's proof.'

'A talent for the drama won't take him as far as a talent for politics or a talent for industry but it will take him far enough for no one to be sorry for him.'

'Oh, not sorry for him now, but before, when we never did a thing for him really. We opted out, Aunt Clara, opted out of a family obligation and told ourselves there wasn't much we could do and he was happier where he was.'

'Obligation, conscience,' Aunt Clara said, as if these were the only words of George's that had resisted instant dismissal and so been set aside for present dealing with. 'Will nothing stop you thinking in terms of an external authority? Unless you are caught breaking the law, which is an artificial authority like the church and an even more splendid means of keeping down excessive competition, you have nothing to answer for to anybody, and the idea of answering to yourself presupposes a state of schizophrenia.'

'But you feel an obligation. To young people. You said so.'

'I did not say so. I said it has always been my concern to give young people help and encouragement. It is a question of force, George. After all, our natural state is one of energy. But you can't expend energy on puddings. It is to do with mathematics, I believe, or is it physics? One force can't avoid seeking out another.'

'But Aunt Clara. That leads to explosions.'

'You have never been a force, George, but with your charm you need not have become a pudding. Force flattens puddings but you could have charmed your way to the kind of power that isn't tough enough to be exploded by a force nor flabby enough to be flattened like a pudding. Are you too drunk to understand fully what I am saying?'

'No. You're saying you're disappointed in me, but you're cross with me too, more cross than disappointed because you must have been disappointed in me years ago when I married a nice but ordinary girl in Cairo, some said to secure my inheritance.'

'Hadn't you better see that Anina's all right?'

'I suppose so.'

He went back to the gloomy part of the corridor, knocked and called out, 'Are you all right?'

'Yes, I'm all right, sweet sweet-George. Like in here I am old Sheba Queen sitting in judgment and wiser than Solomon.'

'Come back soon little Sheba.'

Turning he half expected to find Aunt Clara gone back to her guests but she still stood there, under the light, close to the stairs that rose angularly to the third floor. From below came the continuous grumble of the party, like that of a rabble half way to being roused. An old lady with her hand on a banister rail and about to return to the press and sweat of social togetherness at least deserved explanations even if those were not what she waited for.

'I didn't come for three months,' George said, when he was there by the banister too, 'because somehow I didn't seem to have anything optimistic to say and I usually have had something to tell you, haven't I? I mean something reasonably jolly. I tried my hand at living in a cottage near the sea because I ought to do on four hundred a year. Tuck myself away, do a bit of digging, grow veg, take up a handicraft, buy and sell things sometimes. But I *can't*, Aunt Clara. I hate small boats and lobster pots. And inland, you know, chickens, corrugated iron chapels. I only stood it for a fortnight and of course I never found one of those cottages you hear about that go for a few bob a week.'

'How long have you been in Queensbury Road?'

'Only a few days. I tried Notting Hill before I went to the country. I didn't fancy Pimlico any more, because it's where I first went when Alice and I split up.'

'What are these two prospects you mentioned yesterday on the telephone?'

'I'll tell you some other time, Aunt Clara. I'm sorry I turned out to be a pudding. Truly I'm sorry. Don't frown. I'm not making a joke.'

All the same he began to laugh.

'You'd better go down the back stairs when you're ready. Do you know where they are?'

'No I don't. I'm sorry.'

She walked ahead of him towards and past the door of the lavatory. Two doors further on she stopped, opened, switched a light on and so revealed a narrow cord-carpeted staircase such as in the old days tweenies heaved coal up.

'It goes down to the basement,' she said, 'but stop two floors down, open the frosted glass door and you're at the back of the entrance hall.'

'Thank you, Aunt Clara. Do I look drunk? I don't really feel drunk. I only feel happy for no reason.'

'I should have thought one was happy too seldom not to know the reason why when one is.'

'It's more a feeling of relief, I suppose.'

'In what way are you relieved?'

'I don't know. The alternatives narrow down. Bless you, Aunt Clara Butterfield. I'll wait for Anina and we'll go down the back stairs.'

'I must return to my guests. Goodnight, George.'

He had both her hands and marked the way she bent her head a few degrees down and to the left to take a nephew's kiss on her right temple. Usually she presented her Elizabeth Arden cheek. And time was, years ago in the prime of his youth, when she had always kissed his lips, even when they met over breakfast on the edge of the Manorlord Mount pool and he was wet from swimming.

He watched her to the main staircase, observed sadly the elderly hesitation, the small gathering of the faculties needed to make the descent with considerations of safety uppermost but those of dignity apparent in the tucked-in chin and the way her free hand, while also seeking assurance, gently held the rope of pearls round her neck. Such high heels for an old lady. Moving before he had quite decided in the cold-sober sector of his mind to move he went after her, curious and concerned, and watched her go down without her knowing; wondered if the initial hesitation at the head had been an illusion or whether the now firm negotiation of the steps themselves was one. Even so she might fall, wearing those elegant shoes. If he called out to her and she looked up she would probably lose her balance, so he must not even say goodnight again. Now she was turning into the last curve of the stairs, looking into the room below, a smile already in position like that of an actress within a few seconds of her cue, or so he supposed, never having stood in the wings, which any day now Guy might do, whispering Good Luck to Antigone, although if the one he had read two or three years ago was anything to go by, in a play by Guy the actress would more likely have to wipe an offstage smile from her face and in the last second before entrance become grave and aching with some kind of responsibility, some obligation to the old or foolish, or the unkind young, the sick, the unhappy or the unloved who in the world made private plays that had no curtains, only a continuance of conflicts unresolved for want of being made plain.

He lit a cigarette. Teddy bears, chauffeur's hats, protégées and wives. He looked up at the third floor, blew smoke and went back, after Anina, remembering her almost visible nipples, outraged by the sudden and unexpected intent to fumble drunkenly with his brother's mistress in the back of a rattling taxi, to put it at its mildest.

'Come on out of there Alice,' he said, and punched the door once with the soft palm-edge of his fist.

'This is not Alice.'

'I know. Did I call you Alice?'

'My name is Anina. Who is that?'

'Still George.'

'Sweet-George. Why do you call me Alice?'

'To bring you out of Wonderland, little lost-girl.'

'Wait for me, sweet-George. Like my *craquelure* is most pronounced in this mirror-mirror-wall.'

He leaned against the jamb, and smoked, and then wondered about the ash. Such concern for the deep blue carpet he counted as proof of basic sobriety. He thought: I must put Anina into one taxi and myself into another and do what Aunt Clara said, go home to Queensbury Road and get a good night's sleep, and in the morning I'll wake up sober and indestructible.

Holding his cigarette at the angle least likely to invite disaster he looked up and down the corridor in search of an ash-tray and, seeing none, which didn't surprise him, he moved cautiously to a door in the wall opposite, opened it, felt for and found a switch, pressed it down, and entered what appeared to be a study.

Thirty-Five

It was a small, square room with walls of Wedgwood blue pricked out into panels by thin white beading. A boudoir suite of Sheraton invited him to sit but with a straight back, and not in those clothes. The crimson carpet felt thicker, more shoe-outraged than that of the corridor and stairs. An escritoire, intricately inlaid, was placed so that someone writing at it during the day would have the light from the window (curtained in crimson duchess-satin) fall over the left shoulder in the approved manner, but the whole set of it implied strictures on correspondence and he could not imagine any letter he was likely to write that could be written from there with any kind of élan. Dear Mick, my cap size is six and seven eighths. Dear Perce, you promised to put in a word for me with Mr. Clissold. Dear Tim, I fear I must ask you for another slight extension of time. Dear Mr. Jones, while I appreciate that we All Live under the Surveillance of Head Office. Dear Gwendoline, have you ever thought of a change and plumping for Seaford? Dear Sam, just a line to let you know that if I thought you were ever unkind to Alice I would knock your block off, yours ever. Dear Doctor Honeydew, I don't suppose there is any likelihood of a mistake having been made but, repugnant though the idea is, I am quite prepared to provide a fresh sample.

On the other hand there was what looked like a tape-recorder on a low table by the side of one of the Sheraton chairs, and even a tape-recorder owned by Lady Butterfield could have such messages dictated into it without being given cause for complaint. He went over to it, picked up the microphone and spoke. 'Testing. One, two, three, four, five. Well it's a fine day here at Epsom although we had some fog patches earlier which threatened to obscure the view. It's Fraser to Nash. Trueman is coming up now and it's a defensive field with Cowdrey out there on the boundary. The question in everyone's mind is can Chataway hold Pirie on this last lap? And there it is! Golden Thistle by a short head and Cambridge the winner in this year's boat race. Back now to the studio.'

His ash fell.

'Damn!' he said, and bent to rub it into the carpet with his hand.

'Like it is free now in there, sweet-George,' Anina said, having come in through the open door. 'What are you doing on the floor?'

'I dropped ash. There's not an ash-tray anywhere.'

'Here is one,' she said, picking up and offering him something exquisite which might two hundred years ago have had a bowl to go with it for drinking thé.

'You are clever! Can you work this thing?'

'Yes, sweet-George. I play the tape-recorder with like considerable aplomb. Do you wish to record or to play back?'

'Oh, record. I want to leave a message for Aunt Clara.'

'I learned the tape-recorder in the room of Clarence Rockefeller Brown,' she said, getting down on her knees and shuffling towards the clear side of the table, which looked difficult in her saree, the material growing tauter and more transparent over a nipple that passed within a few inches of his eye. He put up his uncigaretted hand and touched her collar bone. She inclined her head so that her cheek touched his hand and said, 'Sweet-George! Like in that room of Clarence Rockefeller Brown I learned the tape-recorder, the music of Noo Orleens and other things more pertinent to a shared affection, and he is gone back Jamaica-side. And that sweet-traitor, your all-the-same-womb baby-boy brother with the black-black hair is chatting up Antigone with intent to lay. Take the microphone in your right hand and when I like nod this is when you start talking.'

He took up the microphone while she shuffled the last few inches to the table. She bent her head close to the recorder and studied it.

'In this model there are refinements,' she announced presently. 'But the husband of my mother was in India to do with railways and I have a mechanical mind. Seek out and press any noticable protuberance upon the microphone in order to become like live.'

She pressed a button-switch and the tapes began to roll with dignity, like hearses. She nodded her head. George cleared his throat.

'Hello, Aunt Clara. This is your nephew George. I was looking for an ash-tray which explains why I am in this room and Anina is working the machine because her father was to do with railways in India. Alice wasn't a mistake, Aunt Clara. I suppose there has been a mistake but I can't pinpoint it, unless it was that I was brought up to be a sponger by my poor old dad and although there was never a question of sides I suppose I felt I took his because mother automatically had Tim on hers and I suppose if I took sides like that I couldn't even think of what he did as sponging. I wish you'd let Uncle Roderick send me to Malaya to plant tin or mine rubber because the alternative turned out to be Chelsea, Regent's Park and Sloane Street which are full of people sponging with more finesse than my poor old dad but without his sense of gratitude. At least I've always thought it was gratitude but perhaps he wasn't any more grateful than that crowd downstairs who've always had the look to me of treating help and encouragement as their right. Perhaps to treat it as a right is the only way not to be corrupted by it, but I've never seen clearly what rights are mine. I don't think I've got any, Aunt Clara, so I've always been open to any stray bits of corruption going and only saved from the worst by basic innocence which is no skin off anybody's nose because you should only be saved from corruption by experience and will-power. But then will-power goes hand in hand with a sense of having rights and privileges whereas innocence degenerates into conscience and a sense of obligation. Yesterday I decided the causes of my ruin were sex and money but they are sex, money and basic innocence. By basic innocence I mean expecting the best instead of the worst, not only of other people but of myself, and in spite of what I know about us. So I expected Alice to go on forever putting our marriage together again all the time I was pulling it to pieces. So I expect Sam to be kind to her even though I know that with a man like that she'll end up listed with his goods and chattels and depreciated ten per cent a year like his other wife whose name was Rose or Anne or both. So I expected Tim to go on waiting for two hundred pounds until it suited me to pay it back which of course I knew it never would so there *had* to come a day when he was driven to press for it. And now I expect him to do the nice thing and let it drift on again even though I know that having driven himself to press for it once he'll find it easy to go on pressing and I don't expect this to drive me crackers although I know it will. So I expect to swallow my pride and work for a man called Mick and not care about the chauffeur's hat because Mick is above board and my style and it will be all right, although of course I know he's not and it won't be and it's because it's something shady and therefore more paying that I'm attracted to it, so on the few occasions I get scared about Mick I pretend I'll get Perce to speak for me to Mr. Clissold about selling teddy bears on commission only I won't because I've got four hundred a year which means I can't starve and Perce and Mick can go hang and after a bit I'll tell Tim to whistle for his two hundred quid. So I pretend I'll tell him to whistle because if he doesn't get two hundred quid it'll make it more difficult for him to do something not nice about Gillian even though from what I know of Gillian she's not the girl to stand for anything like *that.* And because I know she'd never let them do *that* to her I pretend to myself that she's really quite content with things the way they're turning out and can look after herself because she's basically existentialist, but I know really that she's not content and might let them do *that* to her after all. So I think of her as unhappy and expect to do something about it like offering to take her away and look after her in the country in a place that's full of depressing people making tax free packets out of small-holdings that look smaller on paper than they actually are, but I'd breathe in all that fresh air which is death on good smoker's lungs like mine and expect Gillian and myself to be happy although I would know I was in one sense only trying to work off the debt to Tim and put Gillian in moral debt because I want to be loved for what I like to think I am instead of despised for what I really am. So perhaps by basic innocence I really mean the basic expectations of a louse who looked after his brother not because he liked his brother but because he hoped that looking after his brother would make his mum, who liked his brother better, like him too or even instead. So perhaps since I wrote to you at the Langham instead of to Uncle Roderick I was trying out my natural charm but also setting you up as my unnatural mum which might explain why I wouldn't call out to you while you were on those stairs in those shoes and wouldn't have done even if you'd left me some money or I thought you had in spite of your always saying you hadn't. Well, Aunt Clara, that's about all except that I think Thursdays are a game you play to make up for the fact that in the old days there probably weren't many Top people prepared to forget your father was a butcher which I could have guessed at the time from the sort of jobs you put me on to, and even those few, if there were any, faded out when Uncle Roderick died and you sold that big, empty old place called Manorlord Mount and came here to St. John's Wood to play this Thursday game and not use the telephone much because there weren't many people to ring or because of people listening in and interfering and not letting you have your way and knowing you don't really know anybody now that Uncle Roderick's not here to know them for you both, but this is about where the situation gets too complicated to talk about even to a tape-recorder, so I'll say ta-ta.'

'Like it was way out that sweet-talk to Spielburg' Anina said, switching the machine off and covering her Nepalese eyes with one hand, in an attitude of private prayer.

'Let's go,' George said, putting an arm round her.

'First we must like play back,' she said, letting herself go limp, either in surrender or to become a dead weight, but because both of them had been drinking George did not know which she intended or which he preferred.

'How do we do that?' he asked, bending his head over hers and not being tickled by her hair because alcohol had anaesthetized his nerve-ends.

She tilted her own head back and this brought their faces very close together.

'You do not know how to play back on a tape-recorder sweet-George? Tell me like why is it the nicest men do not have mechanical minds? How do I work this thing is what Clarence Rockefeller Brown said to me, which is how I came to learn the tape-recorder in his crazy apartment. How do we do that, you say, sweet-George. But apart from changing his ribbon there is nothing mechanical I am like required to do for genius-man who can fix anything that needs fixing from a shelf that falls down to a geyser that like threatens to explode. And —' she touched his nose with her fore-finger, '—not only does he fix geysers but also writes serious and beautiful plays about them. Fix the geyser for me Joe, is what you said, like fix the geyser, Joe.'

'What are you talking about?'

'I saw it in the machine before we came.'

'I never see anything in the machine.'

'This is because you have not got a mechanical mind. Now I will play back because you must not make free of my bosom, reserved as it is for genius-boy who may not appreciate it any longer but pays for its keep.'

She pressed switches. Fascinated, they watched the tapes whizz in reverse.

'Have you ever heard your voice recorded, sweet-George?'

'Never.'

'Then you will get a kind of shock.'

She pressed more switches.

'To achieve success through charm.' Aunt Clara was saying, in a voice several tones lower and slower than George at once found familiar, 'it is necessary to remain penniless. He will get no two hundred pounds from me. Does this sound heartless?'

Anina stopped the machine.

'We have gone too far back,' she said, 'and it is rude to listen.'

For a few moments the tape revolved in silence. Then she pressed a switch again.

'—not endangered,' Aunt Clara continued. At least, George assumed it was Aunt Clara, but these days you could rely on nothing so why trust the Grundig? 'I have never believed in God except for the poor, nor in charity except as an expression of force, which is to say —'

'I am sorry,' Anina said, stopping Aunt Clara at her recorded source, and trying again, further along the tape.

'—much more sensible. For instance his younger brother Guy who was born just before the war, an inefficient arrangement which showed why the Spruce side of the Butterfield clan had fallen so low —'

'No, leave it,' George said, restraining Anina, and losing a few words because he had interrupted.

'—of fish; but then he was brought up in a wholly different environment by foster-parents in the country and would sell his grandmother for thirty pieces of silver if he knew where to find her. I have some hopes of Guy as a protégé and am not blind to the fact that he thinks me a stupendous and superannuated bore who may nevertheless leave him some money and provide him early on with the financial security from which, in his plays, he can more comfortably attack standards of civilized conduct. How disappointed he will be! But I fancy he is a force. When you recognize a force it is ridiculous to ignore it or contest it. George, I quickly saw, would never become a force.'

Anina, escaping from George's hold, stopped the machine.

'But I want to hear,' George said. 'I want to know.'

'This is like despicable,' she said.

'Go back to the bit about two hundred pounds.'

'Where was that?'

'It's the first bit we heard.'

Anina got the tape going round in reverse.

'Like here,' she said, stopping it at what looked like its beginning, then turning and pressing switches.

Aunt Clara sounded like a duck.

'What have you done?' George asked.

'It is playing faster than it was recorded.'

'Make it go slower then.'

Anina did so.

'—the - whole - secret - of - living - is - to - be - required - by - other – people —' Aunt Clara said with the voice of a man talking under duress, with his whole metabolism changed by an intentinal obstruction of long standing.

'I want to hear it properly,' George said. 'I want to *know*.'

Anina made another adjustment.

Aunt Clara continued in her normal voice – 'Not precisely needed by them because the last thing others wish to feel towards you is gratitude. Actually a bit of old-fashioned fear does no harm, providing it is only a dash, enough to make them consciously square their shoulders before they come into your room —'

George took Anina's hand in his.

And in this manner like old babes in a frosty wood they heard nearly everything that Aunt Clara had said into the tape-recorder during the past thirty-six hours, but when her voice stopped and it was time for George's to begin nothing happened because, as Anina discovered, he had not pressed the button on the microphone after all and even if he could remember what he said he didn't have the heart to repeat it. So he bequeathed Aunt Clara no last message and they left the recorder neatly where they had found it, turned out the light but forgot the ash-tray on the floor. They went down to the hall by the servants' stairs. And while Anina looked for and found, with the help of Lady Butterfield's maid Hilda, her coat of nylon-fur, blue-grey and hip-length, a present from Guy on the afternoon of the day they left Islington forever, George thought of his own handsome ears, what he looked like in a bathing-suit, the poor prospects for a man who wasn't a force, the Sungei Labong Five per cents, his narrow escape from the Marble Arch, the disappointment Guy was in for, the experience you might have of cows, and pure power in roughly that order. And when he had thought of them in that order, and then in another, and then all jumbled up, he thought of them as a totality and from that totality there emerged the kind of thought that was really an image without words, and sad in its way: the image of an old lady talking to a Grundig because there was no one else to talk to, even on Thursdays.

Thirty-Six

George went all the way to Camden Town. They had no difficulty in finding a taxi because one drew up just as they came on to the pavement and the taxi driver said, 'Taxi for Mr. Spruce?' and only when they were settled in the back did they realize they must have taken a taxi Aunt Clara had rung for on the telephone for Guy, or Guy had rung for, for himself and Antigone. In the taxi Anina began to cry and George had a sad, gentle time drying her eyes and trying to find out why. In the flat she shared with Guy she began to cry again but stopped when George found a bottle of gin more than half full in the kitchenette cupboard.

The time was twenty-one minutes after nine.

Half way through their first glass of gin from the bottle that had been more than half-full he kissed her nipple. She brightened up a bit then, and after a certain struggle exposed the breast because, she said, she did not think it fair to keep him in suspense, but once it was exposed she cried again and made haste to the bathroom to be sick. So he held her puky head after the manner of Clarence Rockefeller Brown, made her a cup of coffee, and poured himself another gin, and felt put off.

The flat gave him the creeps. It was a bed-sitting room on the first floor of a mid-Victorian villa in a street of similar villas, some with lighted porches and their doors painted puce or yellow to prove disengagement from old conformities, and lights showing through plastic Venetian blinds. Guy and Anina's room (kitchen, bathroom and lavatory attached) was covered in cord-carpet of a dark and durable fawn. Three walls were distempered grey like the ceiling and the fourth, against which the double divan bed had its bolster head, was papered in crimson paper broken up with embossed silver fleurs-de-lys. The woodwork (skirting board, picture rail, window frames, doors) was painted glossy gun-metal grey, and the venetian blinds (slats down and *de rigueur*) at the twin sash windows were silver-grey. The fireplace was black and monumental like something salvaged from the Duke of Wellington's funeral carriage. The divan bed had a brown candlewick cover. There were two fireside chairs in grew tweed with brown arms and legs. There was a studio couch of the kind that always reminded George of the bed of the True Princess, being very high and lumpy, with rust-coloured upholstery that would be scratchy to sit on in short trousers, wretched if you were a scoutmaster planning the seduction after cocoa and seed-cake of a member of the troop who needed practise with his knots.

'I'm sorry I was sick,' Anina said, putting her coffee down on the bedside table and tucking her breast back in: so that was that. 'Have some more gin.'

'What would you like with your coffee darling?' Tim asked Sarah directly she had finished her pêche flambée which in Their restaurant had always fascinated them but until tonight had not been afforded.

'There's some brandy left in the sideboard,' Mrs. Wallingford replied to her husband's question, when their dinner of soup, shepherd's pie and prunes was over.

'I fancy a dairy, don't you, Mill?' Con said with the lights up in the interval between *The Brand of the Beast* which had been nice and *Paranoia* which they hoped would be nasty.

'Where's that boy, Ma?' Mr. Clayton asked from behind *The Evening News*.

'Out with that Rod Starling again,' said Mrs. Clayton from behind nothing.

'I thought you was going out with that bird from the Nun-House,' said Rod.

'What if I was? Birds is just birds ain't they?' said Click.

'Hello, anyone at home?' Rick Wragge said, grinning.

'Just me. Come in Ricky,' Sandra Hardcastle said.

'Brandy I think,' said Sarah, 'if things will run to it.'

'The chap on the rank says he doesn't know anything about it,' Guy said, putting the receiver back on to Lady Butterfield's telephone rest. 'But he's coming himself right away.'

'I'm sorry that Z wasn't here,' Lady Butterfield said. 'Good luck with the Antigone. And Guy, I hope Anina has got home safely.'

'Like he's tired of me that little lost boy, sweet-George. But until he shows me to the door I have not the heart to walk out of it. Nor am I like capable of extra curricular relationships which according to Clarence Rockefeller Brown is due to my one track mind, and my one track mind according to the same sweet crazy gone back Jamaica-side source is oh very more than likely due to the fact that when I was but a little girl and lonely and crying because small and grandma black and born in Railway Cuttings, Nehruville, I was frightened by a multiplicity of tracks and points and up lines and down lines and lines that had to be cleared to like ensure the Calcutta Mail did not come to grief by finding in its path the slow train to Benares running behind schedule. Please refill your glass.'

'—if I may call you Alice, after such a brief acquaintance.'

'Of course. Mr. Kennedy.'

'Do call me John.'

'It can't be helped, Cyril,' said Mrs. Wallingford. 'If it comes to it we can always sell the Plot.'

Or we might go to Falmouth, thought Mr. Stainsby, pouring another cup from his flask of tea, although Falmouth is a long coach ride and there's always sickness on such outings and a coachload of sick children is not an especially pleasant prospect nor yet a fitting memorial for poor Miss Lisle, who if I may say so is taking an extraordinarily long time to Let Go and at this rate I shall have to go down for a sandwich.

'You've got a spot of ice-cream on your chin, Con. No. Yes. It's gone now.'

'How's the enemy?'

'Just gone half nine.'

'We'll be late out. I hope it's good.'

'It had better be.'

The lights began to dim.

'And just what do you think you're doing, Ricky Wragge?' Sandra Hardcastle asked from the depths of the sofa in the dark of her living-room.

'How much longer are you going to be?' Andrew Spruce called through the closed bathroom door.

'You're supposed to be in bed,' Gillian called back above the noise of running water.

'I am in bed but I want to go.'

'Use the one downstairs. I'm having a bath.'

'Oh, Lord.'

'And see that you've got your slippers on. You know *what*

you are.'

She tested the water in the bath for heat, took off her dressing-gown and felt through the steam for the hook on the door which was wet and clammy. Naked, she groped for the tap end of the bath, turned the tap off, checked that the cork-topped bathside stool held everything she was going to need, and then put one leg over the side and lowered it slowly until it was immersed to half way up the shin bone and touching bottom.

Four minutes later she was sitting upright with her mouth open like a fish, not daring to move even to wipe the perspiration out of her eyes.

Presently, though, she was used enough to the heat to turn gingerly half right, raise her arms, wipe her hands on a towel, open the square green bottle and pour a glass of gin.

She waited until she heard the cistern go in the downstairs lavatory and the sound, half a minute later, of Andrew on the landing, opening and closing his bedroom door.

Then she began to drink.

After the cannelloni Antigone said, 'Shall we do it now?' So they had done it then; and were now enjoying a second bottle of Spanish claret.

'No, I'm not a Nuclear Disarmer,' Guy said. 'I don't see why I should go to prison for Lord Russell. Mind you if I were well enough known it might be worth thinking about. The point is that nobody is going to give up more for Ban the Bomb than he thinks he can afford in terms of his career. It's the poor sods you've never heard of who'll get the long stretches and before the long stretch is over nobody will even remember their names, and by the end of 1963 or 1964 it won't be fashionable to be a Nuclear Disarmer because if the campaign goes on much longer somebody like Lord Wolfenden will get attached to it as a sort of sponsored observer and that'll kill it stone dead. Or perhaps Tony will be caught photographing a demonstration in Trafalgar Square and that will move the whole thing on to the level of a sketch from *Beyond the Fringe*, and only John Gordon in the *Sunday Express* will care.'

'But something's got to be done, surely?'

'Why?'

'Don't you think I ought to ring?' Sarah asked.

'It's only just gone ten,' Tim said, and nodded a thank you to the waiter who had brought them two more brandies.

'I said we'd be back by eleven.'

'We shan't be much after. We'll get a taxi all the way.'

'Oh well, if we're sprazzing out!'

She settled back again, weight gone from her mind and from her houseworked shoulders which had begun to ache half way through the *pêche flambée* because of the tube journey ahead which had suddenly seemed squalid like the prospect of taking her best dress off to do the leftover washing-up with a pinny over a petticoat. The ache was cancelled out by his loving spendthriftery, his casual but firm protectiveness, his full pocket worked so hard for. His leg was hard against hers and warm with blood capable, when the moment came, of engorging him for the last act of a night on the town.

'There is something I want to say,' she said. 'Lean closer.'

He did so. 'What is it?'

'I'm very proud of my Tim.'

'Are you?' he said, embarrassed, and wondering why she should choose to say so just at the moment when the causes of self-congratulation were turning opaque, as if they were windows that gave on to a prospect and were being breathed on by brandy fumes and people who weren't visible but had names and feelings, like Wallingford; or plans, like Curtis Jackson; or attitudes which might, on closer acquaintance, prove condescending, like Vernon and Minerva Bell's. And Minerva Bell would never say to Vernon Bell, Lean closer; or lower her voice in a public place; or ask, What shall I wear on Sunday?

He smiled at her and increased the pressure of his leg against her, having just become aware of it again, and felt he owed her a corresponding pride, but could not summon it as pride exactly because of her best dress which had had to do for so many occasions that were special without gracing any particular one. So it came to him as love, not pride, this thing he felt for her, but having come like that he couldn't be sure he felt it quite as love because the feeling that came to him was a feeling he had grown very used to, like the feeling of working at Bartle Wallingford.

'Nothing's going to make you change your mind, is it?' she said, meaning about the job.

'No,' he said, knowing what she meant.

'Why do you take it so calmly Lesley?' Cyril Wallingford

said to his wife.

'I'm a calm person,' she said, threading a needle with wool for her tapestry.

And have money of your own: Cyril Wallingford said without actually making a sound. And have never taken my work seriously, nor me seriously. Because you have never depended. Never depended, I say. If I had had someone depending on me I should have been as dynamic as young Spruce. I'd have asked Fred Bartle who he thought he was talking to instead of just letting it go when he called me a fool and Matilida Poole heard, because she had stopped typing, clack-clack-clack.

'And we have always lived calm lives,' Lesley Wallingford said, picking up her frame, and frowning slightly because of the brandy bottle caught in the corner of her eye in the raised position; and being tipped.

You weren't at Gallipoli, Wallingford said as before, and drinking his third brandy. Nor did you even pick your way over glass. Your father never lost twenty thousand pounds between 1914 and 1918 and the two thousand it cost me to buy in with Bartle never touched your pocket. Even your bank account has always been calm. Never a ripple, Lesley. Never a ripple, I say.

Lesley Wallingford said, 'We have lived calm lives in troubled times, Cyril. We have launched a steady daughter and married her to a steady man in a steady profession. You took in what you supposed to be a steady partner in order to achieve equilibrium in retirement.'

You should have warned me against him, Wallingford said without moving his lips.

'He has proved unsteady,' she said.

Now tell me you knew he would.

'But our lives will continue calm because you will sell the business as Timothy Spruce proposes,' said Mrs. Wallingford. And you are getting too old to play at going to business, she added: silently, because a quiet husband went so well with the house. 'Unsteadiness need not be catching.'

'Everything is catching except money and peace of mind,' Wallingford said aloud before he could stop himself and because of the brandy and thirty-five years of holding his tongue.

'Your steadiness is no way impaired,' said Lady Butterfield's old retainer Hilda to her friend Mrs. Braithwaite, drying the last of the glasses in the kitchen with the radio playing well-mannered but below-stairs music. 'It is a marvel to me, your steadiness. Although do please be careful with what you're washing now. I shouldn't fancy answering for either of us if one of us broke it.'

'I've washed better in worse places,' said Mrs. Braithwaite holding up the something exquisite that might have had a bowl to go with it for drinking thé two hundred years ago, and letting it drip before placing it steadily in a draining position on the damp tea-towel Hilda always placed on the enamel draining board when washing up *objects*, to save chips.

'I can't think how it happened,' Hilda said, watching the Lux Liquid bubbles slide slowly across the fat pink bottom of a cupid up to no good with a lady and gentleman disposed in a position, while neglected sheep and an abandoned shepherdess's crook decorated the background.

'Someone was in there smoking,' Mrs. Braithwaite said, taking off her apron and looking at the clock.

'But who would do such a thing? She was in quite a state. Can you explain it, Hilda, she said, and when I said I couldn't she said, Please take it away at once and wash it most carefully. Someone's Been In, she said.'

'Well, I'm off now,' said Mrs. Braithwaite, going for her coat. Hilda went to the crock for fifteen shillings.

'It quite spoiled her Thursday, I reckon,' said Hilda. 'And poor old thing, she lives for her Thursdays.'

'Is it like true my lost-boy was abandoned by you and your brother, sweet-George?'

'There was the war and we'd both gone to it, if you call that abandon,' George said, and tilted the gin bottle because she held her glass out.

'Of course Tim never went overseas,' Guy said, putting his shirt back on while Antigone, in white dressing-gown, poured more Spanish claret. 'He and Sarah came down to Dorset once or twice when their leave coincided because they wanted mother's linen and cutlery. Sarah was a WAAF, or an AT. I must have been ten before I consciously remember George. He'd married this girl Alice he met in Cairo. They were stuck in Cairo the whole war and came home in what, 1946? Anyway they paid me a duty visit and George tipped me a fiver. Then I never saw them together again except through cards at Christmas and birthdays, and sometimes a letter. I got a scholarship to the grammar and then to Reading. After that I went to see Tim and Sarah but they looked dead from the neck up to me. Then I did two years in the army and at the end of that when I called on George he looked dead from the neck down and Alice was out at work. I frigged around in advertising for a spell, lived in poky rooms, wrote stories that didn't sell, did a broadcast or two on that old people's What Are Young People Thinking sort of programme, joined an expedition that was going to the Amazon but got stuck at Gravesend, which at least meant I kept the money I'd saved to buy time to write plays. That's my acquired Welsh streak, of course. I can be as mean as muck. But I never cost anyone a farthing because although mum and dad left no more than paid for their funerals these people who looked after me got paid by the government for my keep, and my education was free, and apart from the fiver from George and the abortive introduction to Lady Butterfield a few years ago I never got anything I didn't earn.'

'It's given you hard eyes,' Antigone told him, handing him his glass. She always made a point of insulting men she had just gone to bed with because it made her feel better and sometimes re-excited them.

'You have masochistic tendencies,' said Guy, making a guess that was random but turned out intelligent. 'Are we going to have an affair?'

'I shouldn't think so,' Antigone said. 'You make me feel too much like a slot machine.'

'The trouble with actors and actresses,' Guy told her, 'is that they want to be loved and not used. Nobody is ever loved and everybody is always used.'

'Am I using you?'

'Didn't you notice?'

'You haven't got the legs to stand round in only a shirt. Pop your trousers on, and then go home and get on with *The Geyser*. You never saw me at the Royal Court, did you?'

'No. And you thought *A Pram in the Hall* was a stinker.'

'Yes. And that silly old woman probably hasn't seen Z to speak to since he was putting on those ghastly little plays at The Gauze in the early Fifties.'

'I've never even heard of The Gauze.'

'It was before your time.'

'Most things were,' said Guy, putting his trousers on and wanting to be loved more than anybody in the world.

'Sometimes it is like love,' Anina said, 'and sometimes it is like afraid, what I feel in this crazy flat.'

'I was brought up,' George said, topping up his gin, 'brought up as I see it not to accept my environment. There were these people next door called Proctor and if it hadn't been for Mr. Proctor and his bicycle I might have come into the world with no doctor and quite on my own in an air-raid, but as I see it I was always taught to believe that in one sense the Proctors weren't there at all because the Spruces, that's us, the Spruces in this same sense lived in a totally different world, a world of titles and connections and privileges that existed even if they didn't actually work, for us, I mean for the Spruces, so that this totally different, this totally illusory world was the real world and the world of Mr. Proctor and the terraced villas and the whining voices and the swank and the bad taste and the loud laughter at night when somebody's door opposite opened to let out neighbours was the illusory, unreal, not there world. Do you see what I mean, Anina?'

'Like here it is illusory and I close my eyes sometimes sweet-George' – and she closed her eyes, her head resting on the crimson wallpaper, her body stretched in its turquoise saree on the brown candlewick cover, and held one hand up with the gin glass in it and the other as if to conjure – 'and make like it is not here but some all-the-same-strange and different and very beautiful and serious world where I am like loved without prejudice to my fine feelings, and everything is clean and tidy and people say, Behold, like it is Anina, and not mucky and they like say, There goes that Annie MacBride to meet her nigger-boy. Or like it is very early on a very fine and not even misty morning and I am standing very high up on the roof of a tall building where it is morning sooner on the roof than it is in the basement and the whole big crazy town is asleep and like neatly tucked up and separately labelled so that I do not have to make with the frown or the quick-bitten nail but can see where everybody is and what they are doing and why they are doing it and not like in my tenement-mind meet only with strangers and a lack of response.'

And my breasts are already beginning to bloom, Gillian told herself, and where I was somewhat concave I am somewhat convex and gin has a very peculiar taste indeed, so that the whole idea becomes slightly fabulous and I don't know why I am doing it although it is very comfortable and somewhat dreamy, so I am lying in this hot water and drinking gin which is an old wives' specific for bringing off a baby and if it works it works and if it doesn't it doesn't and that I'm doing it is sufficient explanation because there can't possibly be a reason for every single thing that goes on because so much goes on some of it has to be unreasonable, although it might have been more sensible to have waited until Sarah is in the house in case I get into difficulties, and nobody can get in without breaking down the door but if I get out and unlock it it might stop things happening just at the moment they are about to happen, and perhaps I shall relapse into a drunken stupor and slide down in the bath like something fishy and floppy in a tank and be drowned and everybody will blame themselves which will be fantastic really because nobody is to blame for me getting into a boiling hot bath and getting sozzled on gin except me.

'I'm glad it's happened,' said Tim. 'We were in an awful rut. Now we're going to get out of it. I'm sick of saving money, aren't you?'

'Heartily,' said Sarah, dutifully, but also meaning it because of the brandy and a sense of internal unbalance that only the thought of merry expenditure could steady.

'Money saved is money idle,' Tim said. 'I mean after a point has been reached. The trouble is we've always been afraid of running up bills, but that's because we both came from homes where the word Bill was used like the voice of doom. Whenever the postman came mother used to say, Is it another bill?'

'And whenever a bill came,' George said, 'I suppose I felt it only came in this unreal world inhabited by people like the Proctors and we'd be protected from it by Sir Roderick and Lady Butterfield because theirs was the world we really lived in and they were never worried about bills. And I remember this time when there'd been a particularly Awful Bill and mother was sitting over the dining-room fire in that way she had when she was at what she called her wit's end, leaning right over it as if there wasn't a scrap of warmth to be lost and young Tim was sitting on the rug pretending to play with his bricks and father was upstairs painting robins and snow and holly, and although I knew there had been The Bill I said, What's wrong? and Tim turned round from his bricks as if he thought I ought to dam' well know and said, there's been a Bill, and he knocked the bricks over because he'd turned round so quickly and I said, Can't father write to Uncle Roderick? and mother said, I'd rather go to the workhouse than be an object of charity for the rest of my life, and your father ought to be ashamed. Which was dramatic, but she made everything dramatic, and

Tim began to cry but whether about the bricks or the Bill or what I had said or what mother had said I don't know to this day because I went out of the room and I don't know whether I went out of the room because I was jealous of my mother fussing Tim because he was crying or because he looked at me as if everything was my fault, or because I didn't take any of it seriously because it was all happening in a world that wasn't real. And I think it was the day my Auntie Ada turned up without writing first and there was a row and she had cherries in her hat.'

'Like I lost my cherry to a boy from The Angel who was the one before that sweet gone-back-Jamaica-side-man and this boy was a very beautiful but not in the least bit serious boy and did not teach me any art that was pertinent to a shared affection because he was like after my cherry and not my puky heart. And I cost nothing then.'

'But now you cost,' George said. 'Given time we all cost something. Because of the investment.'

'It was a good one,' said Sam, meaning the investment of dinner for four at a cost of fifteen pounds fourteen shillings and sixpence, and who now sat in the back of the shiny black car with Alice, having established accord in regard to the preliminary steps in a small matter of take-over which would bring dollars to a second-rate power that was still a force because it had patience and a long experience of colonial administration.

'I like John Kennedy,' said Alice.

'I like you,' said the young man with the Brando haircut who had not yet reached the stage of climbing stairs in front of his ape shadow and obviously was never going to because he was already upstairs in this poor girl's room and the film was about over which meant that the scene on the stairs had been cut out or the poster was just made like that to get you in, but it thrilled Connie Crayfoot to hear him say: I like you, because he was in very close close-up looking straight at her, but at the same time she was glad that it was not really her he liked because the picture seemed to be about to prove that girls he said 'I like you' to tended not just to get raped but stabbed and have their bodies covered in cobweb designs with the point of the knife, which was all to do with the fact that this nice big young man had been locked up by his no-better-than-she-should-be-mother for days and days when he was a nice small boy in an old room filled with cobwebs, and if there was one thing that made Connie Crayfoot's blood run cold it was even just the thought of a spider and she remembered how Matilda Poole who was always kind to her once put one out of the window on a newspaper.

'There's only hard centres left,' whispered Mill, offering the bag of chocs.

Five minutes later they were in the crowd in the foyer and Mill said, 'Well I didn't think much of that,' in a voice loud enough for the Management to hear if it happened to be there or interested in what she thought, and Con thought that you had to hand it to Mill for speaking her mind.

And it was ten minutes to eleven.

And Guy was walking along the Brompton Road on the side opposite Harrods on the first leg of his journey back from his evening with Antigone but thinking obliquely of George, not only because George had seen Anina into a taxi and probably taken her home if the way he had looked at her at Aunt Clara's was anything to go by but because he associated the Brompton Road with the kind of life George lived, in a certain style on long credit in the lanky shadows of fringe debs, bouncing his anti-social way from week to week with his own cheque book and somebody else's gas ring: which might make a play if if he could find its contemporary equivalent.

And it was at half-past eleven that Andrew Spruce came out of his bedroom on to the landing and found the bathroom door still closed. He knocked at it and said, 'Surely you're not still in there?' but got no answer so knocked again, and then again, and was cross and then worried and then frightened because he and Gillian were alone in the house.

Thirty-Seven

It was quite simple really, George told himself. All he had to do was drop dead.

'Is there any more gin?' Anina said sleepily, with only one eye open, her head still against the crimson wallpaper, one hand holding her empty glass on the candlewick cover at one side and her other hand at rest on the other side holding nothing. She closed the one eye that had been open. 'Is there any more gin?'

'No,' said George, having focused successfully on the bottle.

'Then you must go home,' Anina said, 'and Guy will think it is I who have drunk the gin. But he will not mind because it is my perk to drink all the gin when he is not here but making love to someone else. So George, sweet-George, cover me up so that in the night I do not wake up cold and alone.'

'What shall I cover you with?' he asked, looking at her, considering her in the cold sober section of his mind that had now diminished to the size and substance of a sapphire held precariously in position behind the bridge of his nose by a conscious pressure of his eyebrows.

'Oh, anything that is warm and loving and not for sale. But not yourself, sweet-George, because of the morning and regret. Once I had a concern to touch this town with a wand and spark up balls of poetry, but the talent did not occur except in bottles, which are soon empty.'

'What?' said George, hearing but not hearing because his brows had lost their hold but now regained it; too late, because she was silent: in all likelihood asleep.

So he took away her empty glass and put it on the bedside table next to his own and then got up from his seat on the edge of the bed and looked slowly round the room. There was nothing to put over her except the candlewick bedspread so he pulled at the unused half and folded her in. She stirred to show that the warmth had reached her, and smiled a bit, and with her closed eyes looked content and capable of fortitude; but he thought she must be uncomfortable with her head against the wall so he pulled her down in her candlewick cocoon until her head lay on the slight bulge which if the uncovered half of the bed was any indication was made by one thin pillow in a case that needed washing.

He knelt by the divan and snuggled the cover around her ears and the top of her head, pulled it away from her chin in case it tickled, and looked at her for a while, testing the shell of a thought for a weak spot and a way into it: a thought of Anina here in front of him, and Alice, where she might be; but Alice was away somewhere wrapped in Sam, and the cold sapphire behind the bridge of his nose was a camera-eye not a crystal ball.

When he stood up again the camera-eye selected objects of its own accord and at random: silver fleurs-de-lys, two glasses side by side, a straight dark line on the floor, but his ears were so tightly screwed into his head from all the gin he had drunk that messages from eye to brain got scrambled and took time to unscramble, and he was half way across the room before he understood that the silver fleurs-de-lys were significant because they were the ones on the patch of wall behind the two glasses, that the two glasses were significant because they would prove to Guy it wasn't only Anina who had drunk the gin, that the straight dark line on the floor was the join between two strips of cord carpeting and he was moving along this line away from the table with the glasses on it leaving evidence behind that ought to be tampered with. But he kept on going because the camera-eye had recorded a machine that was a typewriter in which there was a piece of paper and by the time he was at the typewriter leaning over it to get a clear definition, the idea of the paper had produced its logical message of the paper being a means of communication with someone who ought to be communicated with, but not Anina, because she was asleep in her candlewick; nor Alice, because she was away with Sam in the dark. Which left only Guy to leave a message for but there was nothing he could think of to say to him and there were already some words on the paper, vaguely familiar. Fix the geyser for me, Joe. Which he was quite unable to, being hopeless with mechanism. So what would he do if the car broke down with the hat on his head suggesting responsibility and the passenger, whoever it was, saying: Well; fix the engine for me, George?

He found his way into the kitchen where the light was still on from making coffee, and drank water, splashed some on his face and stood by the sink dripping and cold. When he looked up from the sink he found his reflection in a small white-framed mirror and after consideration of it turned away to walk the broad corridor of his private feelings which was portable and had to be taken everywhere to be laid like a strip of matting across the bog of other people's rooms in order to enter them from outside or get out of them from in, with dignity.

By the bedside he turned off the table-lamp and seeing the two glasses remembered an earlier intention so took one and went back to the kitchen where he washed and dried it and found a sliding cupboard into which it did not seem especially glad to go because the cupboard was obviously reserved for cups and saucers.

He turned off the light allowing his hand to linger for a moment on the switch and was then in the living-room again with Anina sleeping and the light coming from a hanging globe in the middle of the high ceiling. He bent over her and said, 'Like I am going, now, and have taken care of the glass,' and touched her cheek that was cool and damp, and got no response and thought of the many times Alice must have touched his own cool damp face and got no response and lain awake, glad he was back and safe, but watching him for cyanosis, dreading the morning and his waking, his remorse, his lying promises, contemptible cornered-rat evasions, and the onset of his long silences which he cast about in his mind for means of breaking without success because in the end you could only talk to strangers or into the telephone.

So he smiled at Anina in lieu of a spoken farewell and at the door turned off the last light of all and went out as he was, having nothing but what he left Bayswater in: no coat, no hat, just his suit, socks, shoes, tie, underwear and frayed-cuff shirt and in need really of a brush and comb. Once down the stairs and out of the house the same warmish breeze that stirred what looked like laurel bushes in the small front garden ruffled him up up even more, although it also blew him clean, and the blowing clean left areas of sensitivity exposed and bare ends to his nerves which had been warmer than the breeze and so presently healed themselves by a quick frosting which made him shiver and then perspire fine particles of ice water on his brow and shoulder blades and in the fleshy patch of leg behind the knees so that in his clothes, walking, he was aware of his skin, slight friction, and pockets of air where contact failed rhythmically. But in himself he was warm and did not mind having no topcoat. He enjoyed both it and the freedom of hands ungloved against the night. He went by pavements and unexpected gutters into a brighter world of High Street and shop-fronts, some dark with doorways sealed off by iron and padlocked lattice and others lit and showing some of the things there would be to buy in the world tomorrow when the blown bits of paper would look less sordid, less lost and there would be other footsteps on the pavement besides his own.

He remembered there was a pub around the corner but within sight of it he knew it was shut and paused unable to account for time gone but not disputing it or bothering to check the hour; returned to the brighter concentration of light which at night in cities even the shortest deviation into a side streed led you quickly away from, and found late gusts of traffic coming through from the West End, a brace of Vespas with twin loads each of boy and girl in white skid-lids followed by a taxi not for hire and going the wrong way, towards Alice country, so that a taxi for hire and willing to go in the right direction into the heart of old Spruce country, not so silky any more, now became imperative. He cast about for one, crossing and re-crossing the barely populated roads that met here in a knot at Camden Town, dismissing the alternative of Tube because the tube brought everything too close too soon, being lit from inside and guarded by nothing except evening paper stands: upended boxes sold out and gone home taking all those coppers and only the placards left to prove them and a Persephone smell coming up from below.

No, certainly it wasn't a question of alternatives. There was only one thing to do; take what had been the fourth alternative, but was now the only sensible course; and under these Camden lights and on this pavement, where he was alone save for a car stopped by traffic lights and a youth like Click Clayton going home on foot in medieval shoes and shiny black jacket, he saw the gesture very clearly as one he had worked towards all day; if not for longer, perhaps from right back to the time he'd spent his pocket money on picture sweets unless it was raining when it went on the tram, that rumbling red chariot he and his brother rode in silent communication of their separateness, silent because they were each other's first experience of the world beyond the womb and in that world talk was small, and thought always at least one step ahead of it, preserving an inner dignity and sense of destiny that could be shared with no one else. And such a dignity and sense was lost but once in a man's life, and then not lost but offered with love to match a corresponding offer from a woman such as Alice in Cairo, loved long before the news of money reached them and ruled out certain objections, certain uncertainties about the future, even of quiet war there in Cairo in the days before Rommel increased uncertainty a small degree and then retreated and lengthened the odds back to the long ones of Shepheard's and a charmed life of gentle staff work for Army George and Red Cross Alice and the slow poison of large mess bills incurred because of increased Income and higher Expectations for their son who would ride no tram, ever, and so be a power, if not a force, because of Winchester or Eton or whatever, the choice being arbitrary more than actual and symbolic of Improvement.

And this gesture, worked towards all day if not longer, and now seen clearly, might be made in any one of several ways, although the ways – because of circumstance – narrowed down to perhaps no more than two: to fall on the line under a late train on the tube or to walk into the path of a late bus: a pretty simple business when you thought about it, although messy, and a bit of a shock to people who did nothing to deserve it, like drivers and casual witnesses – homegoing youths or West Indian porters without talents but handy with brooms and pails. And after the people to whom his action would be a shock would come those to whom its aftermath was no more than a job of work: police and ambulance crews, hospital orderlies and morgue attendants, a night reporter, whoever they were who in this drowned city must come with casual flicks of fin and tail to investigate and deal with bubbles rising in the wrong way and in the wrong place.

But before the gesture was made more gin was needed to halt the flowing downwards from his head all through his body of the dull increasing ache of soberness, and put it in reverse until the sapphire was back there on the bridge of his nose, a point of concentration for his purpose, so that the act itself would be isolated, intensely personal, not to say more authentic in the eyes of at-the-time onlookers and later doctors as the act of an unwitting drunk whose end hadn't been at all intentional; because the act had to be seen as the bound-to-come end of Wastrel, and he must go to it properly cloaked, in a manner Sarah would recognise as likely, for he did not want any of them worried (beyond, perhaps, just once or twice in the next few weeks, a prick of conscience in the privacy of their breasts which might pass for a brief warming of their hearts for him), neither did he want Doubt to enter as Mr. Jones might say or Complication in case there turned out to be some frightful Legal Impediment to the passing to Gillian by suicide of her proper inheritance when the time came four years from now and she reached her majority and the ten thousand pound fruit which the Spruces had earned by investing in their connection instead of in their environment which was a polite way of saying sucking-up. Spruce by name but oak by nature, their father used to say. Now why did he say that? And why, George wondered, should he think of it now for the first time for years when, metaphorically anyway, he held an axe ready to lop off his own particular branch?

But there couldn't be any such legal impediment and thoughts of it he knew were prompted by the coward in him who did not want to be basically a mess on the road or the railway line and possibly not wholly gone but unpleasantly still alive if only for a bit and by a shred and having a nasty time. So there you were, he thought, you mustn't fail but do it exactly as if it were real and you didn't know or saw too late and simply lost your balance.

And in a day or two they would break it gently to Gillian that Uncle George had had an accident and say that this was very sad because he had had a sad life in spite of all his advantages over father, and had let himself run to seed, nobody quite knew why, because everybody else in the family had always worked hard to improve themselves, although they wouldn't say worked hard to improve themselves because that was an old-fashioned lower middle-class idea. They would simply say it worried them that she should only shrug her shoulders because that was what Uncle George had always done, and the time had come for her to pull herself together and be alive to her responsibilities as a member of society, especially as Uncle George's death meant that she would be quite well off when she was twenty-one and she wouldn't always be sure whether a man wanted her for herself or only for her money, and she could only learn to distinguish one man from another by mixing with the right sort of people. Except that they probably wouldn't say anything like that to her at all, not only because nobody talked any more about class, money and the right people but instead used words like status, income-group and I.Q. which meant the same things, but because they knew there was virtually nothing to be said or done except to leave the situation to develop along the rigid lines laid down by tradition from which there was no breaking away except by an exception proving the rule that Spruces could rise only to whatever point they had fallen from or to the point to which their class as a whole rose with them into a world of wider horizons.

So the situation would develop like that along lines not much different from those Gillian herself had described over coffee and cream bun. But there would be the difference made by money, because with ten thousand pounds looming ahead and the income from it either accumulating or being applied by trustees for her education, or used as collateral against a loan, Gillian would get the maternity thing taped with what might pass even in her estimation as panache, even in Wales, and Tim need take no hasty step but continue true to his nature and Mr. Wallingford's old age. And in four or five years time, unencumbered by anything but money, Gillian could select with greater care a suitor with a background just that much better than her own so that their children would stand a better chance of being exceptions and seeing people like Lady Butterfield on days other than Thursday.

This was the logic of the gesture to be made: not letting all that money go to waste as it would if he didn't drop down dead but lived for another thirty or even forty years when Gillian would be nearly fifty or sixty and the ten thousand pounds would buy next to nothing because it would be worth what two hundred pounds was worth now, for even in the twenty years that had gone since he had first heard of his private income, Four Hundred a year had changed from meaning a life of pick and choose to one of pinch and scrape if you decided to live on it, which is what he supposed he had decided once and for all when Alice went with Sam and there was no longer any need for him to pretend to have any ambition other than to stay alive and be liked for what he was.

And suddenly a taxi appeared, coming from Holloway where there was a gaol for women, with its roof For Hire box lit up and he raised an arm and stepped into the road and thought of the thin dividing line there was between getting knocked down by a taxi and getting into it which now he did telling the driver to take him to Old Compton Street and getting called Guv'nor and slamming the door and sitting there on the cold leather leaning back tired because he was off his feet and aware of a continuing capacity for drink and of there not being much time to reduce it because some time soon the tubes would stop running and the last buses would be difficult to intercept.

It was twenty minutes to midnight when the taxi carrying George Lisle Spruce in the direction of the Charing Cross Road went past the dark Egyptian front of the old Black Cat cigarette factory twenty minutes behind another taxi going in the opposite direction carrying Timothy and Sarah Spruce to the neat white house they were now reaching, just as, a little earlier, Sam had reached his house and made it home again by restoring Alice to it and dismissing the car from its door with instructions to be back at nine tomorrow, which was another day, a day for exercising skill and judgment with a dignity complete because Alice completed it just as she completed a room she was in as now, the bedroom, sitting in front of the glass, taking the necklace off and putting it on its velvet pad in its leather box that closed with two little clicks, one for each clasp.

And then, before she was aware he watched her, he saw again in her eyes the look he had seen earlier, and so came behind her and put his hands on her half bare shoulders, and said, 'Is anything bothering you?' because nothing must.

She said, 'George rang.'

He considered this from a safe distance and from that same distance thought an autumn holiday would do them no harm especially with long and complicated negotiations between London and New York likely to come to a head in December: Rome perhaps.

'Did his ringing bother you then?' he asked, smiling at her in the mirror.

'I suppose it did, Sam. He's in some kind of trouble.'

'Hasn't he always been?'

'Yes, Sam. He has.'

He bent his head carefully, and kissed her right ear, noticing from the reflection how she closed her eyes.

'Would it help,' he said, addressing her closed eyelids first and then the reflection of himself, 'if we let George have some money?'

He felt no pain at the suggestion. It had always been in reserve.

For answer she felt for and took his hand and pressed it to her cheek but did not open her eyes, and he smiled again, pleased for her, and for himself, and for the two of them together, able in this simple way to give pleasure to others.

'No Sam,' she said, still with her eyes shut, still pressing his hand. 'It would help me but it wouldn't help George. Nothing has ever helped George.'

'You helped him,' said Sam. 'For as long as it was possible.'

'Did I?' she said, and opened her eyes then and stared at herself in the glass as if her face were strange to her. 'For as long as that?'

Thirty-Eight

'Would you like to dance?' George said.

'You're too drunk to dance,' said the girl.

'The crowd'll hold us up.'

'Why don't you go home?'
'Who's this?'
'Silky something.'
'He doesn't look so silky to me.'
'Have you seen Mick?' George asked. 'Sometimes he's here. Sometimes not. But Perce wouldn't come here. It's not Perce's style.'
'You're spilling your drink.'
'The lady says you're spilling your drink. Go and spill it over somebody else.'
And from somewhere a shove that brought him up suddenly against the bar so that he turned and contemplated the ruin of his gin, the glass empty but still clenched in his hand. He pushed the glass slowly towards the barman and when their eyes met he smiled and asked for another gin and added, 'Has Mick been in?'
'Mick? Which Mick?'
'My Mick.'
'And who are you?'
'Spruce.'
'I don't know any Mick,' the barman said and asked for money. There was nothing in his wallet, but his pockets were full of copper and silver. He took a handful and let the coins out on to the counter. He stared for a while at those the barman left him.
The barman went away. Beyond the counter, at the end the barman had gone to, there were pillars and beyond the pillars less light and more smoke and more faces. The room was very small and the ceiling very low. The music seemed to be all from drums and the drums were toneless because there wasn't enough space for them to be heard in. They came at the ears as a feeling. It might be The Gorgon, or it might be The Apocalypse.
'How did I get here anyway?' he said. 'I was just thinking how I got here,' he said, and the girl he said it to said, 'Does it matter?'
'Have I been talking to you?' he asked her.
'If you have I wasn't listening.'
She had a zip in the back of her dress all the way from the neck to just above her buttocks. A pillar intervened. The band got louder. He apologized to somebody. When he got to the other side of the floor he heard himself laughing. There was an alcove with a seat in it. He sat down. Someone sitting there

said, 'Hello, love. Haven't you gone yet?' Her face was vaguely familiar.

'No, not yet.'

'You've had it for tonight, love.'

'Had what?'

'The tube train or the last bus.'

'I've forgotten your name.'

'I'm Maureen and you're George. You're an expert of something called Cracky Loo.'

'May I put my hand up your skirt?'

'It's not worth it, love. It's all much of a muchness.'

'I suppose it is. Where did we meet?'

'At The Gorgon I think.'

'Where's this, then?'

'I don't know, love. I think we came together and I think you signed me in unless that was Reggie.'

'Who's Reggie?'

'I don't know, duck.'

'Do you know Mick?'

'No.'

'I've worked it out about Mick. Why else should he ask me that?'

'I don't know, love.'

'It's to pick up call girls.'

'You want to be careful, love.'

'You get these people down from the north or the midlands for conferences and conventions and when the business is over at night they go back to these service flats on expenses and some young executive smoothy who is personal assistant to the chairman of the board that is entertaining these executives from the provinces rings someone who rings someone who rings Mick and Mick rings me. And I put on this chauffeur's hat and drive over to Notting Hill or Paddington and out she comes. And I drive her into town to wherever these people are staying. And in the morning someone else drives her back or she gets a taxi. And there are pornographic pictures and books on the side which is where the export and import and wholesaling comes in.'

'You want to be careful what you say, love.'

'It's what you come to, you see. Driving crumpet up to Mayfair. Or selling Teddy Bears on commission in Widnes. Do you know Perce?'

'No, I've never met anybody called Perce.'

'Do you know Sam?'

'No, love.'

'He's married to my wife. He paid for the divorce, it didn't cost me a penny. She never needed to ask for alimony because Sam was there. He'll be there at his own funeral to make sure it goes without a hitch. And that nobody speaks out of turn. That the parson knows the words and that all the pall bearers are the same height. She worked, you see, and I didn't. That's how she met Sam, not worked for Sam, she never worked for Sam, she worked for a man Sam ran out of business only it was called acquiring patents. And all the time he was running the man out of business he was making passes at Alice. She used to tell me all about them and laugh at him a bit. But not really laugh because she never would admit Sam ran her boss out of business and mostly there was never much to laugh at anyway. She used to say I was unfair to call it running out of business even when it had happened. But she must have thought there was something in it mustn't she, because she didn't go on working in the business Sam had run her boss out of, didn't work for Sam. She got another job, and he kept on making these passes, sending flowers and theatre tickets. Tickets for the two of us. Taking us out to dinner. Very dignified about it. Don't you think? Don't you call it dignified to take both of us and not always just her? But sometimes it was just her, not often, just sometimes. And it went on for months and months and she was making over a thousand a year in a job she needed clothes for only she couldn't have them. She made them herself. Because she had to keep the two of us most of the time. And all my money was beginning to go on drink and sometimes horses if Mick put me on to one.'

'You want to steer clear of horses, love.'

'Or I'd wake up in the morning and find I'd signed a cheque to somebody for twenty quid. But not remember why. On what. I never can remember what the money's really gone on. Can you? Just like the two hundred quid that's caused all this trouble. I can't remember that, what it was all for, what it went on, what I got out of it. I couldn't even make a list any more of all the jobs I've had or nearly had. Except you couldn't call any of them jobs. What Aunt Clara trained me for. Not jobs. More like propositions. Good things, that never really got going. Never got beyond the point of doing something once and getting a cut. A sort of commission. Helping somebody who knew somebody to sell something somebody else had got and somebody else wanted.'

'You're getting confused, love.'

'Once it was a houseboat at Henley and another time it was a vintage car at Leatherhead. At the time it looked like going into the estate agency business or the used car business. But of course that was only what it looked like from the drinking side of a bar. And then there was once something not clear to me that was connected with altar cloths and vestments and what was called Church Equipment. Run by a chap who'd been a Colonel in the Indian Army who didn't believe in God. And then I nearly got into the Army Surplus racket but the big stuff is all a closed shop. It's always a closed shop, isn't it, the big stuff, the thing that's financially worth while? And time and time again you come face to face with that. But time and time again you think the key to the closed shop can be found by two or three of you gathered together in your one good suit. But the teddy bear and fringe-grade call girl, that's what's really ahead. And before that Alice saying, What's the point of going on? And me saying, None that I can see. And Sam coming to see me and saying he'd pay for everything. And when a man like Sam comes into your room it looks so bloody shabby and sad and eaten away. And eating Alice with it. And so you say, Yes, get it over with, take her out of it.'

'Don't take it too much to heart, love.'

'And then it's all over and you can't look at each other. Because of the waste, you see. Do you see that? The waste? The awful waste. Years of each other gone. Years you've spent not looking at the truth. Not talking to her any more because there's nothing you can say. Only something you can do, and might do tomorrow when the gin and the slim luck have run out at last and you've got to face the fact. That you're a louse. But the gin never does run out. Or the slim luck. Because there's always these Four Hundred bloody stinking pounds a year that keep you on that bloody great long list of people who know they can get something for nothing. So you wonder what kind of trick it was Old Uncle Roderick pulled on you. And why. Whether it was because he lost his only son and heir more or less the same year you were born. Or because he liked the colour of your eyes as a kid. Or the cut of your jib when you were seventeen. Or because he wanted to help you to live like a gentleman because he set store by that sort of thing. Can you beat that? Or because he didn't like what he saw Auntie Clara was trying to turn you into because he didn't like Aunt

Clara. Or because he never thought anything about it at all but just left you the income from a spare ten thousand quid because it was good form to look after poor relations. Or because he wanted to spite Aunt Clara. And when you think of Aunt Clara you wonder whether she helped you to develop your bloody charm only to spite Uncle Roderick. And whether this was because no matter what she says people still think of her as a butcher's daughter. So that she's got to pretend something that's bigger than class power. And does so and calls it Force. Force. What sort of a word is that? But none of it is the real answer, is it? Because there's a limit to the amount of blame you can put on other people for what kind of man you are. Even if it all plays a part. And suffer from delusions. Of Grandeur. That old thing.'

'Excuse me, love. There's someone over there I know.'

Thirty-Nine

'I'll tell you the causes. Causes of my ruination.'

'Don't dwell on it,' the young man said.

'Are you as young as you look?'

'I'm twenty-three.'

'What are you doing sitting here?'

'I'm buying you a drink.'

'Why?'

'You wanted one but found you were skint.'

'What place is this?'

'The Apocalypse. I met you on the stairs trying to use the telephone. You borrowed fourpence.'

'Who was I ringing?'

'God.'

'God? How do you ring God?' George said.

'You dialled GOD 1961. The number was engaged.'

'Was it?'

'So you tried Heaven. You dialled HEA 1961 but that was out of order. I brought you down because you said you were going to kill yourself but wanted a drink first and to warn God you were on the way. But I don't think I'm sympathetic to you any longer.'

'Why aren't you sympathetic to me any longer?'

'You said you were going to kill yourself. I thought you

were in trouble. But from what you've been saying it's just the same old thing. Money. If you want to kill yourself because of money go ahead. But don't forget your drink.'

'Oh, no,' George said. 'It was more than money.'

He leaned his forehead in his hand and tried to remember what else more than money. The darkness inside his head was full of convolutions. His eardrums were too tight. Only the higher registers of sound were getting through. His skin had thickened and the arm of the hand that held his forehead fell away under the weight of its own thickened skin. He brought his head back into balance by opening his eyes so that light could flow back in and fill the empty convolutions. He stared at a chair back to help it in its attempts to get back into itself. He had been talking to someone who sat in the chair. It may have been some while back.

He got up.

People were in the way. He didn't know any of the people.

'You're leaving,' a man said.

'I know.'

There were too many stairs.

'I said you were leaving,' a man said. It might have been the same man.

Forty

He had silver buttons on a blue uniform and a cap with a shiny black peak and came at George diagonally from across a road in the full light of a shop front.

'Where are you going?' he said.

'To the tube,' George said, hopefully.

'A bit late for that aren't you?'

'Am I? Then I'd better get a bus.'

'There aren't any buses, either. Where do you live?'

'Bayswater.'

'You'd better get a taxi. You can't walk round here in this condition. If you walk round here in this condition there are people who might take advantage of it. You'd better get off the street. You'd better take a taxi.'

'Yes. I'll get a taxi.'

'Otherwise you'll be committing an offence.'

'I know.'

There was a taxi coming. George went to meet it, stepping into the road which without thinking about it he knew was Charing Cross Road and in the same way, as the taxi stopped, knew he hadn't any money.

'The police have told me to get off the street,' he said, 'but I haven't any money.'

'I'll take you round into the circus and leave the flag up. He only wants you off his street,' the taxi driver said.

In the back of the taxi George searched through his pockets. There were some coppers.

'It's all I've got,' he said, giving them to the driver, standing on the pavement outside the Palace Theatre where the driver had let him out. The driver took the coppers and said, 'So long as you're off their beat. They don't mind,' and drove away, and George set off to walk up the second leg of the Charing Cross Road, keeping close to the shop fronts, most of which were lighted. When he reached Oxford Street he should have turned left for the long walk to Bayswater, and he knew this without thinking about it, but crossed over without looking and went on up the Tottenham Court Road which was not so well lit and led to Goodge Street and Warren Street and Camden Town and Belsize Park and Alice country, and later to Tim country.

'I've left it too late,' he said, 'unless I can find a car coming fast.' But he felt almost too tired to look for one. He walked with his head down, not seeing much in front of him beyond the coming and going of the pavement between patches of light and his shoes pushing the pavement away behind. To his waist his body felt heavy but from the waist down it felt nothing at all. His arms moved backwards and forwards above this feeling of nothing. He was an immensity of flesh ending at a waist and held aloft from the pavement by nothing in shoes that moved on their own, pushing the pavement away. But the pavement kept coming, matching the immensity of its stone to the immensity of his flesh, and sometimes jarring his shoes and filling the nothing connecting shoe to flesh with a body feeling of leg.

Forty-One

Miss Lisle felt her years running away, scattering, as if she were a stone lifted away from them. Someone was picking the stone up: a great weight, lifting; so heavy at the moment of lifting; with air whispering back into the revealed space, and her years running away to find new hiding places to dream their histories in. My years, she thought; who will provide for them?

One of her years was a sea. She stood in the shallow rim of the sea, her feet growing out of the sand, her hand in Arthur's. And it was as if, closing her eyes and holding her child's face to the warm flame of the sun, she had risen blind from the ocean and the sun opened her eyes like blue flowers that had a scent so deep and strong she saw with them in a way that was stronger than seeing with sight. The sea she saw, and the violet creamy line where the sea went on beyond itself, and where the pale blue sky came up from below itself, spreading, arching over the sea. The wind she saw and the children behind her whose voices were blown away by the wind like seeds in a thin sowing. The children's voices would fall from the wind and root themselves in days. She saw how the seeds would fall and root themselves and bear voices like blooms. And was happy, standing there in the sea, safe from mortality, her hand in Arthur's and her mother sleeping under the same sun and sky on the shingle behind that ran down to the sand, and the sea with its smell like no other smell. And the year that was a day at the sea with her mother and Arthur was the only such year there had ever been. And who would provide for it?

One of the years was a wakefulness in the dark, the boys awake, and only Vi of the children sleeping. A climbing of stairs and threads to be unpicked from under a sash: these were a year. A hat with cherries in it was a year. Vi was many a year. And Harry seeing her to the tram – that was a year she thought had died long ago under the stone, but it was here with the others running wild into the dark to dream its history. She was glad to find it still there with the others, Harry seeing her to the tram, and then not kissing her his brother-in-law goodbye, but standing away in a fashion new for him, and she not approaching him, in a fashion new for her, but helping him build a sturdy silence between them that was a beginning and also an end.

She thought: I have never been in love and tried always to do what was right, and look after Vi because she was not very sensible. Now all my years are running away. I am being lifted away from them. But it is all right, Mr. Stainsby. I know who will provide for my years. Miss Bright will provide for them.

Forty-Two

Everyone is asleep, he told himself, drunk-sober from long tramping, everyone of them asleep – behind dark windows above dark shop fronts or in dark houses lying back in dark gardens behind stucco walls.

They were asleep the whole length of an empty road where orange light from tall lamp standards was wasting away in small hours that found him bowling along large, like tumbleweed: weightless but carrying his years; in a town of sleepers who carried nothing because they had stored their years in dreams as if those dreams were warm barns that could be stocked against hard winters.

They were asleep, he told himself, in barns as tight locked as the doors of their cars parked in the open at the edge of the pavements. There were no buses, no tubes, no cars coming fast. But there were plenty of empty cars which had nothing to do but wait for morning and offer him temptation. He would drive one fast, hatless, out of the areas of light and London flood, into the dark dry countryside of Hertfordshire, riding behind main beams that would kindle the cats' eyes in the road until they illuminated a tree-trunk for Gillian's sake.

But they were a cautious, suspicious lot, the sleepers behind dark windows. He crossed and recrossed the road from car to car, looking for an unlocked door and a careless, dangling ignition key.

'We'll take him now,' said the man at the wheel of the black saloon that had the word Police on it front and back and was moving slowly two hundred yards behind, following George Lisle-Spruce as he crossed and recrossed the road from parked car to parked car, trying door handles.

The man at the wheel accelerated gently and his companion lowered a window and threw out a cigarette end. The suspect was now walking up the hill on the right which meant that when they reached him and drew up the sergeant would be first out, being nearer. The sergeant would probably have been first out anyway, even though he was driving. It was that sort of night, dull, with an ache to it, and with the sergeant in a curious mood that fitted the night's dullness and ache and might even be responsible for it: silent and unsmiling as if there was something wrong at the sergeant's home and sitting at the wheel on a dull aching night was one too many, altogether one too much.

'Right, here goes,' the sergeant said, and swung the car across the road, braking quickly but smoothly, just ahead of the fellow who had been trying door handles. They both opened their doors together but the sergeant was there first, saying loud, 'All right, now. You've tried every car door along the road for the last half a mile,' and had the beam of his flash on the man's face, having first flashed it briefly on what the man was wearing: a crumpled but decent suit, white shirt and quiet tie. The man stood very still and was looking not into the beam of the sergeant's flashlight but above it, trying to make out the sergeant's face.

'I know,' he said, 'but it wasn't to pinch one.'

A gentleman's accent, the sergeant's companion noted: natural, not put on. Usually they said, I ain't done nothing, or, You're making a mistake.

'Get in,' the sergeant said, and opened the rear offside door. The suspect got in. The sergeant slammed the door. No charge for resisting arrest.

'I'll be back in a sec,' the sergeant said and walked back down the road, to check – his companion supposed – the last few cars for damage or doors unlocked or because anything was better than sitting in the car, aching and unsmiling.

I've done it now, George thought. From here we can drive in this big comfortable car to a place that smells like a barracks inside, but isn't. And I'm charged with loitering with intent to make off with somebody's car to drive it into a tree-trunk. But I didn't mention the tree-trunk, which is a worse reason to pinch a car for than just pinching one to drive away somewhere. It would have left a nasty taste, wouldn't it? Because of the damage and the repair bill if it wasn't beyond repair. A bill for the insurance company to foot, if it was properly insured, which perhaps it wouldn't have been, and then there'd have been an awful mess for someone to be in and get out of. And even if it had been insured it would have been a mess, leaving this nasty taste, your car disappearing from outside your dark window and being found in Hertfordshire a bloody wreck, and I should have thought of that before.

The door by the driver's seat was still open. The driver had gone somewhere. There was only one policeman in the car, sitting in front with a note-book out and a light coming from a hidden source, perhaps from the pen or pencil that was already writing something on the paper: time of arrest probably, and place. Where was the place?

He wanted to say: Where is this? but did not because he could not talk to the man sitting there at the front who showed nothing of his face except an ear and an unfriendly line of copper's jaw. He could not talk to anyone now, even to strangers. He leaned back on the upholstered leather seat and bent his head close to the window, watched the blue-grey tarmac of the road and an oil stain on it that looked like the map of an island, so that he thought of ships and voyaging.

There was a readjustment, a displacement. A door shut. The driver was back. George saw three stripes and thought: A sergeant, a hard case, out for an arrest, any arrest, this one, to meet a quota. I've had it.

'Right,' the sergeant said. 'What's your name?'

'Spruce,' he said. 'Initials G.L. George Lisle.'

The sergeant's companion wrote it down.

'Address?'

'Fifty-one Queensbury Road, Bayswater.'

'Bayswater?'

'Yes.'

The sergeant was turned sideways in the seat, one arm over it, the other resting on the wheel.

'What are you doing here if you live in Bayswater?'

'I was going to see my brother.'

'At this time of night?'

'It was earlier when I started,' George said, humbly, because suddenly he felt humble in the face of so much authority.

'Where does your brother live?'

George told him.

'You still have a long way to go.'

'I know,' George said.

'How old are you?'

'Forty-three.'

'Married?'

'Not any more,' he said.

'Widower?'

'No. Only divorce,' he said.

'Any children?'

'No.'

'Occupation?'

'None, I'm afraid.'

'Oh? Why's that?'

'I was left some money by an uncle. Not much.' Then he added, 'But too much,' and smiled, because if you were locked up it was better smiling.

The sergeant was silent for a bit. Then he said, 'Why were you trying car doors?' And, when George didn't answer, 'To find a place to kip down?'

'What?'

'I said: Why were you trying car doors? To find a place to kip down?'

George tried to see the man's face. Was the sergeant helping him? Offering him a loophole because to arrest him was too much trouble?

'Yes,' he said. 'To kip down.'

'Been on the beer?'

'No. Gin, I'm afraid.'

'And then you found yourself skint, I suppose?'

'Yes.'

'So you had to walk. Where from?'

'The West End.'

The sergeant's companion seemed to have stopped writing things down. He was staring at the empty lighted road ahead.

'Is your brother married?'

'Yes.'

'What does *he* do?'

'He's a chartered accountant.'

'Children?'

'Yes. Two.'

'Why were you going to see him?'

'To sort something out. A family thing.'

'He'll hardly expect you at this time of the morning, will he?'

'No.'

George leaned back. He wasn't being helped after all. The next line for the sergeant would be: So we'd better tuck you up for the night, hadn't we? Which meant arrest: drunk and disorderly, suspicion, loitering with intent. The book. Thrown at him. He wanted to say: Look, I haven't been telling you the truth. I wasn't going to see my brother. Perhaps when I got to a certain road I might have turned down it, knocked on Alice and Sam's door. Perhaps not. I was looking for a car I could get into. For a kind of kip. But the kind that goes on into what they call eternity because I worked it out I was more use dead than alive. I still am. But if you let me go I won't go looking for a kip. I'm sober again. I'll go the rest of the way to my brother's house and doss down in his garden shed until it's late enough in the morning to knock. It's too far for me to walk to Bayswater. And Tim will let me shave and give me a cup of tea and lend me the fare. I think he'd do that for me. All you have to do is let me out of this car.

But the sergeant had turned away and settled himself properly in the seat to deal with mechanism. The engine started. The car moved out into the road, crossing it, then moved up the hill he recognized now as a landmark of Alice-country. He also remembered that there was a police station a mile or so ahead; so closed his eyes and sank back into the corner of the seat. And prayed.

Gentle Jesus (he said, without moving his lips). Speak to your servant. But not on the telephone. Tell me something or give me something to take with it when I come out of this dark corner and have to show my face. My old ma would have died of shame. Where am I to look, she would have said, when I go out of this house and down the street. I don't want to die of shame, only of old age. I meant it about the tube and the bus and the tree-trunk, but I don't mean it any longer. And I'm not praying for this arrest not to happen, just for something to take with it, because it must be happening to make me face facts. It's happening here and now and it's happening to *me*. Like the street we lived in and the people around us happened to us and were real. This car is a real car and the two coppers in front are real, and it was *me* trying car doors. And if you try car doors one after the other at this time of the morning anybody watching you would be a fool if he thought you weren't going to pinch one, and so it's a cinch you get caught. And it isn't that a man like me ends up driving crumpet to Mayfair and selling teddy bears on commission in Widnes, so much as he ends up getting arrested for acting like a fool and committing an offence so trivial it lacks the dignity of a decent crime. And those two men in front probably feel nothing but contempt for me, not just because I made a muck-up of trying to snitch a car and they'd prefer any day to deal with professionals, but because they can tell I've had advantages and opportunities in life, and they're probably getting a kick out of locking up a middle-aged drunk who speaks with a posh accent but hasn't two pennies to rub together, because it ranks as a small victory in the class war which goes on and on and on and will probably go on for ever because none of us believes that what he's got is as much as he wants and the damnable thing is he's right because what he really wants is love, peace of mind and the respect of friends and strangers, and all of them cost. And just as it is a terrible thing not to have talents so it's a terrible thing to be praying, because I don't believe in you, I only believe in the idea of there being some kind of you, and I suppose that's only because, like everybody else, I like the idea of having what we can't get enough of here, somewhere else.

The car was slowing down. When it stopped he kept his eyes closed, imagining the light that would be showing in the doorway and one of the windows of the station, and the blue lamp above the porch.

When he opened his eyes they were shocked by darkness, a feeling of wind and stars and isolation. And this, too, he presently recognized, another landmark of Alice-country. From here, on a clear day, the whole of London might be seen, drowned in shallows and pale pink, grey and violet pools of air, low-lying, weighed down by the invisible weight of square mile after square mile of noise that with height and distance had acquired density and inaudibility both. Sometimes there were gulls. Beyond where the car was parked the road led down and down, making for Tim-country.

He looked at the sergeant who had resumed his earlier position right arm on the wheel, left on seat back, face turned to look at his passenger.

'I don't think,' the sergeant said after a while, 'that I need to arrest you. Do you?'

'No,' George said, automatically. But his mouth was all at once parched, his belly empty. In such darkness and isolation perhaps, for the hell of it, they might follow him out of the car and punch him up just to relieve the monotony. You heard such stories.

'This is as far as we go this end of our beat,' the sergeant said. 'You've still got a tidy step to get to your brother's. I'm relying on you. Not to do it again. Trying the door handles. You just go straight to your brother's. Bed's the place to kip down. Not somebody else's car.'

'I know. I'm sorry.'

'All right then. You hop out here.'

George felt for the door catch. Emerging, the air came at him like silk. The soles of his feet that had tramped so far ached as they stood once more in contact with the hard free ground. He had nothing to offer the sergeant: not even a cigarette, only his thanks. But then the sergeant knew this. The sergeant knew more than this. The sergeant knew the difference between the stupid and the culpable. And had not learned it in a night.

'Thank you,' said George.

The sergeant said, 'That's all right. Just mind how you go.'

'Yes, I will. Goodnight.'

'Goodnight.'

Forty-Three

It was getting light when he turned the corner and saw the telephone box. He looked at his watch but found if stopped at twenty minutes to four. His watch was old and, like his pen, a gift from Alice. It needed cleaning and oiling and wouldn't last the night if you forget to wind it at bedtime. He wound it now, standing at the corner, and turned the hands to point at half-past five, there being a feeling of half-past five in the chill air, of an hour to go before sun-up.

Tim's road was curved. Its pavement was edged by grass and trees which bore, in April, pink blossom. The houses stood in pairs, no pair quite the same, behind privet hedges well-trimmed after a good gardening summer. The gardens and the houses were darker than the growing daylight so that it hurt the eyes to look too closely at them.

Now that he was here he wondered what he could do, how he could face knocking, even after an hour or two. And where, decently, could that hour or two be spent? In the telephone box? In Tim's garden shed? In the back porch, like a tramp? And what excuse could he offer for appearing at all, other than the excuse of having not a bean in his pocket and being in need of a shave? And a fare.

There's no end to it, he thought; meaning degradation once it had set in. The ten pounds had gone. On what? He had nothing but a hangover to remember them by, nothing to live on for the rest of the month, no money for his rent or his food. From this kind of rock bottom a man could only climb by casual, menial labour. And that was what he must do. Once he had had a cup of tea. And a shave. And a fare. Perhaps a fiver. Or only a quid. If Tim wouldn't cough up Alice might. Or Sam. Even Mrs. Poulten-Morse. You couldn't write off Mrs. Poulten-Morse. She understood there were difficulties a man of his class could get into. She wouldn't like him to come home dirty from a job he'd taken just to earn her rent. And he had collateral. He had his four hundred pounds a year from the Butterfield Estate.

Tim's gate was made of wood and painted white. It creaked on a high note when opened and on a low note when shut. The front door was half-paned. There was a light in the hall, not a direct light but a reflected light: a light coming from above, from the landing, and a light coming from below, through an open door, the kitchen door. Looking up George saw another light, shielded by closed but unlined curtains that had a stripe in them, the window of Sarah's and Tim's bedroom. His eye told him he had seen the lights before he opened the gate but he only understood them as lights, now, when he was half way up the path and making ready to go round the back to find the shed or the back porch to wait there until the house was awake, but it was awake already. Why? Was it closer to half-past six than half-past five?

He approached the front door, stood on the step and looked into the hall. The kitchen door opened wider, the light in the kitchen was turned out and Tim emerged in pyjamas and dressing-gown, carrying a tea-tray.

George tapped on the glass.

Tim looked up. For several seconds they stared at each other. Then Tim put the tray down on the hall table and came to the door, and stood hesitating before, at last, with an oath George felt rather than heard or saw from any shaping of Tim's lips, he bent down and reached up, unbolting the door bottom and top, and opened it, but blocked the way, standing in it square and looking as bad as George felt, his hair ruffed up, holding himself somewhat curiously, sagging from the left shoulder, with the left arm looking not quite but nearly out of commission; dangling almost.

Without saying a word he stepped back, and George stepped in and waited, making himself small to one side while Tim shut the door and then, still without a word, turned and went to the table where he had parked the tray and with his right hand picked it up gingerly and only when it was picked up bringing his left arm slowly into play until the left hand was there, under the tray, taking part of the weight.

At the foot of the stairs he paused, looked at George, jerked his head in the direction of the living-room and said, low, 'Wait in there. Perhaps you want to talk to me. Well *I* want to talk to *you.*'

So George went into the living-room and sat in one of the overstuffed chairs, listening to Tim's footsteps, the creak of a floorboard and then Sarah's voice, followed by Tim's, followed by the kind of silence so heavy and skilfully fashioned it was beyond anyone's means to keep in the manner to which it was accustomed. A bedspring creaked violently and Tim's voice came clearly, saying, 'No, leave it to me,' before it became jumbled up with Sarah's voice, which seemed to be protesting, and the bedsprings which creaked heavily and were then still, their twanging giving way to someone's brooding. Sarah's.

After a while the same floorboard went again. A door shut. Tim was coming down. Another door opened and shut, this time outside in the hall. Tim had gone into the kitchen. A kettle lid clattered. A tap gushed.

Five minutes later Tim came into the living-room with a cup of black coffee. There was no need for the light. In the gloom of half-day he gave the coffee to George and sat on the other overstuffed chair to watch him drink it, which took a long time, because the cup weighed and was difficult to hold up let alone keep still, and the liquid in it was scalding hot, although even so it did not easily melt the dry-baked gum on his lips and tongue and the lining of his mouth; and when at last it had done so it began to burn a raw groove in his throat, down into his chest, where his heart was punching his ribs hard and monotonously.

'We have things to discuss,' Tim said, and stood up, rubbing his left shoulder. He lit a cigarette but did not offer the packet to George.

'When you appeared just now,' Tim said, 'I was going to bed for the first time tonight, after the kind of experience that has been an absolute bloody nightmare. The fact that so far as I can see it happens to be all your fault makes your sudden appearance significant. Yes. I think significant is the right word.'

'What's all my fault?'

'What Sarah and I have been coping with, while you from the look of you have been up to God knows what. Now. What did you say to her?'

'Say to whom?'

'Gillian. You know dam' well who.'

'Say to Gillian?'

'Don't pretend you didn't talk to her. Don't pretend you

didn't see her. Don't try to make out you didn't deliberately disregard my very clear instructions that Gillian wasn't to be bothered and didn't want to see or talk to anybody.'

'What's happened?'

'She damned near killed herself. That's what's happened. Now. Why? That's what I want to know. What did you say to her?'

'Where is she?'

'Upstairs in bed.'

'Is she all right?'

'What do you mean all right? How can I tell whether she's all right until I know what you said that made her all wrong?'

'What does she say I said?'

'That Uncle George was very kind but she thought it was for the best.'

'What was for the best?'

'The gin, you bloody fool! The bloody hot bath and the gin! Half a bottle of gin and the water practically up to her neck, and her nearly under it.'

'When?'

'Tonight, last night, when Sarah and I were out. And if we hadn't sprazzed out on a taxi and got back as soon as we did she would probably have drowned. Look at this! See this? Have you ever tried to break down a locked door with your shoulder? Have you? No, of course you haven't. I damned near broke my arm off. It looks easy on the films, doesn't it? Well, try it. Just try it and see. And I can tell you this. You're getting the bill for that door. You can add that to the two hundred quid when you pay it back next week. And when you've paid it all back and told me exactly what you said to Gillian, well that's the finish. As far as Sarah and I are concerned we're finished with you. If you want to know, it's taking me all my time not to punch your bloody nose right here and now and chuck you out of the house.'

After a while George said, 'Did the gin work?'

Tim stubbed out his half-smoked cigarette before he answered.

'No.'

'I see.'

'What do you mean, you *see*.'

'I see why you're so annoyed. If it had worked that would have been fine, wouldn't it? It might still work though, mightn't it? How can you tell it won't work?'

'Because it hasn't and it won't. You can tell. Sarah can tell, I can tell, Gillian can tell. It's stuck tight. She's got hips on her like hams.'

George considered this. Tim had seen his daughter naked, probably for the first time for years. Sarah alone couldn't have managed. He would have had to take most of Gillian's weight, even with his bad arm, getting her out of the water, unconscious presumably, passed out, drunk: the seed of his loins grown from reprimanded child to a woman no longer open, somehow, to reprimand, being pregnant with gin bottle, and the water in the bath cooled down, gone sour like the end of a night out; to say the least, unpleasant to come home to.

'I think,' said George, 'she was worried about giving the baby up.'

'She wasn't before you disobeyed my instructions and said God Knows What to her.'

'I don't like that, Tim.'

'Don't like what?'

'This idea you have of instructions. Disobedience. She's my god-daughter. I have certain rights and certain obligations. Punch me in the nose if you like. Chuck me out of the house if you want. But I shan't ever stop trying to get in touch with Gillian. And if I suffer too much obstruction I shall go straight to the vicar of whatever parish she's living in.'

Tim stared at him, his mouth half open.

'And apart from being my god-daughter,' George continued, 'she's my heir because I'm as sterile as a lump of old cheese and have been ever since I had the mumps, only I didn't know for sure until a few months ago and if you don't believe me you can take me round to the hospital of your choice and watch me perform into a test tube and then wait for them to analyse the result. Then you can come home and start treating Gillian like a woman instead of a child, which should be easier for you because you'll know she's worth ten thousand quid the moment I snuff out. And if I'd had any real gumption I wouldn't be here now but in the morgue, which is where I was headed for until I had the one gin that changed me from suicidal to maudlin. I've no idea which one gin it was and even so I might still have managed if I hadn't been arrested an hour or two ago for trying car doors to drive one away and plaster myself over a tree-trunk somewhere in Hertfordshire.'

'Arrested?'

'It wasn't really an arrest. But only because the man who

stopped me and put me into his patrol car was the kind of man who does his job but doesn't get bent by it. Tomorrow he mightn't be so lucky, might he? I mean tomorrow night he might climb out of his patrol wagon to stop a man trying car handles and end up with a bullet or a knife in his gut, and that would bend him permanently, and probably bend the young chap who's with him and doesn't say a word but just makes notes and probably rubs them out afterwards. And it would bend me too, just thinking about it, just as it would bend me to sit and listen to the chap who fired the bullet or stuck the knife talking about his lousy life from childhood on. Like it bends me to sit here, Tim, and tell you all this, and see you sweating at the idea of me nearly being arrested when according to Gillian you're within an ace of earning five thousand a year and getting a seat on a board.'

And (he thought, watching Tim's face), like it bends me to see you sweating a different kind of sweat at the idea of me being sterile and Gillian getting ten thousand quid, and sweating yet another kind of sweat at the idea that it might not be for another thirty years, and even another kind of sweat at the idea you can sweat about things like that when your own flesh and blood's involved. And like it bends me to think that tonight it was nearly young Andrew who got ten thousand quid, what with me being suicidal and Gillian trying for an abortion in bathwater up to her neck.

'What else do you know about my private affairs?' Tim said, but sitting now, having done so about half way through what George was saying; and, George thought, marking like that, without either of them noticing it at the time, the moment when the balance of power between them had shifted and gone over, ostensibly to George's side, but in actuality getting lost in the process, leaving them caught out in the middle of what sounded like a quarrel but wasn't, there being nothing really to quarrel about: simply facts they had to consider and situations each of them must make the best of; so that from the brief drama, the flash and clash of high dry combat, they were back again in the wet, the flood, eyeing each other because they had unexpectedly come face to face, and were about to blow bubbles before flipping away to look for a bit of weed or a pile of stones to hide behind.

'I only know you aren't very keen on leaving Bartle Wallingford,' said George.

'It seems my private talks with Sarah have been overheard.'

'It is true?'

'Is what true?'

'About your not being keen even on five thousand a year because of Mr. Wallingford's old age and Bartle Wallingford being safe?'

'Safe?'

'Safe.'

'No.'

George considered this too. There were contexts in which the answer No was meaningless. Are you happy? No. Are you unhappy? No. Are you suicidal? No. Are you looking forward to tomorrow? No.

'In that case,' he said, 'it's a good thing I didn't plaster myself over a tree-trunk in Hertfordshire, because I was going to do it not only to help Gillian with ten thousand pounds but help you to stay at Bartle Wallingford *because* of Gillian and ten thousand pounds.'

'Yes, it's a good thing. If that *was* behind your reasoning,' Tim said, 'because I resigned from Bartle Wallingford yesterday afternoon.'

'Couldn't you unresign?'

'No,' said Tim (thinking of certain words spoken to Wallingford: I'm sick of it and sick of you: and of certain images: Miss Crayfoot behind the partition, not typing any more).

'Why?'

'Because I don't want to.'

'What do you want?'

Tim bunched himself up in the chair. He gave George the impression of being about to burst bonds by main force in spite of his hurt shoulder, or possibly because of it; or if not exactly because, burst bonds in full awareness that the shoulder was hurt because in this house he was confined in a way that among other things could cause him, if only once, to have to break down locked bathroom doors to save pregnant daughters from death by gin and water.

'What do I want?' Tim asked, repeating George's question. 'What a dam' fool thing to ask. One answer's as good as another, isn't it? You could say I want to be back in August with Sarah and Gillian and Andrew in Seaford watching the boats, because that's the last time I remember really enjoying myself. On the other hand, although I didn't know it, Gillian was already pregnant, so I hadn't any real call to be enjoying myself, had I? And this other job had already been mooted, so I had that to think about, even though I thought I was going to turn it down. I'm assuming you've wormed all the details out of Gill. So perhaps June or July would be better. But I expect if I thought hard enough I'd be able to remember some bloody niggle even in those months. And in any case, what's the good of being back in June when August and September are still due to come up? You could say I want to get stuck in at this new job and prove myself, or that I want just to go on waiting for Old Wallingford to die or retire because then I can get stuck into a job I've already proved myself in. And each answer would as true as it's false. Of course there's another answer, too. That what I want is for you to tell me truthfully why you are here.'

'I've told you.'

'No you haven't. You've told me not very directly about being arrested for trying to pinch a car to commit suicide in to help Gillian with ten thousand quid. And you've told me you can't have children.'

'Don't you believe me?'

'You've got to the stage where it's almost impossible to believe a word you say.'

'Yes. I see.'

'But if you tell me what you're here *for* I have a feeling I'm going to believe that.'

George said nothing.

'Years ago,' Tim said, 'I used to envy you. I was as jealous as stink. And to tell you the truth I still envy you a bit because you're once again about to get something for nothing. What is it, George? Shall I see if I can guess? A wash and a brush up? A spot of breakfast? The fare back to Bayswater? A few quid to add to the two hundred which you know and I know you're never going to pay back, especially now that I'm about to earn five thousand a year and you're broke to the wide until the first of the month?'

George said, 'I could do with a shave. There's a man I ought to see about a job this morning.'

'There often has been. And you may see him. You may even get the job. And you may even keep it until the next time you get drunk. It's happened before. All right. You can have a shave but you'll have to do it in the kitchen. And while you're shaving you can make yourself some coffee and fry yourself an egg if you're capable of doing it without making a clatter because between now and half-past nine I've got to get some sleep. So when you let yourself out, please close the front door quietly.'

'Thank you.'

'How much is the fare?'

'I don't know. A bob. Couple of bob.'

'And how much have you got?'

'Nothing.'

'So what do you live on for the rest of the month?'

'Oh, it'll work out. If I get this job.'

'You may not get it.'

'No. But I've got another iron in the fire.'

'You usually have. How much rent do you owe?'

'I've only just moved. I'm paid up until next Monday,' George said, and added, 'but then it's three pounds twelve shillings and sixpence, in advance.'

'Next Monday is, let me see, the eighteenth of September. After that it's the twenty-fifth. Then the second of October, by which time you can draw cheques again.'

'Yes. Something like that.'

'So the known difficulties are rent on the eighteenth and the twenty-fifth. Two lots of three pounds twelve shillings and sixpence. Which is seven pounds five shillings. Add to the seven pounds five shillings the fifteen days to the end of the month at say ten shillings a day basic food and you've got seven pounds five shillings plus seven pounds ten shillings which equals fourteen pounds fifteen shillings, or fifteen pounds in round figures, if we're going to be devils. So if your tale about committing suicide was true you were going to do it for fifteen miserable bloody quid.'

'I suppose so. Put like that.'

'How plainer can it be put?'

'No plainer. You could fancy it up a bit, though.'

'That's where you're always coming unstuck. Fancying things up.'

George said, 'You're forgetting two things.'

'What two things?'

'Two hundred pounds and ten thousand pounds. It was the only way I could repay you – making the bigger sum available to Gillian.'

Tim said, 'That's moral blackmail.'

'It wouldn't have been if I'd pulled it off. It's only moral blackmail because I didn't pull it off and have been dam' fool enough to come and tell you, come here like a bloody beggar because there wasn't anywhere else I *could* go, while you sit there playing cat-and-mouse, with your brain ticking over like a lousy book-keeping machine.'

Tim looked at his gold watch and got up. 'All right,' he said, 'a straightforward non-cat and no-mouse question. If I give you a few quid will you promise to leave Gillian alone?'

'What do you mean alone?'

'Just that. Alone. You know what I mean.'

'What do you mean, a few quid?'

'What I say. A few quid. And I suppose an understanding that no matter how often I ask you to pay back the two hundred pounds you just laugh.'

'Supposing she wants to see me? Supposing she writes to me or rings up and says Uncle George, I've got to talk to you?'

'No matter what. I meant refuse to see her again in any circumstances unless I give permission which I won't until long after the adoption has gone through. Refuse to see or talk or write to her in any circumstances.'

'It's not a thing only I can decide.'

'Let's make it plain. The two hundred pounds gets written off, here and now, if you agree. I give you some petty cash. And a cheque to keep clear of us.'

'A cheque?'

'A cheque. Say Fifty Pounds. Sarah will say I've gone mad. I think I've gone mad too. But that's what I'm prepared to pay if you promise to keep your nose out of my private and tricky and damned precarious affairs.'

George shook his head: not trusting himself to speak.

'Fifty Pounds,' Tim said. 'A cheque for fifty, and a fiver in your pocket to go home with.'

George stopped shaking his head, but still said nothing.

'A cheque for fifty pounds,' Tim repeated, 'a fiver in your pocket, and a receipt from me acknowledging repayment by services rendered of the two hundred quid. That's what it comes to, George. What it's worth to me to stop an undesirable influence undoing all the good work we're trying to do for Gillian.'

'No, Tim,' George said, feeling himself tremble. 'I've been bought in hundreds of indirect ways. But never direct. Come to think of it nobody has ever offered to buy me quite as crudely as that.'

'I'll bring down my soap and razor then. You can put your own kettle on.'

'Thanks. Can I have the fare money without strings?'

'Yes. I suppose so. I'll give you a couple of bob if I can find it.'

'Thanks.'

Tim held the door open. 'Get your kettle on now, will you? And try and be out of the house within half-an-hour.'

The kitchen had been redecorated since George had seen it last. Apart from some piled up crockery that was waiting to be washed up there was nothing out of place. There was a gas gun to light the ring on the stove. The kettle looked like something a finicky surgeon might boil swabs in. He filled and put it on, then tested the hot water tap. It ran scalding within a few seconds. He took his coat off, his tie and undid his collar. The louvres of the venetian blinds were open. He could see into the garden. The lawn was close-cut, the edges razor sharp; not a weed visible in the flower beds.

He looked in the cupboard under the built-in sink for a bowl and found one that was made of yellow polythene. In a blue plastic rack there was a cake of soap. He rolled up his sleeves, filled the bowl and soaked his hands. In the hot water his knuckles felt tight and lumpy, his finger nails chewn. The worst of the night's grime came off with the first soaping. With the second they were nearly clean. He changed the water and began on his face. It felt like a skull under his hands.

'There's a towel and a shaving mirror,' Tim said, coming in.

'Thanks,' George said from behind his hands.

'I can't find any small change, so I've had to give you a ten bob note. It's here with the shaving stuff.'

'Thank you.'

He bent over the bowl anew and rinsed. Straightening up he heard the door close and, turning, found himself alone. On the formica topped table was an injecto-matic razor, a tube of Yardley holding down a ten shilling note, toothpaste, towel and shaving mirror.

He looked at himself in the mirror.

Fool! he said aloud to the awful image. When he had finished shaving the kettle was boiling. He opened cupboards looking for a coffee tin, found it, and some milk in a half-used bottle in the refrigerator, and some brown sugar in a brown pot. After his coffee he drank a glass of water, and then another, washed up, dried, put away, laid the shaving tackle neatly on the folded towel on the draining board, put the ten shilling note in his pocket, paid a visit to the downstairs lavatory which was in the hall near the front door and then let himself out.

It was still too early for a bus, which meant that he would have to walk all the way to the tube, but this involved a saving of fivepence even before the day had begun.

Forty-Four

'I do beg your pardon, Mr. Spruce,' said Mrs. Poulten-Morse, her chin held by the invisible swimming instructor who helped her to keep her eyes off George's pyjamaed legs, 'but I thought you were up hours ago. I was waiting for the kettle to boil and I saw you come in and thought Mr. Spruce has been for an early constitutional.'

'Well no, Mrs. Morse. I was just coming home.'

Her eyelids flickered once, but she kept her chin up.

'And actually I shall sleep in a bit,' he said, viewing her with mixed feelings of gratitude for her friendly interest, irritation at her knock when he had had one foot in bed, and alarm for them both, with Monday not far off and no assurance that it would pass off peacefully. 'I had a pretty restless sort of night one way and another,' he went on. 'I was at my Aunt Clara's, the one who used to live next door —'

'Oh yes,' she said, and smiled the smile of returning consideration.

'—and then I went on to my brother's to discuss some business.'

She nodded a nod of general approval.

'—and found them having a rather worrying time with Gillian. That's their daughter. My god-daughter.'

She tilted her head with sympathetic interest.

'But it was only a bad tummy and not what we feared.'

'I *am* sorry. And here I am interrupting your well-earned rest. But there was a call for you last night at about eight o'clock and of course I was hoping it was the one I wished for you of pleasant tidings. I kept an ear for you until gone eleven.'

'Oh? Who was it from?'

'I thought he said Nick but then it seems it was Mick. I hope that makes sense to you.'

'Yes, it does. Thank you for telling me.'

'I'm afraid he left no message, although he seemed anxious to know how long you would be and I promised to tell you the moment you got in. Perhaps I should have left a note under your door? Not that in the circumstances much time has been lost, but for future reference perhaps this is what you'd prefer?'

'Well, last night was exceptional, Mrs. Morse, but a note would save you keeping an ear open for me, wouldn't it?'

'Oh, that is no trouble, Mr. Spruce. I am constantly on the qui vive for my people and the telephone. I hope the name Mick spells out good news for you in some connection?'

'I'm afraid I don't anticipate anything special.'

'In that case if he rings again before you are up I shall tell him you're sleeping in?'

George hesitated.

'Or that you're out? Would that be better?'

'Perhaps if you'd knock me up, Mrs. Morse. Whoever rings. If it's not too much trouble. Not that Mick is likely to ring until later. It's no good my ringing him now. He keeps late hours.'

'Very well, Mr. Spruce. Now I'll leave you in peace.'

Not, he thought when she had gone and he sat on the edge of his bed with the bright light of a sunny September morning poking its way through the net curtains in the gaps left by heavy plush curtains where they failed to meet, not that peace was anything anyone could find the means to leave him in, unless by peace was understood a planned withdrawal into unconsciousness. He took off his dressing-gown, climbed in and turned his face where he could see his assets on the bed-side table: his note-book of addresses and telephone numbers, a packet of ten Bachelors now holding only nine, and six shillings and sevenpence, change from Tim's ten shillings after an expenditure of one shilling and sixpence on fares and one shilling and elevenpence on cigarettes bought at an early-open shop.

And something else, he thought, closing his eyes with lids that felt lined with scraps of emery paper; something other than the assets assembled on the table, something other even than a mental note, still lingering in his mind after a store-cupboard check, (a tin of baked beans, half a tin of Nescafé, a churned little mess of luke-warm butter, a tin of sardines, a packet of mushroom soup, a few days' supply of Co-op 99, about half a pound of granulated sugar in its Tate and Lyle bag screwed up to keep the contents in, a tin of condensed milk, an almost new pint from yesterday morning's shopping run; only faintly cheesy; a nob of cheddar, a bit sweaty and tending to crack, and three-quarters of a wrapped cut loaf with the first piece only a bit curled at the edges); something else connected to and yet separated from notions of what steps might be taken after sleep towards Mick or Perce or Alice or Aunt Clara or (a new thought) that man, what was his name, met in the Queen's Head the other day who was in something that sounded interesting because it was unclear and likely to expand; something else that accompanied warmth coming at him from under and from on top, from all round, so that once or twice he shivered, getting the contrast, the bed warmth nudging the body-cold away, and the cold escaping to find someone else's bones to hide in, and setting up small draughts as it went, going wherever there was an outlet afforded by bedclothes not quite touching his limbs; something else added to all these things that were not liabilities but, looked at square, sleepily, almost blessings; something not new exactly, but with a freshed-up feeling to it, repaired and renewed; something else (he thought) emerging, emerged, and now going with him into his sleep to make his sleep dreamless.

But failing in the end, being not strong enough in the face of memories of arrest and drunkenness which shocked him into life as if they were the sting-tail ends of nightmares; but weren't, and proving they weren't by wriggling on through minute after minute of his being awake, and aware of the damp pillow under his open mouth and the chill that had crept into his toe-ends and the fingers of his right hand which was outside the sheet and blanket.

But then again (he thought) perhaps, truly, it was sleep, long sleep, cats'-eye led and tree-trunk born, all actual problems shattered into the patterns of permanent windscreen *craque-lure*, disrupting the bland face of the sitter behind the screen now as dead as the old master who had painted him; part of a totality of canvas and pigment that lacked only a frame and a place on someone's wall, although still capable of watching regarding from close-at-hand-distance assembled assets, relics, souvenirs; and capable of remembering: store cupboards, what they contained that might nourish bodies still in need of it, names, and the people names caught a likeness off, like Mick and Alice, Sweet-George, Anina, or even descriptions like sergeant, hard-case, lost-boy; even of hearing: a car passing, a telephone bell that had just ceased ringing, footsteps, even a Morse-like tread and knock, and her voice.

'Mr. Spruce? Are you there Mr. Spruce? Telephone.'

Forty-Five

'For me?' he said foolishly, still tying his monk-gown cord, his bare feet penitent on the cold strip of lino by the open door. 'I suppose it's Mick.'

'No, this is someone else. Mick rang at three o'clock, but you were dead to the world.'

'What's the time now?'

'Nearly four, Mr. Spruce. I told her I'd only see if you were awake, so if you don't want to bother —'

'Her?' he said, but was already out, and going down, stumbling a bit; and picked the receiver up as if it were her hand.

'Alice?' he said.

'Is that you, George?'

'Yes? Alice?'

'I'm sorry to wake you. This is Sarah.'

'Oh. Hello, Sarah. How's Gillian?'

He leant against the wall, defeated, but he smiled at Mrs. Morse as she passed him on her way back to the ground floor from whence stale music came.

'She's all right now, thank you, George.'

'Nothing's happened?'

'Nothing's happened.'

'And she's feeling all right?'

'Yes. She's feeling all right except for a hangover. George, I want to talk to you.'

'I'm sorry about last night.'

'Do you mean last night or this morning?'

'Both, I suppose. It was all one to me.' He lowered his voice. 'I'm not quite alone here, if you see what I mean.'

'Oh.'

'I don't mean that.'

'You mean you might be overheard?'

'Yes. Why have you rung anyway? I've been through it all once. Hasn't Tim told you?'

'Yes, he told me. I've been discussing things with him. Look, if you can't say much at your end just keep it to yes and no and let me say what I have to say.'

'Yes, all right.'

'I'm terribly unhappy about Gillian. I mean I feel responsible for what's happened, as if it's all been my —'

Presently he said, 'Hello? Sarah?'

'—all my fault. I blame myself, George. Tim won't have it, but it's true. Well, that's that part of it. The other thing is I believe you really were trying to help. I'm taking Gillian down to this place we found, on Monday —'

'Where is it? Wales?'

'Yes, Wales. How did you know?'

'Gillian said so.'

'Do you remember Mrs. Williams?'

'Williams?' George repeated.

'Who looked after Guy?'

'Yes of course. That Williams. I only saw her once.'

'Tim and I went down there several times during the war —'

'But that was in Dorset, not Wales.'

'She moved back to Wales when her husband died a year or so ago. Actually we don't think he ever really was her husband, but the point is we always kept in touch because she and Mr. Williams were kind to your parents as well as looking after Guy like they did. Tim used to send her a couple of pounds every so often to help with Guy.'

'I didn't know that.'

'He thought it was the least he could do, especially when Guy was older.'

'Yes, of course.'

'Not that he ever cost them anything. But the point is it's through Mrs. Williams we've got this cottage. She knows all about Gillian's trouble and doesn't mind. She lives near by but it's pretty isolated. She's letting the cottage to us quite cheaply. I think she owns a bit of property here and there and it's she who has this cousin who knows the matron of a nursing home that sounds just right for when the time comes. And of course she knows the local GP very well, so I think it's going to be all right, George. Except for one thing. I've got to be with Tim much more often than we expected because of this new job he's going to. We wondered whether you would come down and have a look at it.'

'Look at the cottage?'

'Yes.'

'Why?'

'Because there's a spare room. To be frank I've never cared much for the idea of Gillian and me being alone together there, and although Mrs. Williams says she'll look after Gill any time I have to be in London I know I should still worry. I've talked to Gill and she says she'd be very glad if you came down and perhaps stayed a bit. I mean as long as you wanted, actually right through the whole business if you felt like it. As her godfather.'

'I see.'

'I should be pleased too, George.'

'Would you?'

'Yes, I would. Does that surprise you?'

'Very much.'

'I'm thinking of Gillian, George. I should have thought more about her years ago.'

'But Tim would never agree, Sarah.'

'Tim does agree.'

'I find that awfully difficult to believe.'

'I won't pretend I didn't have to work on him. In the end he said he hadn't any real objection because you gave him the right answer this morning. When he offered you money to keep away from Gillian and you said No and left with only ten bob.'

'Why was that the right answer?'

'Tim thinks it showed you really cared what happened to her. Which of course is what I thought directly he told me, but it takes him longer to know what he thinks than it takes me. And if you cared that much you probably really did think about pinching a car and trying to kill your silly self. George. I don't want ten thousand pounds for Gillian. Not that way. I want her to be happy. And I want Tim not to have so many worries and to succeed in this new job. The new job means a better chance for Andrew who isn't bright like Gillian. I mean Andrew works like a little black but it's such an awful uphill plod for him, and he lacks what Tim calls an examination mind. A better school would be the making of him, give him a better chance in life, and if we can just cope with this awful thing that's happened to poor Gill – entirely through my own lack of care, I admit that – then everything will be all right. And if you help us out it means I can devote more time to being Tim's wife just at the one moment in his career when he really needs one.'

'Yes, Sarah. I see all that. I know what you want for Gillian and Andrew and Tim.' He hesitated, because they had never really got on. 'But what do you want for yourself?'

After a moment she said, 'But these things *are* myself, George. I don't add up to anything alone any more. I'm terrified of the new people I've got to meet. You'll be helping me as much as anybody because if I know Gill is being looked after while I have to be away I can put everything into pretending to be what I'm not. The capable wife of a clever young director.'

'Yes. I understand, Sarah.'

'Will you come down, then?'

'Next month? I could manage it early in October.'

'One thing I forgot to mention. There's a letter in the post to you from Tim.'

'What about?'

'Putting all this officially as a kind of proposal and adding something.'

'Money, you mean?' His ears tingled. He couldn't help it.

'A small cheque. To help with the fare down.'

'It's very decent of him.'

'He's a decent man, George. I wish you two got along better. Of course if you decide to stay you can give up your room and save the rent. Tim says your only expense would be your share of the housekeeping, I mean about two pounds a week. You could save a bit then, couldn't you George? And give yourself something to fall back on next year.'

'Yes, that's true. But I owe Tim two hundred.'

'Oh, I think that's all to be forgotten.'

'I see.'

'Of course it will be pretty isolated, but you've always liked Gillian and it's not as if you'll be on your own, stuck away from everything.'

'Oh no, of course. It's quite different.'

'And perhaps Alice could pay us a visit. You and Alice are still friends, aren't you?'

'Yes. We're still friends.'

'George.'

'Yes?'

'*Please* do it. I'm sorry I've often been such a pig to you.'

'You haven't Sarah. Honestly you haven't. If you have I've deserved it.'

'And perhaps Guy could come down. Mrs. Williams would love to see him again. It's so long since she's heard, apparently. And it's years since Tim and I have seen him. Do you know how he is?'

'I saw him yesterday as a matter of fact. He's getting his plays on.'

'Is he? But that's marvellous! On the stage?'

'No. Television.'

'But that's wonderful, George! Do tell him about the cottage. Mrs. Williams says there's a studio couch in what she calls the downstairs, which makes it sound like one room only on the ground floor, but there are three bedrooms and a bathroom upstairs. I gather the loo's outside but it's flush, not the other sort. And I expect the views are out of this world.'

'It sounds terrific.'

'Then you will come?'

'Thank you, Sarah. Of course. I'd love to.'

'Bless you, George. Ring us tomorrow when you've had Tim's letter. Perhaps you can come over for lunch. Or supper.'

'That's awfully kind of you, Sarah. I'll do that. I'll ring you tomorrow as soon as the post has been.'

'That's fine, George. We'll be a bit at sixes and sevens here because of the packing, but you won't mind, will you?'

'Of course not. Thank you for ringing.'

'All right then, George. We'll see you tomorrow.'

'Yes, tomorrow.'

'Goodbye, then,'

'Goodbye, Sarah.'

He replaced the receiver, and waited there, feeling instinctively for fourpence, but not having it in his monk's gown; so he climbed back up the stairs and entered his room, and felt, in that room, the briefly tangible presence of the curious enchantment that was always there, in the air, but was not often felt, stood still long enough for, or touched, except momentarily, in tiny spasms that come richly like air almost too good to breathe. He thought: It's nice here, I shall be sorry to leave.

Then, with fourpence gone from his assembled assets, he left the room in which the happiness that did not have to be pursued had suddenly been encountered, and went back down the stairs thinking: It's all right. It *will* work. But I didn't remember to ask what happens when she sees the baby. Which is the point, I mean, isn't it? Basically the point? But I mustn't think too closely about any of it, because it may seem then less that suddenly I am loved and more that I am being used, even though it saves my life. But it is there, rising like the faint Morse-music up the stairs, all the things it is *for,* apart from my temporary peace of mind, I mean like Tim's higher income and improved position, and Andrew's new school, Sarah's long weekends away from Wales, and old Wallingford's creepy old age to keep it creepy; the old firm gone, scattered like children from old houses, and Gwendoline unable more, maybe, to think of Corsica.

He dialled, listening to the purr, and the click, and the blessedly short ringing and her voice saying: Hello? as if wondering who else on earth might ring except himself.

'Alice?' he said. 'George here. I've got some rather good news and I wanted you to be the first to know.'

EPILOGUE FOR MINOR CHARACTERS ON A COLD DECEMBER DAY

'You must have misunderstood me, Stainsby,' said Doctor Barr, standing over the grave to which the curate had led him in order to inspect the wooden cross just erected, 'I'm sure the words were not my suggestion.'

'Oh, but they were, doctor,' Mr. Stainsby replied. 'She had a wish for a line or two of verse and these were the ones you spoke when I sought your help.'

Here Lies

ADA LAVINIA LISLE

Born Feb 1 1882 Died Sep 15 1961
Benefactor of the children of this
Parish and remembering the Fallen
in the war 1914–18.

'Does the road wind up hill all the way?
Yes, to the very end.
Will the day's journey take the whole long day?
From morn to night, my friend.'

'I must have spoken them in some other context,' said Doctor Barr. 'I must have been thinking of Those Stairs at The Grange.'